The Candle of God

For Judy,
a dearest friend -
love,
Donna
October, 2012

DONNA SPECTOR

This is a work of fiction. The events and characters described herein are imaginary and are not intended to refer to specific places or living persons. The opinions expressed in this manuscript are solely the opinions of the author and do not represent the opinions or thoughts of the publisher. The author has represented and warranted full ownership and/or legal right to publish all the materials in this book.

The Candle of God

v3.0

Outskirts Press, Inc.
http://www.outskirtspress.com

ISBN: 978-1-4327-8886-5

PRINTED IN THE UNITED STATES OF AMERICA

Ladies in Waiting

The three ladies
in Parisian hats
buttoned up
to the lip
with laces
in this photograph
are dead:
Grandmother,
sweetly brushing
long white hair
dark Sundays;
Aunt Leah,
her lonely head
severed
from her watchful body
by an erroneous car;
Aunt Dena,
burning years of candle
to her son
whose lung collapsed
when I was too
young to cry.
All wait wistfully
for deliverance
from this moment,
and I, voyeur,
am heavy with memory
I cannot deliver.

Jessamyn Singer

Part One

Pasadena, 1951-1952

He carried the boy out of the house and down the street. It was a warm day, the beginning of summer, but he held the boy close so he wouldn't catch cold, because you never knew, even on a day like this when the sun was shining. There were shadows as he passed the live oak trees, brief bursts of cool air, anything could happen. How light the boy was! Surely no more than sixty pounds. He brushed the boy's hair out of his eyes. "Don't be afraid," he said, "I'm taking care of you. We're just going for a walk. I'm going to tell you everything now."

The dream was always the same. First, piano music ripples through the night house. Then a woman is yelling, but he can't make out the words. His mother? A glass shatters against a wall. "Don't tell me I have to stay here!" a man shouts. His father? Someone pounds the piano keys, and Danny flinches in his sleep. Footsteps running. A door slams somewhere in the house. Silence, as though the house is holding its breath. "Daddy?" Danny moans. "I need you."

Outside in the driveway a car's engine roars, tires crunch over gravel, a screeching of brakes, then nothing but a woman weeping and palm trees rustling in the wind. Danny tries to open his eyes, but he can't move, his body is paralyzed, someone is pushing him down, down into the bed, he's gasping for air, and then, laughter. A voice: "Come now, this isn't necessary. Just leave it behind," and he rises up, out of his body so easily he's amazed. He glides through the house like a ghost, past the forlorn piano, his mother huddled on the living room sofa, his grandmother standing like a grim sentinel in the kitchen, and out the open door. "Good-bye," he whispers as he floats over lemon trees, past the pyracantha, its flame-colored berries blue in the moonlight, and up into the clouds toward Mount Wilson. Then he looks down and sees his father carrying him in his arms.

Dena was counting Danny's pennies again. He could hear his mother drop them into the jar, as though each one were a drop of her own blood, to be collected like a magic elixir. A protection against harm.

He opened his eyes. What time was it? Six a.m.? Seven? His mother kept his Venetian blinds closed so he could sleep late and get well.

Mama, he whispered, tasting his penicillin breath. *Mamoushka.* He sat up and pulled back his sweaty satin comforter, quietly, so the bed wouldn't creak, so Dena wouldn't rush in with her tray of pills. Let the day wait, he thought. Let it begin later, after Mama has brushed the cobwebs from her beige hair. Sitting in her room like Miss Havisham, because her bridegroom deserted her. Only Mama doesn't wear a wedding dress.

He saw the cans of peanuts stacked like an Eiffel Tower in the corner of his room and stifled a giggle. A year's worth of peanuts he'd won for his mother. Another gift ignored. But tonight he would play the piano sonata he wrote for her and Gram, and maybe he'd dress up for them. Yes, in Gram's red silk shawl and his mother's black high heels, so he could read them his new play about a girl who ran away from an orphanage and became an opera singer.

Why were his arms so thin and white, like the arms of those plastic skeletons in doctors' offices? Was he wasting away, like Uncle David said, calling him a Hanukkah candle? But Gram said this was a joke Uncle David made to cover the guilt of his Christian wife.

It was last Christmas, when they had gone to Uncle David's house, and his uncle was embarrassed by the Christmas tree Aunt Kathleen had bought. A pagan ritual, Gram had said, when they were hanging ornaments and lights on the tree. "I don't know why you invited us," his mother had said. "Maybe you don't know that Jews don't celebrate Christmas?"

Aunt Kathleen had turned paler than the Christmas angel she was holding, and Uncle David, to divert her, said, "Where are all the cookies and the fudge? Danny needs sweets! I won't have my own nephew thin as a candle of God."

"Was my father thin too?" Danny had asked. No one answered him but the radio. "Silent Night," it sang.

In her bedroom Dena counted pennies like minutes and waited for Danny to wake up before she got ready to visit Rabbi Saltzman at the Healing Center in Pasadena. Danny had coughed very little last night, though perhaps she had slept and not heard him. What if he'd died, and she'd been dreaming of something stupid, as usual?

No, she wouldn't think in this way. She and her mother alone in this little stucco house with Danny all these years since Earl left to play the organ at Woody and Eddy's and never came back. Leaving his one good suit, his orange toothbrush and his black underwear like an insult. She knew Earl never believed

Danny was his child. That last night he sat in the kitchen waving his cigar and yelling, "He's no child of mine. I've got lungs like an ox, and if he can't breathe, he's somebody else's."

Thank goodness she had Rabbi Saltzman, who was a good man and didn't care that she was a woman whose husband had left her. Dena shivered with rage, remembering the way Earl's smoke clung like soot to the counters, tables and chairs, black-outlined her lace doilies on the davenport, made their house an ash bin. No matter how much Lysol she used, or Mr. Clean, that smoke was sneaky like Earl himself. It lay over her bed, a veil of death, trying to draw the very breath out of her.

She had even hired an exterminator. Twenty-seven years old that man was, very sincere. Said he never went after smoke before, rats were his usual line.

And Dena had said, "Never mind, Earl was a rat and all I'm asking is for you to clean up his trail." When the man laughed, Dena glared and said, "You think that was funny?" It wasn't then, but now, remembering, Dena laughed with her hand over her mouth, so the laugh would stay inside. So Danny could sleep.

While the man worked, Dena took her mother to lunch at Bullocks' Tea Room with nice finger sandwiches, egg salad and watercress, and a double feature at the Academy in Pasadena.

When they got back, the smoke was gone, except for one place that she didn't find till the next morning. Seven o'clock sun drifted through the kitchen when she came in to make coffee, and there was Earl's face, drawn in smoke on the yellow refrigerator. Grinning like a Cheshire cat.

The phone began to ring. Dena raced into the living room to answer it before the noise woke both Danny and her mother.

"Dena," Rabbi Saltzman said, "can you be here by nine?"

"Oh, yes," Dena whispered, his voice warming her to the very soles of her frozen feet.

"Why are you whispering?"

"Danny and Mother are still sleeping. What time is it?"

"Eight o'clock. I've been meditating for an hour, waiting to call you."

Dena smiled, remembering how handsome Rabbi Saltzman looked when he folded himself into a lotus position. "All right," she said. "I'll see if Danny's awake. I promised him he could spend the day at my brother's house in Alhambra."

"Good. I need you. It's Monday and we have work to do."

Yes! He needed her. "I'll be there." She kissed the receiver as she hung up, knowing it was a silly thing to do, but how could a woman stop herself when a man as wonderful as Rabbi Saltzman said "need"?

"Bring Danny to my house," David had said. "Let him play outside with the kids. Fresh air, some exercise for his muscles, a rare steak for his blood. What does he want with a couple of old ladies in a dark house up in Altadena? And besides, your latkes are too heavy."

That was a joke so bad Dena couldn't laugh, knowing David's silly wife Kathleen made latkes out of Bisquick. But even though her brother thought he knew everything, she would let Danny go to David's house, only because of Rabbi Saltzman.

She tiptoed to Danny's room and opened his door slowly.

"Mama?" He was sitting on the edge of his bed, his face glowing in a sudden slant of sun. "Am I really going to Uncle David's?"

"Yes, darling. If you feel well enough."

"I do," he said. "I'll get dressed."

Dena's whole body fizzed with joy.

Danny liked being at Uncle David's clean, white house, where he could play with his cousins Jessamyn and Melissa. They pulled him out of himself, into the world of palm trees and purple bougainvillea, wagons racing along uneven sidewalks and catapulting down hills too steep for him to contemplate later, but each time he felt himself caught in the swish and rush. His cheeks and fingers tingled with energy as he tilted into the warm October afternoon. Alhambra with its modest Spanish-Moorish houses protected by hedges or low walls with scrolly iron gates became golden-domed St. Petersburg, the wagon a sleigh soaring over hills blue with moonlit snow. And he was the family patriarch, bearded and ruddy.

After dinner, after they'd reassured themselves that he ate everything, didn't hide his vegetables under his potato skin, they played a game Jessamyn invented: they crawled down both flights of stairs head first while Uncle David and Aunt Kathleen were at the neighbors' playing canasta. It was a dangerous game, they knew, even though the stairs were carpeted, because Danny had so many headaches at home, and what if he hit his head?

But Jessamyn loved danger, so Danny thought if he could live this way just for a while, if he could ignore the headaches, stomach aches and pains in his chest and try to be like daredevil Jessamyn and little, laughing Melissa, his world that curled in on itself like a snail might open into unknown possibilities.

Danny went first down the stairs, while Jessamyn followed, teasing him because he always farted. "It's your mother's Gentile cooking," Danny said, though they both knew that wasn't true. It was because Danny was the runt, last of that line. If his mother's family hadn't escaped from the Ukraine, his tattered body would never have been dragged from her womb. Thirty-six hours, and when on January 2, 1938, he finally emerged, drugged with twilight sleep, he smelled his father's cigar smoke.

"Impossible," his mother said. "While I was in the hospital, your father was playing the organ at a Pasadena restaurant."

Danny's grandmother Esther sat in the kitchen, in the gray, predawn light, with a cup of tea and her memories to protect her from the loneliness that seeped through her body and settled like a stone in her heart. So many years since she had come, by the grace of God, to this country because, her father said, the Czar was eating the Jews. How different her life was then, when they lived in Chicago, and she was given the limited education proper for young ladies.

Now she was old, her body tortured by aches and pains, her fingers twisted with arthritis, living like a mummy in this house with a sick grandson and a daughter who sneaked away, heaven knew where, every day.

"Tell me again about when you were young," Danny had said last night. "Tell me about Grandfather."

She had let herself float back through the years till she was sixteen again. "I was plain as a weed, flat-chested, my heavy brown hair pulled tight into braids, when I married Benjamin," she said. *Who touched her, and she became a white rose bush, flowering with children.*

"And Grandfather was…" Danny prompted, to draw her away from daydreaming.

"An intense young man," Esther said. "With black hair and eyes, and a a black mustache hiding his sensitive mouth." *"Esther," he said, his voice trembling with love. "Esther." Oh, she heard the unspoken promises, so out of place in their conventional parlor. Her mother, who pretended not to listen, was startled from her crocheting.*

"Although your grandfather was quite serious in the daylight," Esther said, "at night there were poems on his breath. Songs as well, melodies of money and children, and tales of the Bal Shem Tov."

"I love those stories," Danny said, closing his eyes. "Now tell me about Chicago."

"We lived in a small, dingy basement apartment in the ghetto," Esther said, her voice slowing into the story she had told so many times. "Those dark nights, thick with the incense of poverty, cabbage and potatoes, although always, even in winter, we opened the door after supper.

"Our eggshell walls were streaked brown with tears from the people upstairs. Twelve steps to one wall, ten to the other, and be careful of the bed covered with my grandmother's lace cloth from the Ukraine." *The bed where Benjamin gave her children in the darkness.*

"Each day after Benjamin left, I climbed on a chair to wash our high, half-window so I could study the feet of the city through a steaming circle in the greasy glass. 'Look,' I would say to the child in my womb. 'Those leather boots belong to an important businessman. See how he hurries along unmindful of the snow and slush? Soon he will gather with other powerful men around a huge, polished table. Mahogany, gleaming in morning sun. As they drink their coffee from porcelain cups, their words will ring with significance. When you grow up, you will be like that.' And that was the right thing to say to Samuel and Nathan, my two eldest."

But to David she said, "See those delicate white boots? That is a young girl with opalescent skin, green eyes and dark curls. That is someone you could love," and she knew now she was a fool to have spoken.

"Mother! Are you daydreaming again?" Dena was standing in the doorway, her arms crossed over her pink quilted bathrobe, like an angry schoolteacher.

"Yes," Esther said. "I suppose I am. What day is it?"

"Tuesday, and I'm leaving early, in case you didn't remember."

"Didn't you leave early yesterday and take Danny with you?"

"You know well enough that Danny went to David's, and you could have gone too, if you hadn't refused."

"Where are you going so early these days?"

"Oh!" Dena's face turned flaming red. "Am I on trial here?"

"It was a simple question."

"Never mind," Dena said, knowing she couldn't tell her mother about Rabbi Saltzman. Not yet. So she steeled herself against her mother's questions. "Will you stay with Danny today?"

"Where else would I go?" Esther gave Dena a sly look that Dena knew was meant to inspire guilt, though all it did was make her itch with fury.

"You could go anywhere. Except for today."

Danny collected stamps and coins, because through them he could travel anywhere in space and time, beyond their beige stucco and gabled bungalow, its sloping roof like the house of the seven dwarves, hiding under pine trees in the foothills of the San Gabriel mountains. He knew there were lions, bears, deer and bighorn sheep in the forest beyond their street, but he'd never see them. He'd never met anyone in their neighborhood, not the old people sitting on porches of their one-story wooden or stucco houses like his or the children calling out from makeshift clubhouses in the ubiquitous avocado trees. Not even the teenaged boys, who sometimes picked the orange and blue birds of paradise in his front yard for their girlfriends while Danny watched from his bedroom window. What did he care?

He imagined himself in Egypt, riding a camel through the desert to inspect his tomb. Tall, erect, his back arched like the handle of a scythe. While he surveyed his domain, the desert glittered with possibilities. Up ahead he could see the workmen, hear their cries as they strained to erect his last house. He had chosen an artist to paint his story on the walls in reds and golds. Everything in his tomb would be real gold and jewels: sapphires, emeralds, rubies. Even lapis lazuli, but no diamonds, because they were much too plain.

He could still be fourteen because pharaohs died young in those days. Rulers of the world, they couldn't control death the way Danny would, because without him, his mother couldn't survive.

He tried to breathe deeply so he wouldn't cough. His mother would come in and see that he wasn't sleeping. "Seven in the morning and you're up," she'd say. "Then you'll have to rest all day, no going outside." But he knew it was lying down that made him cough.

Danny opened the drawer of his bedside table, took out his flashlight and shined it under the bed to catch the cigar smoke. There it was, hiding in the corner. His father sent it at night, like a messenger, to comfort him.

He turned off the flashlight, skimmed his fingers over the coins in the book he kept under his pillow, counted to ten and flicked the light back on.

"You're looking at the coins again?" It was his grandmother, in her green velvet robe, bringing him tea and toast and medicines. She set the tray on his bedside table and turned on his lamp. "May I join you?"

She sat on the edge of his bed. "That Indian head penny was from 1922, when your mother was a girl with long red sausage curls and fat cheeks. And that franc was from one of my trips to Paris when your mother was young."

"You took Aunt Leah but you never took my mother," Danny said without reproach.

"Yes," Esther said. "And your mother was very bitter about that. She said Uncle Nathan and Uncle Samuel were hateful when I was away."

Danny couldn't imagine his proper uncles in their rich suits being young and mean. Teasing their little sister until she cried and refused to learn the French songs Gram and Aunt Leah sang when they returned.

"Gram," Danny said. "Remember when you sang 'Frere

Jacques' to me when I was in the hospital?"

"A nice man taught it to me in Paris," she said, "when Aunt Leah and I sat in a café after shopping in the Latin Quarter."

Danny wondered if that was the time she bought the silver dresser set, the comb, brush and mirror. Tonight, he decided, he'd write a song about Gram brushing her long, silver hair with her silver brush. That would be a nice thing to do. Then just as she'd begin to brush her hair, he would play it for her. There would be a hush in the room, and Mama would weep.

On Sunday afternoon, as usual, David came with his family for dinner. Esther made potato kugel and Kathleen watched, saying, "This time I'm going to get it right." She rolled up the sleeves of her silky red dress, took up the knife and began to peel potatoes.

"Stop!" Esther said. "You're taking too much potato away and leaving the eyes."

Dena felt a surge of evil triumph over David's Irish whore. "I'll do it," she said, "I know how." Kathleen walked out of the kitchen trying to hide her tears. "I feel sorry for her," Dena said, "She can't do anything right."

"Be quiet," Esther said, and the precarious balance in the kitchen was tilted toward Kathleen, until Jessamyn brought in a picture of the baby Jesus.

"Will you look at this!" Dena said, snatching the picture from Jessamyn and waving it in her mother's face. "Another example of Irish Catholic idolatry!"

"Give it back to the child," Esther said, averting her eyes from the offensive image as David entered the kitchen.

"Do you see this, David?" Dena said. "What your child brought into our kitchen?"

"I'm sorry." David said, taking the picture and stuffing it into his pants pocket.

"Really?" Dena said. "I'm surprised you didn't become a Catholic yourself, even though everyone knows the Catholics force people to make these agreements because they want to take over the world, it's a plain and simple fact."

"I'm tired of telling you, Dena," Esther said. "Be still."

After dinner the children gave a play Danny wrote about immigrants. In Esther's coats, sweaters and babushkas, they looked like three little bears remembering their days in Kiev. Then Danny put on David's hat and coat and became Great Grandfather the wine seller.

"I thought he was a rabbi," Kathleen said, kicking off her high heels and crossing her legs in a way Dena felt was too provocative. Sick with jealousy, she watched Kathleen rearrange the silver combs in her naturally curly hair as she thought of the nights she suffered, trying to sleep on pin curls.

"This was the other grandfather," David said.

"Oh," Kathleen said. "So what kind of wine did this grandfather sell?"

"Grape," Melissa said, from under the table.

"Kosher," David said nervously.

"Leave it at grape," Esther said. "For only seven years, it's a good answer."

"Oh, they're so cute," Kathleen said, her green eyes wide and innocent.

Dena watched David lean back on the couch in his smug way, so delighted that he, the poor Jewish poet, could possess such a classy- looking shiksa. "Are you," she asked Kathleen, "speaking of your own children?"

"And Danny, of course," Kathleen said, smiling in a way Dena knew was condescending.

Danny, who had never been called cute, began to laugh, and soon Melissa and Jessamyn were laughing so hard they were snorting, all three of them rolling around on the floor.

"Why are you laughing?" Kathleen asked.

"Because," Jessamyn gasped, "Danny is so cute."

David hated these scenes, endlessly repeated, as though his wife was on trial and Dena the judge. "Mother," he said, "where have you hidden the cigars?"

Esther looked startled. "In the wooden box on my dresser."

"Cigars!" Dena shrieked. "You would smoke in the house when Danny can't breathe?"

"No," David said, through clenched teeth. "I am going outside to smoke my cigar."

Cuban cigars, Esther thought, turning restlessly in bed. Benjamin knew what men wanted. When Leah had begun to grow in her womb, Benjamin came home one spring evening and threw a handful of dollar bills down the steps. "This is only the beginning," he said.

Next came the silver dresser set with her initials engraved on the handles. She polished the silver every day until her initials gleamed as though she were somebody. *E.S.*, a person with a right to initials. Brushing her hair, she watched herself in the mirror. Saw, in the dim bedroom light, that her body had changed, from severe angles to soft curves. Astonished, she dropped her shift down over her shoulders. Breasts. Not only was she a wife and mother; she was a woman.

When they moved into their upstairs apartment by the lake, Esther sat by the huge window with Leah in her arms. Indulging in radiance, the sunrises and sunsets, they could now afford. How she felt the morning dazzle from lake and sky! She remembered the way they became transfixed, as they looked down on the city and watched people's heads. "Look at those hats," she said to Leah, for it was no use trying to interest Samuel and Nathan, who had been nurtured on men's feet and were following their father.

Then Benjamin began to make business trips to Cuba. Esther was alone too much with four children, including Dena, the new baby. The walls receded; even the thick carpet and elegant draperies could not absorb the echoes of her loneliness. "Benjamin," she would cry, as he hurried past.

"Yes, my darling?" he would say. But before Esther could answer, he was gone to find more money.

By the time David was a child, she could afford a governess. She left Dena with all the boys and took Leah to Paris each spring to buy gowns and shoes and hats, her passion. "Ah, you are lovely," she said to her daughter's reflections in the mirrors of hat shops. "Such a delicate head, in that hat. How perfectly those flowers frame your high cheekbones. Those ribbons cascading down your slender neck."

And she had done it, another mistake, like bewitching her baby David with the charms of Irish girls. She had praised Leah's beauty when Death was listening. She should have known. At twenty, a lyrical girl, romantic in pastel picture hats, Leah was adored by men. But she married Myron, a foolhardy, pretentious fellow, who lured her with gold jingling in his pockets. He would not be her husband, only her driver. On their honeymoon he raced Leah down the highway to Florida, skidded into the arms of her impatient lover, Death. Who didn't want Myron, no, not then. But who took him a bit later, as an afterthought.

Perhaps, Esther thought, she should have taken Dena to Paris. Dena would not have fallen in love with hats. She knew nothing of heads or feet, only the space between her legs. Dena never loved anyone, except Danny. And no one, except Danny, ever loved her.

Until now. Someone was calling Dena early mornings. And where did she go, day after day, so secretively? Could she have a lover after all these years? Why else would she leave Danny, when he was so ill?

"Rabbi Saltzman," Dena said, "our house is moving uphill every year. The first time I noticed, it was only a couple of inches, but now it's speeding up. Last year it was a foot and a half. I've talked to nobody but you about it."

"Please, don't call me 'rabbi,'" Rabbi Saltzman said. He and Dena were eating Ritz crackers with cream cheese and avocado slices in the anteroom of the rabbi's healing temple in Pasadena.

"Oh, I always forget," Dena said, rolling her eyes. "Because to me a rabbi once is a rabbi forever."

Rabbi Saltzman smoothed his sleek hair. "When I became a faith healer, I left my religion behind, lying in the dust."

"If you say so." Dena licked cracker crumbs from her lips. "Although to me..."

Rabbi Saltzman interrupted her. "This business about your house. I think it's a sure sign Danny will be cured. And within ten years, you'll have the best view in Altadena. All the way to El Molino Mills on Valley Boulevard."

"You think so?"

"Yes," he said, "and if you have great faith, the house might make it to Mount Wilson someday. And Mount Wilson, for anyone's information, is going to be the summer home of God." He got up and brushed off his satin pants. "Excuse me. Nature calls."

Alone in the anteroom, Dena practiced smiling at the gold-flecked mirror while she remembered El Molino Mills. That was where she and Laurette experimented with vegetables when she was pregnant with Danny. She was pretending to be a virgin so Earl would want her. She knew even then it wasn't true, what people say, that when you're pregnant, your sexual desire goes away. Not at all. Of course, she had just found hers that crazy night in Arizona with Clyde. One night and that was it, then she was carrying around what would have to be Earl's baby.

She was waitressing with Laurette, who showed her how to alter her uniform so it would be tight and sexy, especially around the bust. The male customers were all giving her a feel, and she was enjoying it. But she was afraid.

"What can I do?" she asked Laurette. "If I fool around and Earl finds out, he'll never marry me."

They went back to Laurette's place behind the Mills and tried oiling up hot dogs. Which didn't work too well, because if you get excited, they tear right in two. That's when they discovered vegetables smothered in Vaseline. Dena was partial to a hefty carrot, but Laurette liked a good-sized zucchini or even a cucumber. That still amazed Dena, but to each her own. Of course, Laurette was much taller than Dena, although Dena's breasts were larger. They still were quite shapely, Dena noticed, lifting them slightly and pushing them together. Dena was sure Rabbi Saltzman had noticed them. She could tell sometimes by the bulge in his pants. And why not? After all, a man is a man.

That morning Rabbi Saltzman and Dena had enjoyed an especially long prayer session. When they held Danny's picture between them and concentrated on healing Danny's lungs, their knees touched, ever so gently. Divine energy flowed between them so powerfully that Dena opened her eyes, just a crack. And there was that bulge, glowing in a heavenly halo.

"What you are, Rabbi, is a Christian saint," she murmured, and she reached out to caress that bulge. But she stopped herself just in time.

"Little Dena," he said, touching her cheek. "I've seen it so clearly. Your son will get worse before he gets better. You must have faith. Danny's breath will ascend to God and return, purified."

"I'm frightened," Dena said. "I couldn't live without Danny."

"These experiences are like messages in fortune cookies," he said, and he smiled. "You may call me Daniel, after your son."

When he said that, Dena was so overcome she had a vision. She saw his bulge rising on a golden platter, right up to God. But she didn't mention it.

"Rabbi," she said, "don't you think it would have been

impossible for Mary to be a virgin? Imagine! All that fuss over a ridiculous idea!" He looked confused, so Dena worried that he didn't understand her. But what did that matter? He was going to heal her son.

Danny was in the hospital again. Propped up in bed by pillows, he copied Dr. Rieger's list of medicines into his journal. *I am now taking*, he wrote in his small, precise hand, *penicillin, terpen hydrate, salt solution, liver shots with folic acid, Folvron, vitamin A shots, vitamin A pills, Aquasol, vitamin D shots, vitamin K Menadione, pancreatin tabs, Stuart's Formula, Aureomycin, Rubrafolin, Terramycin, brewer's yeast, Gantrisin, Streptomycin (shots), Ephedrol, Aminophylin, Crysticillin, Pyribenzamine syrup and Neopenil.*

All these medicines make me a little dopey and sick to my stomach, he wrote, *but I don't mind because I've just gotten two stories published in the Pasadena City College magazine. One about Rascal, my last dog, who was taken away April 23, 1948. The other about Miss Hermione Pascoe, the red-headed nurse with a big birthmark on her left cheek, who gave me my first pair of guppies when I was in the hospital last time.*

Susan, the original female guppy, had twelve babies. Seven survived. Then Freddy, her husband, died, so I bought a new male, George, and another pair, Dinah and Drake. Susan had another dozen babies, but Dinah, who was very prolific, had more than thirty. Most of them died. Of all the children of Susan and Dinah, I have only three large and five small ones left.

A fit of coughing overtook him and he buried his face in the pillow, so the nurse wouldn't call Dr. Rieger. When the coughing subsided, he continued: *I bought a set of barbells, and*

I'm going to build my strength up so I can take math classes at the college. I was admitted last fall, but I had to stay with my home teaching because I was so tired from malnutrition. Dr. Rieger says these new vitamins will help.

This would be Danny's first time in school. He had taken a Latin correspondence course from the University of California at Berkeley last year, but he had never been inside a classroom. Mr. Winans, his latest home teacher, said he could do it, but he worried whether the students would accept him. He knew he was odd, his head too big for his scrawny body. No matter what his mother said.

Danny leaned back, let his journal fall onto the bed and closed his eyes. Last night he, Jessamyn and Melissa played birds with Gram's jewelry while she listened to Jack Benny. They made castles and furniture of necklaces, bracelets and brooches. Fortunately, Danny thought, Gram has three bird pins, so he and Melissa didn't have to fight with Jessamyn, whose temper could be terrifying. Danny's bird was green (and really the prettiest), Jessamyn's was red and Melissa's blue. Gram didn't mind if they played with her things, as long as they stayed in her room, which was dark, but they set up her lamps on the floor, so the jewels would gleam. Gram had said they were real, smuggled out from the Ukraine.

"Why don't you put them in a vault?" Aunt Kathleen asked once. "I wouldn't let the children play with them."

But Gram just smiled, and, remembering, his eyes still closed, Danny smiled too.

When they first entered Gram's room, Melissa smelled the cigar smoke. It was being playful in the dark. Just as Danny turned on the light, it vanished. "Does Gram smoke cigars?"

Melissa said, and Jessamyn giggled.

"No," Danny said, hoping she'd be quiet, even though she was only seven.

"Where is Uncle Earl?" she said.

Jessamyn said, "Shhhh."

Yes. Danny knew it was always better not to talk about his father. He didn't mind that Earl had gone, he reassured himself for the thousandth time. He must have had a good reason. But his mother got very unhappy whenever she thought about him. "He took my soul," she said.

So Danny cheered his mother by winning another contest. Last month he won her a refrigerator with his knock-knock joke. "Knock, Knock. Who's there? Winifred. Winifred who? Winifred--fred robin comes bob-bob bobbin' along." They didn't really need a refrigerator, but they needed some place for most of the Circus peanuts and the ninety-six bars of Sweetheart soap, because the guest closet was full of Campbell Soup cans from last July's contest.

If we can't be happy, Danny thought, at least we'll be clean and well-fed. He began to laugh, and suddenly he was choking on his laughter.

"Mother," David said, as they paced the glaring hospital corridors while they waited for Danny to wake up. "Where is Dena?"

"I wonder that myself," Esther said.

"The desk nurse told me Dena has only been here a few times, and she doesn't stay very long."

"I think she has a lover."

"A lover!" David's face contorted with pain. "Why now, of all times?"

Esther took her youngest child's hand. How dear he was! Gentle like her husband, but a dreamy poet with a bright, inventive mind. Although his high cheekbones, downward-slanting eyes and sensual mouth kept him from being handsome in the usual way, David wooed people with his charming unconventionality.

"She lets her body rule her, as usual," Esther said. "Let's not talk about Dena. Do you remember at Sen High School, when you played Puck in *Midsummer Night's Dream*, edited the school paper and were elected senior class president because you recited a humorous poem?"

"Mother, please. This is no time for memories."

Esther smiled. "What else is there? You may be small, but you won that fight with the school bully by stepping aside at the right moment. How proud your father was! That huge, dim-witted fellow slammed his head into a wall and knocked himself out. And he thought you had hit him, so you were never molested by anyone after that."

"Yes, yes," David said impatiently. "Now listen to me. When Danny gets out of the hospital, I want him to come and live with me."

"No," Esther said. "It will never happen."

"Why not? If Dena is too busy with a lover to care."

"But she does love Danny, even though she is preoccupied at the moment."

David pounded the wall so hard a nurse looked out of one of the rooms. "I can't stand it!" he cried, as he turned and walked away. "I'm going home."

"I'm sorry," Esther called after him. She didn't say, How could you afford another mouth to feed, because she couldn't bear to hurt him. He would never work in the cigar business, like Nathan and Samuel, who had distinguished gray hair at the age of fifteen. No, it was always poetry for him, and the study of literature. Esther would awaken at night, see a light in the kitchen, and there would be David, hunched over, dark hair hiding his eyes, reading or making notes.

"Go to bed," she would say, shivering in the pre-dawn chill blowing from the lake. "You'll be tired tomorrow."

He would raise his head bemusedly and smile. "Yes, I probably will."

Sometimes she wondered if he slept at all, in college or afterwards, when he worked on the newspaper. Imagine, she thought, someone with his creative intelligence, a copy editor! Still, it was better than some jobs he he'd had. Better by far than the job he had now.

"Please, David," she would say, "don't be proud. Work for your father, like Nathan and Samuel."

"It's not pride, Mother," he would say. "But I see how hungry that business is. If I want to write, I must work at a job that won't devour my energy."

Yes and no. He was proud, but he did need the time, even though he lived at home much too long.

When he was older, a reporter for the paper, he married Kathleen. Met her in an evening poetry course, although she knew nothing of poetry and must have gone there to meet a man. Such things happen in this country, Esther knew, where people have the time to be dilettantes wearing red dresses. How could she stop him, so inflamed by Kathleen's pale skin and green eyes, her dark curls, that Esther knew he would burn himself into ashes without her.

"A Catholic?" she had said. "Not only a Christian but a worshipper of saints and idols?"

Benjamin was outraged. "Will you deny your heritage?"

"Please," David said to his father. "Don't turn away from me. I must have her, never anyone else."

Benjamin left on a business trip, his way of avoiding unpleasantness. While he was gone, David married Kathleen, in a civil ceremony on the top floor of a bank.

"A compromise," he said. "Neither priest nor rabbi, but a justice of the peace."

But there was no peace after that, not with his father, so David and Kathleen moved to California.

Now Jessmyn and Melissa, her grandchildren, brought home pictures of Mary and Jesus. And Esther knew she could say nothing, because she came here to be near her son, the one who still had time for her now that Benjamin was gone.

Nathan and Samuel had piles of gold and no families to care for. David, with a wife and two children, sold cat litter during the day and wrote novels in the evening. Which might never be published.

Esther decided to sell another bracelet.

"I have a special project in mind." Rabbi Saltzman was drawing elaborate astrological calculations on a blackboard with colored chalk when he heard Dena enter his office. Her heels clicked across his Egyptian tile floor.

"What?" She rested her hand lightly on his arm so her

scarlet nails would glimmer at him.

"I'm going to round up all the West Coast healers I can find for one massive session for Danny at the summer solstice. But we'll need some money for publicity."

"Well, that's easy enough," Dena said. "We can sell some of my mother's jewels. She has so many she won't miss a few."

"What sort of jewels?" he said. Dena saw his bulge swell with interest.

"Oh," she said slowly, teasing him so the bulge would continue to rise, "there's a diamond bracelet, an emerald pin, a turquoise and garnet brooch, one with rubies and seed pearls, several strands of pearls, an amber and gold necklace..."

"Stop!" he moaned. "I can't stand it. The amber necklace you must keep for yourself, and you should wear it as often as possible. Amber is a direct conductor of healing vibrations. But some of the other pieces I think we should sell. Could you bring in the diamond bracelet tomorrow? I have a reliable outlet."

"Why not?" she said, leaning forward so her crack would show above the scooped neckline of her dress. *There is a devil in me*, she thought, *but after all, my breasts are my one real asset, and I am a woman raising a child alone in the world.*

Dena and Danny were looking at old photos. There was one of Leah, Dena and Esther, all wearing the most outrageous hats. Dena's had a big satin bow nestled under the brim. It was green, she remembered, to set off her red curls. Leah had a pleated velvet hat piled on top of her head like a lampshade masquerading as a soup tureen with fringe. Blue, like her silk dress that Dena had envied because it was from Paris. With three baby white roses tucked into the pleats. Esther had a picture hat, like those Leah wore before she married Myron, only the brim wasn't as wide. On top were two giant feathers, drooping down like wilted grass huts or weeping willow trees.

But what interested Dena more than the hats was their heads, and not because poor Leah lost hers later, although for years she had dreamed of Leah's head flying across Miami Beach and landing in the ocean among the bathers.

No, what fascinated her was the expressions on the faces. Leah was twelve in the picture, and Dena was ten, the baby. They both stared straight into the camera, Leah as though she was challenging death, and Dena with a wounded look as though she knew someday her husband would leave her. But Esther stared away from the camera, off into space, refusing to acknowledge petty problems like love, or time or death. Dena had always wondered what Esther was looking at over there. She didn't like it when she didn't know what was going on.

Danny pored over this picture of his mother. "You were such a pretty little girl," he said.

"Yes," Dena said. "I was pretty." But never as pretty as Leah, she thought, even though every night she stretched her eyes to make them bigger, pushed the end of her nose up while she studied and developed a mysterious, closed-mouth smile, just like the Mona Lisa.

She missed Leah, of course, but it was nice to be the only girl left. Now she had her mother all to herself.

Unlike Leah, Dena was a distasteful child, Esther thought.

Plumply self-satisfied and self-centered. Even as an adult, she wore the same terrible smirk on her pudgy face. She thought it was a look of acceptance. Ah, poor Dena! Her walls were still papered with old movie stars: Lillian Gish, Ruth Stonehouse, Mary Minter, Marguerite Clayton, Theda Bara, Mary Pickford, Edna Mayo, Billie Burke, May Allison. All the beauties of the age, their eyes dark and dreaming, surrounded the young Charles Chaplin, who watched Dena at night and woke her in the morning.

"Good morning, Dena," Esther imagined him saying. "Too bad you never looked like these women on your wall. You might have had a different life--Hollywood glamour, the shimmer of stars. Instead of a sickly child, an aging mother, a dark, smoky house."

Well, no. Esther had to admit that Chaplin was serious and brooding, but not mean. He would tell Dena he loved her. And poor Dena must regret that she married Earl and not someone like Charles.

But Esther knew that Earl was not a mistake. Dena was lucky to find him after that night in Arizona with the gas station man. They were on their way across the country, Nathan driving, all of them cranky from the desert heat. The way Dena eyed that scruffy fellow when they stopped for gas, Esther knew there would be trouble if they didn't move on. Nathan, oblivious as usual, said of course they could stay in the motel behind the station.

Twilight. They ate their first Mexican food in a dingy café, and there was that man, tall and cadaverous, a stringy mustache, watching Dena from the next table. What could Esther say? She often wondered at the fools who throw their truths like pebbles at a concrete wall of denial.

That night Dena put on red lipstick, fixed her hair and took a walk. She came back disheveled to their room at three in the morning, and Esther knew Dena's girlhood was gone. Probably, being nearly thirty, she had waited too long for a man, and by then there was no stopping her.

But when they were settled in California, in this house Nathan and Samuel bought for them, and Dena insisted on working as a waitress, she found Earl, playing organ in some local bar. Found him before she was wretched with morning sickness, so he never knew. Nor did Danny. Probably Esther was the only one now who knew, because Dena was so good at forgetting. Earl was a weak man, Esther thought, but he served his purpose. Now they had Danny.

Danny was glad that he had inherited his musical talent from his father, and he knew if Earl were still here, he'd be proud of his son's ability. He dreamed that his father had given him a book of music. Eleven symphonies, one for each year he'd been gone. But in the dream Danny was Earl's wife and the music an anniversary present. Wearing a white hat, he looked like Aunt Leah, who died in a car crash. His father was so handsome, when he touched Danny, he couldn't breathe. He woke up gasping, and his mother had to give him oxygen. Then he was calm, like a child again nursing at his mother's breast.

"You have to sell the bicycle," his mother said that afternoon. "And stop with the barbell exercises."

But he'd only won the Schwinn last month from a contest

on KTLA, dark red, model D 19, and it was worth seventy-five dollars. His mother didn't understand that the bicycle and the barbells would make him strong for his father.

Danny was sure his father still loved them. His mother had never told him this, but Danny had finally figured out why Earl had left. He was given a job conducting an orchestra, probably in Europe. He was never satisfied playing the piano at Woody and Eddy's, and how could he be? Danny knew conductors made a lot of money, wore tuxedos and performed in big halls where thousands of people listened and applauded. Woody and Eddy's was crowded; his mother said people paid more attention to their steaks than to his father.

In Danny's dream his father was tall, and thin, like Danny. He had a long, drooping mustache, although Danny didn't remember that. How could he? He was little when his father left, and his mother had burned his pictures. But Danny felt his dream was a sign that his father would return before too long and would probably buy Danny a grand piano. By then he'd be ready.

Danny's math teacher had introduced him to Mr. Meyerson, the head of the college music department. He looked at some of Danny's music and chose a piano concerto for their May concert. "Amazing," he said, "writing music like this at your age."

"But I'll be fifteen soon," Danny had said, which made Mr. Meyerson laugh. People take age so seriously, Danny thought, because they believe in numbers. They don't understand that numbers, like words and music, are to be played with.

"Thirteen is an unlucky number, and I'm not going to

play with you any more until you understand. You don't mess around with thirteen." Jessamyn and Danny were sitting outside in his back yard, while she ripped up handfuls of grass. Danny didn't say anything, even though he knew his mother would kill Jessamyn for ruining her lawn. Whenever Jessamyn got excited, she did things like that, even though it almost always got her in big trouble.

"Why," she said, "do you think they don't have thirteenth floors in buildings?"

"Of course they do," Danny said, laughing gently.

"Just go into any elevator," Jessamyn said, "and look. Twelve, fourteen."

"But the floor's still there. They've just changed the numbers."

"No," Jessamyn said. "The numbers tell the truth. You've got to believe the numbers or you'll go crazy like that man on our street who bought all those hamburgers and threw them at his wife until he ran out of hamburgers. Then he ran down the street absolutely bare naked, except that he was covered in ketchup."

"I suppose you think broken mirrors and black cats are bad luck," Danny said.

"Well, everybody knows about broken mirrors. Let's not be too stupid. But black cats, if they don't have yellow eyes, if they even have one blue eye and one yellow one, are all right."

"Okay." Danny lay back on the grass and stared at the sky as a large, hippo-shaped cloud drifted past.

"It's a good thing you said that, or we wouldn't be friends anymore, even if we are cousins."

Danny sat up abruptly. "What?"

Jessamyn felt a sharp pang of guilt. "Let's face it, I'm mean. But I wouldn't really be that mean, because you don't have any other friends."

"I know. The kids at the college think I'm funny- looking."

"Boy, if I were there, I'd punch their faces off."

Danny giggled at the idea of little Jessamyn punching one of his tormentors.

"It's because you're new," she said. "Kids don't trust new kids. When we came to Los Angeles, I was a new kid in first grade and kids hated me. I got stuck on the merry-go-round going faster and faster, all of us bunched up on the platform. 'Hey, let me off!' I shouted. But nobody would, so I threw up on the kid next to me. That was no fun, let me tell you. But you'll get over it,"

"No, they don't trust me."

"That's because you're too smart. And what can you do about that, take stupid pills? You take enough pills already."

"I know. That's why I fart a lot."

"Daddy says you should quit taking pills and spend a month with us. Which would be fine with me. I want to teach you to climb trees. We could start easy with the avocado tree; it has all those nice, flat branches for sitting on different levels. It's pretty low to the ground, so even if you fall, like Melissa did last week, you don't get more than a bloody nose. Then we could work our way up to the fir tree in the Heltons' front yard. From there you can see everything, if old lady Helton doesn't catch you."

Danny looked down. "I don't think I could."

"I might have to pull you a little where the branches get thick and say, 'Close your eyes, watch out for the needles!' But even Melissa can do it, and she's only seven. My hands won't be sweaty, so I'll go first, with you in the middle and Melissa last, in case you slip. When we're as high as we can go, we'll eat peanut butter and bologna sandwiches and dare each other to look down."

"Okay," Danny said. "As long as we'll always be friends."

"We have to be friends," Jessamyn said. "We're family."

"Not this family," Danny said.

The next Sunday night Kathleen called Esther *Mother*. Esther kept silent. How could she say, "I would never choose to have an Irish Catholic daughter"? Still, if it were not for David and his celebration, Esther might not have held back the truth. But Kathleen was saying it in the way of thanking Esther for the money, *such a constant flow*.

"And now," Kathleen said, "you'll see, we won't need it any more. David has sold his first novel." Her cheeks were flushed with the champagne, and she looked pretty in her red dress.

"You always wear red for Sunday dinners," Dena said. She was in a blue polished cotton wrap-around, which she had pulled much too tightly around her plump body, forcing her large breasts to billow up over the edge of her neckline with every breath she took.

"Oh, do I?" Kathleen said, wrapping an apology around herself until she almost disappeared.

"There is nothing wrong with red," Esther said. Dena sniffled and snuffled till Esther said, "Stop it." Then Dena ran wailing away from the table.

"Mother," David said, "this is my dinner of triumph. Can't

we all be happy?"

"Now I apologize," Esther said. "I am an old woman, cranky with the ebbing of life."

"That's not true," Kathleen said, "you're very generous of spirit."

"We love you, Gram," Jessamyn said.

Gram. The word lay heavy on Esther's heart, reminding her that she was their only living grandmother, now that Kathleen's parents had died.

"The sweetest woman in the world," David said, "who has always believed in me." He put his hand gently over Esther's in a way she could never resist. So sincere and reassuring.

"That's because you're a poet, like your father." Esther gave him that, just as she could give him anything but the total acceptance of his wife and children.

"A novelist now," he said. Laughing, in Benjamin's white suit that gave him a rakish look, with his olive skin and careless, dark hair. "And in my book people have learned the way to Heaven. Well? Don't you want to know the way?"

Esther was watching Benjamin move in behind his features. *Oh, Benjamin,* she thought, *if you were here, would you love me even though I'm old? Would you say, your hair has become silver with moonlight? Would you see the softness of my skin, so threaded now with lines, and call it beautiful?*

"Up a golden ladder," David said.

Do they think there's a fountain of gold in my closet, Esther thought, *and that's where the money comes from? No one ever asks, not even Dena who has not worked a moment since Danny arrived. Except for the caring of Danny, which is, as she always tells me, a full-time job. Of course, Benjamin left a great deal, although not as much as he thought*. Esther was glad he would never know how quickly money goes nowadays. He would feel foolish not to have left them more.

But with Samuel and Nathan's help, Esther knew they would be fine, she and Dena and Danny. Which was why she didn't mind having such busy sons, who expressed their caring by working hard in their father's business. Nathan and Samuel, the tobacco tycoons. Yes, someone needed to keep bringing money into the family.

But when David needed money and didn't ask--Esther loved his pride, so much like his father's—but when she saw David's face tightening and his shoulders bending, she dressed herself in her best black taffeta and took another piece to the jeweler.

"Are you sure, Mrs. Singer?" he always asked. "These are so fine. Such settings you don't find nowadays, not to mention the stones."

"No," Esther wished she could say, "I'm not sure. These are my inheritance, from my mother and grandmother, each piece secreted away in coat linings when we ran from the Czar. Their beauty shines with the hopes and tears of my ancestors. This ruby brooch with the tiny pearls hanging, I remember my grandmother wore it on her lace collar when we lit the Sabbath candles. I would have liked David's wife to have them. Now here she is, this Christian woman and her children who have no idea of the jewels they might have had. Sold for rent and hamburgers in a country where the streets were to have been lined with gold."

Esther turned away from the jeweler's kind eyes and looked at the case filled with wedding rings from the old country. At least she still had Bernard's engraved gold ring on her crooked finger, his pearls around her neck.

And her son David had sold a novel.

On March 16, 1952, Dena's Gem of Gold Tappan Gas Range, model CPAV669, valued at $375, arrived. Danny had won that, the ukulele, and the seven-piece silver tea set, valued at $250, from the TV Time contest. The night before, Mr. Wormser of KTLA took Danny and his mother to the station. Danny appeared on the show at 7:15 p.m. and received a magic book and souvenirs. After the show Mr. Wormser and Dell O'Dell took Danny and Dena to dinner. They had roast prime ribs, fruit cocktail, ravioli, salad, baked potatoes, peas, milk and spumoni at $3.75 each, which Danny and his mother could never afford.

At his doctor's insistence, Danny had sold his barbells and his Schwinn. "None of this exercise!" Dr. Rieger had said, frowning and shaking his head. Danny was depressed for a week after that, even though he made ten dollars on the barbells and fifty dollars on the bicycle.

But Danny began to feel better when he found out that he was going to be on "Time for Beany" next month, and he'd won three gallons of ice cream and five large bags of Fritos for Jessamyn and Melissa from Handy Hints, three Paper Mate pens (just for entering) for Gram, four bottles of Par-T-Pak for Aunt Kathleen, and for Uncle David a Voit basketball in a Quaker Oats contest.

On Tuesday Uncle David took Jessamyn, Melissa and Danny to the record store on Main Street in Alhambra. They went into a listening booth and played Miles Davis's "Birth of the Cool." Danny had never imagined anyone could write beautiful music like that. But he was going to try, even though Uncle David said jazz was very difficult.

After a while Melissa and Jessamyn were bored, so Uncle David took them all for chocolate ice cream cones. And then, when they came home, Uncle David gave Danny the Miles Davis record.

Uncle David said he was going to be rich now, that's why he could do such things. He sold a novel, *The Golden Ladder* he called it, and he said he would let Danny read it. He and Aunt Kathleen were so happy, Danny thought they looked taller, and their faces shone.

And that night Uncle David told Danny a secret. When he got the money, he was going to invest it in a special invention: a piggy bank that tipped its hat when you put money in. Danny wasn't as fascinated as he pretended to be, because he wasn't interested in saving modern coins.

When David and his family arrived the following Sunday, he was excited about something. He picked Danny up and spun him around. "Air and light," David said. "That's what you need."

"What are you talking about?" Dena scowled at David. But he just smiled. "We're going to experiment. First the mountains, then the ocean."

"No, you're not," she said, wiping her wet hands on her apron. "It's getting harder for Danny to breathe lately. He might have to go back in the hospital."

"No," Danny said. "Please don't let me go back there."

"No, no," David said, "we're going to Mount Wilson tomorrow to see the snow and, if we're lucky, a few stars."

Esther folded a smile away and harumphed at the idea of snow. "I thought we turned our backs on snow forever when we drove those many days to California."

"Snowballs," David said, "snowmen and"--he tipped his hat at Jessamyn and Melissa--"snowwomen."

"Count me out, I'm busy tomorrow," Dena said. "And you'd better check to see if the mountain roads are clear."

"Busy again, Dena?" Esther said. "You've been going out every afternoon. Where, I wonder?"

"To the moon," Dena said. "To the sun. Why this sudden interest?"

But one day Dena came home with a book on Theosophy, and Danny could tell by the grim line of Esther's mouth that she was upset.

"Why?" Dena said. "Do you think I'm not a good Jew? I go to Temple, observe the Sabbath, and I didn't marry a Christian."

"All the good it did you," Esther said.

Whenever Danny's mother and grandmother fought, Danny wanted to hide under his bed. But this time he felt sorry for Aunt Kathleen. And now he knew something for certain that he was afraid to ask: his father was Jewish.

That was another fact to write in the notebook he was keeping about his father: He'd written "Dreams and Facts about Earl Norman" in black ink on the cover. So far there were more dreams than facts, but someday, when he had enough information, he would write his own novel, with his father as the hero.

"Which do you like better," David asked, "snowflakes falling on your face or ocean spray?"

"Snow, snow, snow!" Jessamyn shouted. "That's a silly question. We go to the ocean all the time, but snow, that's something else."

Danny liked the snow too. He was grinning when Jessamyn pushed his big ears under his wool hat. Then she grabbed him around the middle and shoved him into a snowbank. They rolled over and over, giggling wildly, until Esther called, "Stop!"

"Okay, Gram, you're next!" Jessamyn said.

"I'm a bit too old, I'm afraid," Esther said, getting back into the car. But she gave Jessamyn her cane to use for the snowman.

When the snowman was finished, it didn't have a hat, so David said, "Let's change it to look like Gram." With a magician's flourish he pulled out of his jacket a pair of Esther's old glasses. He and Kathleen worked on the face, and Danny, Melissa and Jessamyn made the hair, pulled back in a little knot.

Esther was cuddled in a blanket in the car, but she kept rolling down the window to say, "That doesn't look at all like me." The corners of her mouth curled up slightly, as though she was holding in a smile, so they could tell she was pleased. Then Kathleen took pictures, one with Esther next to her own snowwoman.

They had spent such a long time in the snow that Kathleen's hands were blue inside her gloves, so they all went to the café that looked like a tiny green and yellow Swiss chalet and had hot chocolate.

As Jessamyn was blowing into her cup, she saw Danny's face through the steam. "Look at you!" she said, "so bright red."

"That's nothing," Kathleen said, "we're all red and sweaty."

But Esther took a closer look. "Not this red," she said.

"Drink up quickly and back into your coats," David said. "We're off." His voice was carefully casual, as though nothing was wrong.

Kathleen bundled up the children, and Esther put her fur hat from Chicago back on her head. Danny was breathing very fast, in and out, in and out, like a hummingbird, as David carried him to the car.

"Good thing we have a Studebaker, the all-weather car," David said. They took off with a loud roar and screeching tires.

"Be careful," Kathleen said. "We want to get home in one piece. You're skidding off the road."

"Let him drive fast," Esther said. She was holding Danny in her lap under the blanket, with Melissa on one side and Jessamyn on the other. "I'll never forgive myself," she said. Danny's eyes were closed.

"Is Danny going to die?" Melissa said.

Kathleen said, "Hush, just watch the snow."

When they were halfway down the mountain, the snow almost gone, a fawn ran across the road. David jammed on his brakes and slid into a baby fir tree. "I almost hit her," he said. Kathleen started crying. "Please," David said. "Not that."

As her father was backing the car into the road, Jessamyn saw the fawn running past the trees into an open space. And there, with the sun shining on their fur, was a huge deer family. Mothers, and fathers, aunts and uncles, cousins and babies, all staring at their car and then at the fawn running toward them. When it got to the edge of the meadow, a grandfather deer with gray in his fur and giant antlers stepped up to greet it.

Jessamyn pulled back the covers. "Look," she whispered to Danny. He opened his eyes. "Over there past the trees," she said in a voice so tiny the grownups wouldn't notice. He looked over at the deer, and just then the grandfather deer looked back, right into Danny's eyes.

Later, before they got to Danny's house and Dena started yelling, Jessamyn said, "Can you imagine walking around with heavy antlers on your head all the time? And never a chance to take them off, not even when you sleep?"

"He must sleep standing up," Danny said. "Try it tonight, with two encyclopedias on your head."

"Let me do it too," Melissa said.

They laughed until Gram said, "Shhhh," but her mouth didn't look sad again until they saw Dena standing in the yellow porch light.

"She looks like a wicked witch," Melissa whispered.

"Shut your mouth!" Jessamyn said. "Remember, Aunt Dena is Danny's mother." *And,* Jessamyn thought, *I'm glad she's not mine.*

"Idiocy," Dena said, "plain and simple. Who was the worst I just don't know. Kathleen you could expect it of because she never thinks of anyone but herself. Possibly David whose head is so full of crazy dreams I'm amazed he can drive a car. Then to hear that he almost hit a deer and skidded across the mountain road with my baby sick in the back, well, it staggers the imagination. I told them straight out they were fools."

"Good," Rabbi Saltzman said, "Hold nothing back, it's bad for your digestion. You should have realized Mount Wilson is no place to fool around with."

"All I can say is, never again. When Danny gets back from the hospital, he's staying inside, except to go to school. He's comfortable at home, safe, and I'm having the piano tuned so he can practice for the May concert." Dena paused in an unusual moment of uncertainty. "Do you think he should play?"

"Why not?" Rabbi Saltzman said. He was staring out the Temple of Health window at the crimson sun floating in his fish pond.

"Rabbi," she said. "I mean, Daniel, don't pick at your ming tree, you've asked me to remind you, and don't you think playing is too much? Having his concerto performed is enough of an honor, without all the exertion. And his doctor says..."

"Doctor, schmocktor," he said. "If you don't put your faith in me, we can call it quits."

"Never!" Dena said, picking up his cuticle scissors. "If you say another bad word, I'll stab myself right in the left aorta."

"What bad word?" he said. "And give me those scissors. They're special German steel."

"Quits!" she shouted. "Quits, quits is the bad word! Let's make no pretenses!" She was pacing around the edge of the Holy Healing Circle, careful to stay on the turquoise rim, and she waved the scissors into the incense, secure in her own special sense of melodrama.

"Dena, my little Dena," he said. "Stop where you are. Freeze your feet on the Green Star of Nature."

Her feet did just what he said. "You see?" Dena said. "You

have such power. And only forty-two, three years younger than I am. What is it, I wonder, that makes some people so wise?"

Rabbi Saltzman said modestly, "It came from working out with weights on Muscle Beach."

"That doesn't make sense," Dena said. "I'm not as dumb as I look."

"No," he said, "that was where I first received the healing call of God. I was a rabbi then in Santa Monica, and two afternoons a week I worked out on the beach. Well, one day I strained my back because I was pondering the nature of the universe and not paying enough attention to my body. As I lay in agony on the hot sand, I saw a young virgin with golden hair and a seashell bikini digging her toes into the wet sand by the ocean's edge. 'Speak to her,' God said, 'of the Imponderable.' 'I can't, Lord,' I said. 'My back is a mess.' 'Well, heal it then,' He said. I did, and ever since, I've had the power."

"Now, that, as far as I'm concerned, is an amazing story," Dena said. "But knowing you, I believe every bit."

Rabbi Saltzman strolled across the healing circle, while Dena watched his thigh muscles ripple under his white pants, and he took the scissors out of her fingers, which had gone limp.

"Let's have no more talk of stabbing," he said. "We have too much work to do to heal our dear little Danny. Now, let's make a list of the faces that you've seen on your fridge."

"Not counting Earl, there were Moses, Abraham, Isaiah, Solomon and one fuzzy Adam. But I don't think we can count him, he didn't come through clear enough."

"We can count him," he said, making a list in his elegant handwriting, indigo ink on pink healing paper. "We need all the help we can get."

"All right," Dena said. "Then maybe you want Ruth, who appeared, God knows how, on the surface of my lime Jell-O. I never mentioned her, because Jell-O manifestations seem to lack authenticity."

He said, "Nonsense," and Dena knew he meant it, which was a comfort to her.

"Splendid! Little Dena, what would you think of the Healing Center making an investment? I got a brochure in the mail yesterday that sorely tempts me. Piggy banks that tip their hats. Sound good?"

"Absolutely," Dena said, although she didn't think so at all. Her mind had wandered down to a warm place between her legs, as it often did.

When he leaned over and kissed her on the ear lobe, she could smell his English Leather aftershave. "Oh, Daniel," she said as she slid her fingers through his black, wavy hair.

Sex. Danny wrote in his journal. *It's something I don't think about. I've been too busy with music, writing, math, or just trying to breathe. So I suppose in a way what happened at the college is my fault. I should've seen, should've been alert when that big, beefy fellow Steve asked me for math help. Should've remembered he laughed at me in class when I gave answers. And not because I was wrong, but because I'm too young.*

What an insult it must be to be nineteen, unable to comprehend the mystery of numbers, and to have some skinny little fourteen-year-old analyzing problems with the professor.

Danny remembered the way Steve had approached him

after class. Grinning sheepishly as he leaned over Danny's desk. "Listen, kid, I'm having trouble in this class, and you're our resident genius. Could you spare me a little time, just to go over stuff?"

"I guess so," Danny had said.

"How about Thursday? I don't have football practice then," Steve said. "We'll meet in the second floor lounge."

Danny realized he must have been flattered, drawn in by the promise of being accepted for once, and by an older athlete.

Three o'clock. Bright sun mingled with dust in the empty lounge, covered the cracked orange plastic chairs and the Pepsi-ringed Formica table with a sad beauty. Danny was mulling over the homework problems when Steve pulled two beers out of his athletic bag.

"Oh, no," Danny had said. "We can't drink beer in here. And anyway, I don't drink alcohol. I'm too young." He didn't say he was sick, especially with cystic fibrosis, because he wanted so much to be one of the healthy people who take breathing and exercise for granted. And was there a warning on one of his bottles that said not to mix alcohol with the medicine? He couldn't remember.

"Don't be a jerk," Steve had said, and he opened Danny's can of beer. What power! What simple, definite movements! He owned the earth and Danny loved it, so he took a sip and gagged.

Steve laughed and slapped Danny on the back. "Tell you what," he said. "Let's play chug-a-lug. It's a game the guys play, only we'll take it slow because you're new at it."

Within twenty minutes the room was spinning. "I'm not sure I can help you now," Danny had said.

Steve rumbled a loud burp. "Oh, I bet you can."

"What did you say?" Danny felt himself falling into the faded print on the wall and saw his voice spin right out of George Washington's mouth.

"Look at this." Steve's math notebook was open, but there were no math problems. Just pictures: women with nothing on and their legs spread wide, naked men playing with themselves, men and women together doing things Danny didn't want to think about.

"Don't." Danny covered his eyes.

"What's the matter, jerk? Didn't you ever watch your mother and father doing it?"

"Don't talk that way. That's ugly," Danny said.

"Ugly," Steve sneered at him. "Maybe you don't like the women, but I bet you like the men, you little fairy."

He grabbed Danny and kissed him on the mouth.

When Steve let him go, his whole body was trembling. He backed to the door, opened it, staring at Steve, at his big, nasty smile, backed out and slammed the door. Clinging to the bannister, Danny stumbled down the shuddering stairs.

"Earthquake!" someone shouted, and as Danny fell to the floor, he hoped the earth would swallow him.

"What happened to you?"

Danny opened his eyes and saw Jessamyn leaning over his hospital bed. "How long have you been here?"

"I just snuck in. We didn't even know you were back in the hospital till today."

"Yes," Danny said. "I got sick again."

"Is that why you quit school?"

"I suppose."

"Did you get in trouble?"

Danny felt a surge of love for Jessamyn because she was so earnest in her efforts to protect him. "I never get in trouble."

"But something happened, didn't it?"

He pulled the covers up to his neck. "I don't want to talk about it."

"Hey," she said, trying to cheer him up. "We did your immigrant play for all the fifth and sixth grade classes. I was Great-Grandpa, the rabbi in Kiev, with a mustache."

A little smile crept around Danny's mouth.

"They wouldn't let me shave my head so I'd look like a man."

This time he laughed. "Thank goodness! That would've been totally wrong."

"Well, at least I remembered to take off my gold cross. Here. I decided to give it to you." She held it out, but Danny wouldn't take it.

"I can't wear a cross. I'm Jewish."

"I'm pretty Jewish, don't you think?"

"No, not if your mother's not Jewish." He closed his eyes. "You wear it."

Jessamyn put it back on, but she was mad, the way she always got when she didn't understand something. "Why can't I be Jewish if I want to? And if I'm not, what's the matter with me and my mother and Melissa? I look Jewish, don't I?"

"What does that mean?"

"I've got dark hair and eyes, like you."

"Don't be stupid."

She could tell he was getting annoyed, but she couldn't stop herself. "Couldn't my mother be Jewish if she decided to?"

"No. You can't just decide. God decides before you're born." He kept his eyes closed, so she kicked the wall and the nurse ran in.

"You'll have to go now, dear. Little Danny needs his rest."

"Hell! " Jessamyn said, watching the bad words march out of her mouth like soldiers. "He does not! He's just pretending!"

The nurse smacked her bottom and dragged her out of the room. "Here!" She shoved Jessamyn at Kathleen, who was waiting in the corridor. "Take her, and don't bring her back!"

Kathleen sighed the way she always did when Jessamyn did something mean. "What did you do this time?"

"I said 'Hell'."

"That's all?"

"No, I said he was just pretending to be sick."

"But you know that's not true, darling," Kathleen said. "He's a very sick boy, and you shouldn't upset him."

Their voices faded away as they walked down the hall, and Danny felt a loneliness so intense he wanted to throw up. "Come back," he whispered. But they were already gone. The room was suddenly filled with shadows. "I want my father," he murmured. "I want..." And then he was asleep.

"Don't tell Daddy, okay?" Jessamyn asked her mother as they were pulling into the driveway. "Danny knows I can't help myself sometimes. Last year he made me a sign: 'PICK THE TOENAILS OUT OF YOUR TEETH.' Which means, Danny says, to keep my mouth shut so I don't get foot-in-mouth disease."

"I won't," Kathleen said. "Your father has enough to worry about."

"Promise? Because otherwise I'm not getting out of the car."

"I promise. But don't do it again. And help me with the groceries."

Jessamyn took the heaviest bag out of the trunk to impress her mother. "Mom? Do you think I look like you?"

"I think so," Kathleen said. "Come on, now, don't dawdle."

As they were putting away the groceries, Jessamyn said, "People say I'm pretty like you so I must be sweet."

"I know," Kathleen said, "but that's before they get to know you."

Jessamyn giggled. "That usually takes strangers about half an hour until I deliver the old one-two punch and kick. Ka-pow! Leave 'em gasping, it's safer that way."

"Someday, darling, you'll learn it's just as safe to be nice."

"It's not, and it never will be."

At dinner that night Kathleen argued with David about his new piggy bank factory. Jessamyn had seen the warehouse in El Monte that her father had bought with the money he got from his novel. There were pink plastic lady pigs and blue plastic gentlemen pigs, and when you put a penny in, their hats bounced up.

"It's a crazy idea," Kathleen said. "Why don't you just write? That's your talent. Do you have to get involved in all these crazy business schemes your friends talk you into?"

"This one is solid!" David's eyes sparkled. "Solid as the earth!"

Jessamyn remembered the earthquake a few days ago, 5.1 on the Richter scale, but she kept her mouth shut.

"Why is it everybody but you gets rich on these nutty ventures?" Kathleen said. "Fountain pen necklaces, a newspaper for the deaf, whatever it is, they walk away with gold in their pockets, and you stand in the big graveyard of ideas like a penniless fool!"

"The difference is this time I'm getting a lawyer to draw up the contract. And besides, I trust George like my own son."

"You have no son," Kathleen said. Jessamyn put her fingers in her ears and walked away.

"Danny is worse, there's no doubt about it, and if it weren't for your reassuring words, I'd be in pieces with terror," Dena said. She and Rabbi Saltzman were drinking ginger tea in the Healing Center office. "I blame it on Earl, first of all, for leaving us, and on David and silly Kathleen, taking him up to freeze and catch his near death."

"They were very careless, no doubt about it." Rabbi Saltzman's face was stained blue, green, red and gold from the sunlight streaming in through the stained glass windows.

"And he so weak, he fell down those stairs two weeks after he went back to the college. But now no matter what David says, when Danny comes home, I'm keeping the blinds closed with no visitors. Especially not those crazy children who get him flushed and excited. Mother reads him Russian stories when he's too tired to do his own reading, and that's fine. He can stay in bed and listen. Should I move his bed into my room?"

"He's too old, little Dena, even if he is sick. He needs privacy."

"You are the only one who could say those words to me," Dena said. Sometimes she felt guilty about taking her mother's jewels without asking. But then she convinced herself that her mother didn't really care about them. After all, she let the children play with them, and she herself never even looked at them, Dena knew, because she watched everything that went on in their house. And who, she asked herself, would ever quibble with the cause they're paying for?

She had only given Daniel a few pieces so far, because she liked to keep the power in her hands while they organized the Grand Healing for Danny. And Daniel was saving them, he said, until he had a pile to sell. In the meantime, he put them in the Holy Crystal Container to catch the sun's power. That way, they would ultimately be worth more.

Since Dena had become the executive secretary of the Healing Center, she had discovered her organizational talents. Sometimes she was amazed by all that time she had wasted being a waitress. But perhaps she needed those years of suffering to teach herself her true worth?

She had drafted a letter to the West Coast healers that Daniel said was worth its weight in gold. And she had perfected her telephone manner until it was irresistible.

"Hello, Healing Center," she would say in deep, liquid tones. "Do your vibrations need rearranging? Come to the source of power."

People were practically beating down the doors to join their workshops, and Daniel said he might let Dena lead "Healing the Rosacrucian Way" in May. She was also painting the In-Depth Room a special silver-blue in preparation for Danny's healing.

"When can I bring Danny over?" she said. "We can trust him to keep quiet and not tell Mother."

"Impatient as usual," Daniel said. "Wouldn't you want the Center to be perfect for him? We still have work to do."

"But he is getting worse," she said "I feel the urgency. Perhaps we'd better hire a couple of painters to help me."

"Nonsense." He nibbled her ears, which left her cross-eyed with desire. "We're working on Universal Time. Where's your faith? And besides, you do such a good job painting."

"It's wonderful to be accepted by someone like you. I never dreamed of such a thing, not even in my wildest." She traced her fingertips down his chest and stopped just below his belt. Very near, but not touching his bulge. Not yet.

"This is more than acceptance, Dena," he said. "I'm beginning to think it may be..." He hesitated, biting his beautiful lip. "... personal love."

Two days before Danny was scheduled to play his piano concerto in the college concert Dr. Rieger released him from the hospital. Dena wasn't sure Danny was strong enough, but Danny insisted, and Dr. Rieger said it was all right if Danny was careful. The morning of the concert Dena gave Danny an extra dose of vitamins, even though he said he felt fine.

That evening, with Dena's reluctant permission, Jessamyn walked with Danny down the middle aisle of the concert hall. When she saw a group of football players looking at them and whispering, she knew there was going to be trouble. Both of them were dressed up, Danny in his brown corduroy suit and Jessamyn in a pink dress with three crinolines, white bobby socks with pink scalloped edges and pink ballet slippers. Dena, David, Kathleen and Esther were all sitting in the front row, reserved for student composers and their families.

Danny played so beautifully Esther found herself weeping, and even Dena wiped her eyes, carefully, so she wouldn't smear her mascara. "He's an absolute genius," Kathleen whispered to Dena and Esther.

After the concert Danny came out to take his bow. The whole audience rose, clapping furiously, but the football players whistled, stamped and catcalled. One huge, lumpy blond athlete yelled, "Hey, honey! Hey, sweetie-pie!"

"Why are they doing that?" Aunt Dena asked. Jessamyn could tell her grandmother was confused too, but her mother and father were turning murderous red, so she knew they were figuring it out, just the way she was.

Don't you worry," Jessamyn said. "It doesn't mean anything. Just college kids." But she started to lay her plans.

When everyone was standing around over the punch and cookies telling Dena how wonderful Danny was, Jessamyn saw the athletes start to move in on Danny. So she moved in on them.

Danny was halfway across the foyer, holding his punch glass in a dreamy way and not noticing anything. The athletes got there first, and the blond put his face down next to Danny's.

"Hey, sugar-puss."

Danny stiffened as though he'd been electrocuted. He dropped his punch glass, and the guy bent down in a mocking way to pick it up. Jessamyn zoomed up like a speeding bullet, kicked him in the rear end and knocked him off balance. He fell over, and Jessamyn poured her punch on his head.

Just as a deep growl was coming up from his intestines, she said, "Good-bye, Shit-for-Brains," grabbed Danny's hand and took off. They zigzagged through the crowd and out the front door before anyone noticed.

"Where are we going?" Danny said when they were waiting for the bus on Colorado Boulevard.

"I don't give a damn. How about Cuba?"

"Don't be silly." He was breathing hard, but he was laughing.

"Well, we'll figure it out when we get to downtown L.A.," Jessamyn said. "How much money do you have?"

"Two dollars. And a seventy-five-dollar savings bond Gram just gave me."

"That should pay for our airplane tickets."

They arrived at the main bus terminal in downtown L.A. just before midnight. "Okay," Jessamyn said, "we've got to make some decisions."

"I'll do whatever you want," Danny said. So she left him on an empty bench and went to check for airport buses.

The downtown terminal was disgusting, Jessamyn noticed, especially at night when the neon lights came on and the bums came out from the sewers. She waited for about fifteen minutes in what she thought was the information line but turned out to be the line for the Cleveland bus. Finally she started getting nervous because people were staring at her cute little pink dress and ballet slippers as though she was the Sugar Plum Fairy in Hell. She found the information booth, and the man told her they had to walk back up to Hill Street.

When she came back to the bench, there was a bearded

bum, in a dirty housedress and lace gloves, hanging all over Danny, trying to get money to visit his mother in Kansas City.

"Come on," she said to Danny, even though she could see how tired he was. "Let's get out of here."

They went outside, into a slimy downtown area. Jessamyn had her arm around Danny's waist to protect and support him, but she was amazed at how heavy her skinny cousin could be when he was leaning on her. She dragged him along the broken sidewalk, trying to avoid the bums, the dog shit and the greasy hot dog wrappers blowing around.

When they were almost to the corner, she felt Danny slipping down. "Jessamyn," he said, "I wonder if I'm dying."

"Oh, hell!" Jessamyn said, as Danny collapsed right into an oily puddle. "Oh, damn it! We need help!"

And suddenly there were two ladies right next to them, as though they were sent by God. Jessamyn was bent over Danny, so first she saw only their spiky-heeled patent leather shoes.

"Hey, kids, what's the problem?" one of the ladies said, cracking her gum nice and loud the way Jessamyn always tried to do.

"My cousin is sick," Jessamyn said.

"He sure is," the other lady said.

"I guess we need a doctor right away," Jessamyn said, "because we're in a rush."

"What's to rush?" the first lady said. "You got your whole life ahead of you."

"Maybe," the other one said.

They eyeballed each other while Jessamyn stared at them. Both ladies were pretty in a run-down way, with teeny-tiny shorts and strapless tops. Even though they dressed the same, they looked different, because one was pale with lots of silver hair piled in a mound on her head, and the other was probably Mexican, with straight black hair down to her rear end.

"I'm Sylvie," the blonde one said, "and this is LooLoo. Come on up to our place, and we'll fix you a cup of tea."

"We don't really need tea," Jessamyn said. "What my cousin needs is medicine. We're on our way to Cuba."

"How cute!" LooLoo said.

Sick as Danny was, he started to laugh, which only made him cough.

"Look," Sylvie said, "you can't leave your cousin on the street in an oil puddle. First thing to do is get him up to our place, and we'll call for help."

So, what else could Jessamyn do? They carried Danny through a door next to a bar named "NITE LIFE," and up three flights of grungy stairs, while she followed. Their room was very clean though, with just a couple of mattresses on the floor. On one wall was a calendar with a picture of a cow in a snowy field and all the past days X'd off in black pencil. They had three windows with no shades or curtains, and in one window there was a big red neon heart flashing on and off. On every third flash a blue word appeared in the center, so the sign went: red heart, red heart, red heart with blue "LOVE" in script.

"That window is nice," Jessamyn said as they laid Danny down on a mattress. "Now, can we call the doctor?"

"Pretty soon," LooLoo said, "but, see, we don't have a phone in here, so we got to borrow the guy next door's. What's your names, so we can tell the doctor?"

"John and Mary," Jessamyn said. She didn't want to give

their real names so they could call Aunt Dena. Not unless she had to.

"John and Mary what?"

"Mullen." That was the name of her last year's teacher.

"Where do you live?" Sylvie asked. She was sitting cross-legged next to Danny and taking his pulse.

"Beverly Hills." Jessamyn wasn't thinking very fast, or she would have known they'd get excited over that one.

"Jeez, Syl, they must be worth a ton!" LooLoo said.

"If you think you can hold us for ransom," Jessamyn said, "you should know our parents are all in France at an unknown resort and they won't be back for a year."

Jessamyn thought that really impressed Sylvie. She looked at Jessamyn, then at Danny. "Get your ass out of here, Loo," she said, "and onto the phone. Try Giovanni, and maybe bring him back with you."

Danny's breathing didn't sound good, so Jessamyn lay down next to him while Sylvie painted her nails.

"What makes your hair stay up like that?" Jessamyn said, trying to be friendly.

"French bread," she said. "I got a loaf inside, one of those round ones, with my hair pinned to it. Then I spray it all over."

Jessamyn sat up and stared at Sylvie's hair: there were tiny bugs crawling around in it. But she didn't say anything and soon she fell asleep.

"Christ, he's blue!" A clown was standing over them, with a bright red smile painted on his face. "Those fucking paramedics better get here fast. You could get charged with murder!"

"Shut your fucking mouth, Giovanni," LooLoo said. She looked down at Jessamyn. "Honey, this is Giovanni, who let us use his phone. The doctors'll be here any second."

"Why is a clown in here?" Jessamyn said.

"Part of my sex act down at the NITE LIFE." he said. "See, first I come out as a clown, tell a coupla dirty jokes, then I..." He screamed, because LooLoo had stepped on his foot in her high heels.

"Accident," she said. "Got any uppers, Syl? I ain't used to helping anyone, it kinda wears me out."

Then two doctors carrying a stretcher came in.

"Always wanted to see a joint like this," one doctor said.

"Shut up," the other one said. "Where's the kid?"

Sylvie pointed at Danny.

"Jesus, Mary and Joseph!"

"You shouldn't take the Trinity in vain," LooLoo said.

"How'd you get mixed up with these characters?" the first doctor asked Jessamyn. "Nice kid like you in a pink dress. And what's the matter with your brother? Is he dying?"

"That's not his brother, it's his cousin," LooLoo said. "And for your information, we are his aunts and his uncle."

"Thanks, Sylvie and LooLoo," Jessamyn said as they left. "And you, too, Giovanni. Shall I call to let you know when he's better?"

"Don't bother," LooLoo said. "I got a massive headache."

In the ambulance Jessamyn told their real names to Dr. Boyd and his assistant, James, who wasn't a real doctor but liked to dress up like one. Dr. Boyd told her this privately, but said not to mention it or James would get hurt feelings.

In the Emergency Room they put Danny in an oxygen tent and called Dena. Jessamyn could hear her screaming like a wild animal.

After Danny was transferred to Huntington Hospital, no one in the family would speak to Jessamyn, not even her parents, who said she would have to stay in her room every day after school until Hell froze over. And she couldn't see Danny, who was sicker than ever.

Lost in his dream, Danny cried, "Over here, Father, over here! I'm on the mountain. Look up, you can see me in the sunrise, black against gold. Like an Indian dancing in the desert, a pharaoh riding across a mirage of sands.

"Oh, see my voice bounce down the rocks! Lost. Why not? There was no substance in that fragile sound. But your name is not Father, is it? Dad? Daddy?

"Why do I know all the answers to the wrong questions?

"In the cave, playing music. In the cave. Well, I can't come in, there's a lion outside. Why is a lion in the desert? Why does he guard your cave?

"I'll wait for you in my striped silk tent on the mountain. Green and white stripes blow like flags. Because there's a wind up here when God breathes. A hot wind, makes me sweat so much I could drown in my own salt water, like a river of tears racing down gold-veined rocks.

"Take your time down there. I've waited my whole lifetime, what's the rush? I'm watching my lungs fill up on an eight millimeter viewer I won from Handy Hints, value $8.00. Mucus deathly white, yet slightly opalescent. We've got jars and jars filled with the slime of your son's life, if you want a closer look at real obscenity.

"I've got a present for you: a wooden bench from the Rose

Bowl, first prize in Easy Sloman's contest in the Independent, December 31, and it was just delivered.

"Cold up here now. God is both hot and cold, something they don't tell you. A refrigerator with fire inside. Frozen flames.

"All right. Father, Dad, Daddy, pick your name, take your ticket, get on the train, in the car, and come to your son. Get up out of that desert and come. Carry me in your arms, close to your heart.

"Oh, Earl Norman, I want you," he moaned aloud, reaching into the night.

Esther had to do it, there was no choice. All her prayers went nowhere; she could feel them hovering on the ceiling at night. Not one ascended to the Holy of Holies, where God had taken Danny's spirit and left his voice murmuring, "Father, Dad, Daddy" till she couldn't endure it.

When she saw the advertisement in the paper, she knew that was her last hope. "Have you lost anything? I will find it for you. Psychic readings, only ten dollars, guaranteed. Call Madame Olivia, AT 7-3993."

She made an appointment for that very afternoon, left the hospital and took the bus all the way down Huntington to South Pasadena. Madame Olivia greeted her at the door of her pink stucco house. A scrawny little thing, surely no more than thirty, gaudy with rhinestones and shawls, but her eyes were bright and clear. When she said, "Now, Esther, whom have you lost?" Esther knew she could trust her, because she had told her nothing on the phone.

"Benjamin," she said, "my husband, but you cannot help me with that. No, I am here to find Earl Norman for my grandson, who is dying of cystic fibrosis."

While Madame Olivia studied her cards, Esther studied the statues in her living room. Some no more than two inches tall, others as large as six feet. Little carved wooden owls and Indians with painted headdresses, poised solemnly on a table draped with a woven black and gold tapestry. Pink glass angels on lighted blue glass shelves. An ebony African dancer, an ivory pharaoh's head. The two largest were a shabby blue and white Virgin Mary, the paint peeling like a skin disease from her unhappy face, and a Saint Francis with missing toes and fingers, smiling blandly as awkward birds perched on his head and arms.

Showing Esther a card with an exotic empress, Madame Olivia gazed at her seriously. "You've never done this before."

"No." That was all Esther could tell her, not the agony which drove her to violate the sacred boundaries of her heritage by visiting a psychic.

"All right. Then I will tell you: you are this woman, and your inheritance is not what you believe. It is an inheritance of power."

"Yes, yes." Esther nodded, impatient with this vaguely mystical way of speaking.

"Esther." She traced circles with a scarlet fingernail on the smoky glass table. "Listen to me. You are changing, becoming transparent, like my glass angels. I would like to help you to understand, so the transformation does not frighten you."

"Please, Madame Olivia," Esther said. "Time is pressing. I am not, at this moment, in the least concerned with myself."

"Yes." She shrugged, impatient now with Esther, and her shawl slid away from her bony shoulders. "All right." She turned over a new card, a jester dancing on the rim of a ball, with "The Fool" printed underneath. "I see the man you search for. He is in the desert," she said. "In Tucson, Arizona. Playing music in a bar called 'One-Eyed Pete's'."

She served Esther musky tea in a white porcelain cup with gold dragons painted on the outside. "Now I am going to give you advice. You must write to him quickly, because he is a restless man who can't stay long in one place. Your letter will be his salvation."

Esther gave her the money and thanked her, although she could see her gratitude was received with indifference. All the way home on the bus she kept thinking, Why not write to Earl? She had, after all, come this far.

Their shadowy house reeked of damp carpet smells, emptiness and longing. Esther rested on the edge of her bed in a sort of trance; then she rose, as though she were being pushed by spirits. She took a sheet of blue stationery and a matching envelope from her dresser drawer into the kitchen.

Faint, very faint, but there it was again: Earl's cigar smoke, which poor Dena had never eradicated.

Esther sat heavily at the table and swept Dena's toast crumbs off the yellow Formica. Her veined and spotted hand picked up a pen, and she watched it write: "Dear Earl, Please come home. Danny is dying, and he needs you."

And she sent her letter out into the desert.

Part Two

Tucson, 1952

Seven o'clock on a pastel evening and Earl lullabied the desert sun. Everyone in One-Eyed Pete's was sodden-weepy from cheap red wine and rum-soaked banana bread, Pete's latest culinary experiment.

"God, I hate this stuff!" Violette, her breasts draped comfortably over the bar, wolfed down her fourth piece. "Especially with tears on it."

Pete glared at her with his one good eye and his one painted eye. "So, leave it for the customers."

"I can't, it's addictive." Violette wiped her big hands on the greasy ruffles of her French maid's apron, then traced a purple fingernail along the edges of Pete's eye patch. "Why did you paint that eyeball red?"

"I told you, to scare people." As he grabbed her wrist, Violette's chin dropped into the bowl of melting butter. "And look, Vi, don't ever touch the art work, it makes me nervous. This is a genuine reproduction of a famous Irish hero's eyeball, Koohoolan, his name was. See the drops of blood at the end of each eyelash?"

But Violette was gone. Her curly head rested peacefully on a tray of maraschino cherries, while butter from the tilted bowl ran down into the crack between her breasts.

"What an angel," Harriet said, plunking her tray of dirty glasses on the bar. "What a complete doll. Vi's got a lover a minute, and it don't even matter if her stockings are ripped."

Harriet straightened her gaunt, gray frame, rested her hands on her hips and thrust her ruffled chest forward. "What'd'ya think, Pete? Could I ever be a sex object?"

Pete turned away from Harriet's desperate parody. "Sure. Only you got to find what works. Maybe if you wore pants instead of that French maid's outfit..."

"Pants don't show off my legs like these opera stockings do. When a girl's got the longest legs in Tucson, she..."

Pete sighed. "Never mind. Do whatever you want. Only maybe you could arrange that Kleenex in your bra so it don't look so lumpy." He resisted the impulse to caress Violette's impudent ass.

Violette was no longer his lover. He had let her go, as he had his two wives, had watched her ride her bicycle, with her white parrot perched on the handlebars, out into the desert.

Pete was a victim of his own indifference, which covered his feelings like a layer of cold fat. Nothing really interested him until he had lost it, this time to Earl, his best friend. And, Pete added to himself with habitual approbation, the greatest musician in the desert.

"Goodnight, Irene, Irene goodnight.

Goodnight Irene, goodnight Irene,

I'll see you in my dreams."

While Earl's baritone led the aggressively maudlin voices of the customers huddled around the piano, Pete studied him in the Budweiser mirror. A small man, slightly balding, fifty years' worth of lines sharply etched on his face, he attracted women the way blood draws mosquitoes. No need to wonder why. Pete knew it was Earl's virile cynicism that kept women panting and sobbing.

"Look," he had said three days after Violette had moved in with Earl, "you gotta let up on the sex. Violette's so tired she's turning into a lousy waitress. She falls asleep standing up while she's waiting for change."

They were outside the bar then, watching the sun trim the

sagebrush with orange haloes. Violette was inside, snoozing on Earl's piano bench.

"Whaddya mean, sex?" Earl flipped his Lucky Strike into the burning afternoon.

"Whaddya mean, sex?" Pete mimicked, struggling with his unruly jealousy. "Whaddya do all night? I mean, you got any special positions?"

"I ain't all that interested in sex." Earl shrank back from Pete's intimidating fake eyeball. "Okay, okay, but no more than one or two fucks a night. The rest of the time we're reading Kant."

"What kinda talk is that? Reading can't? Can't what?"

"Kant. This guy who proves there ain't no God. Didn't ya ever read *Critique of Pure Reason?*"

At last! A chance to release his self-torture in a righteous cause. Pure joy surged through Pete's body as he punched his best friend in the gut.

Earl crumpled into the sand. "You bastard! Another move like that, and I'm quitting, taking Violette and all the customers with me, over to Freddy's." One of Pete's two major rivals, Freddy had no live music, but lured his customers with free cactus hors d'oeuvres and a pair of dancing snakes.

His energy was spent. "Okay, okay." Pete helped Earl up. "Lemme buy you a few beers and fix you a steak."

"None a that shoe-leather variety." Earl knew how to milk a grudge. "I got my pride."

That evening after the bar had closed, as a conciliatory gesture, Pete attended his first meeting of the Atheist Society. Twelve people, eleven of them women, were crowded into the living room of Earl's duplex apartment.

When Pete entered, one of the women giggled. "Oh, no, that makes thirteen! Who's gonna offer to leave?"

"Nobody." Earl, like a tiny Buddha, sat cross-legged on a bar stool, an open book on his lap. "We ain't superstitious here. This is," he gestured grandly at his devotees determinedly smoking and sipping black coffee, "the place of pure reason."

Pete had never seen more voluptuous women, including, of course, his dear, lost Violette. Most of the women wore peasant blouses, pulled artfully off the shoulders, full skirts and wide, glittery belts that cinched their waists and rearranged their flesh. Pete thought of juicy sausages, tied with string.

Violette herself wore yellow silk pajamas and perilously high heels. She tottered about, serving bitter black refills, while Earl droned on and on.

The women were amazingly bright-eyed, but the single male devotee, gray-bearded and wildly hairy, sat propped in a corner and snored. Halfway through the evening, Violette wrapped him in a Navajo blanket. Without opening his eyes, he reached out his hand and caressed her breasts in thanks.

By four in the morning Pete was exhausted from sitting too long in one position and overindulging in sexual fantasies. Furthermore, he had the caffeine jitters. Time to bid the old atheist crowd good-bye. His joints popping and snapping, he began to unfold himself piece by piece. His feet were numb.

"Hell!" he said.

"Well," Earl said, closing his book. "Time for discussion. Let's go back to page one, okay?"

Silence, profound and looming.

"Who wants to start?"

Pete looked around. Everyone, including Violette, was now unabashedly asleep. Draped over cushions and chairs, mouths open, they were covered by the beauty of hazy dawn light. Sadness crept up from Pete's tingling feet and settled heavily in his chest.

Prompted by a habit so ancient it surprised him, Pete raised his hand.

"Ha!" Earl said. "Look, everybody, our most promising student!"

"That was great stuff," Pete said, "but I got to take a leak. How about chewing over this God business in the fresh air?"

"Sure," Earl said.

As they carefully picked their way through the limp bodies, Pete noticed Earl's windows covered with photographs of the ocean. "Any reason you got photos on your windows instead a curtains?"

Earl shrugged. "Yeah. I hate the desert."

Outside, they stretched and blissfully sprayed the pink and white flowers growing three-dimensional in the rising sun.

"Too bad those folks fell asleep," Pete said.

Earl's face was radiant. "They always do. Being a thinking atheist is hard work. But each time they last a little longer."

Hands in their pockets, eyes squinting into the morning, they strolled past the inner-tube fence surrounding Earl's flat adobe building and leaned against Pete's blue Ford.

"So," Earl said, "are you convinced that the power of the mind is all that's important?"

Pete thought of the litter of sensuous flesh in Earl's living room. "Nah, I really ain't so sure."

"We gotta trust in reason, not faith. Know what I mean?"

"Faith, yeah, that's something else. I ain't so hot for the church. Not since I started havin' those Jesus dreams. I got sick and tired of Jesus comin' down off the cross every god-damn noon and trying to make me lunch with those nail holes in his hands. Nothin' worse'n a bloody burrito, and I told him so, too, for Christ's sake."

Pete was working himself into a frenzy. Hands clenched into tight little fists, he pounded the hood of his car. "But he's some kind of smart guy, lemme tell you that. Two nights ago he said, fine, he'd take me to lunch at a fancy restaurant. 'So, big deal,' I said. 'You think I wanna sit there while you embarrass me by gettin' blood all over the cloth napkins?'"

"That ain't exactly what I was talking about, but you got the right attitude. Come back next week," Earl said. "We're starting Spinoza's *Ethics*."

The next afternoon Pete was polishing the bar when Joe Karp, the mailman, peered into the gloom.

"Hey, Pete, you in there?"

"Yeah," Pete said. "Whaddya got? Any love letters for me?"

"Nah, but I got a letter for Earl. He comin' in today?"

"'Round six." Pete continued his polishing, moving on to the brass cash register, his pride. "Lay it on the piano, where he'll find it."

At five p.m. Harriet, in a stiff orange wig and yellow flowered overalls, began her shift. She hid her orange plastic purse behind the bar, admired her lavender lips in the Budweiser mirror, then started to pick up last-night's litter from the tables.

"What a mess, what a goddamn mess," she muttered as she

dumped mounds of cigarette butts into a grocery bag.

Saloon area cleanup was the sole responsibility of Harriet and Violette, a fact Pete had made clear when he hired them. "The bar area is mine, and I keep it shiny. You dolls take care a the rest."

"Fine with me," Harriet had said. "I'm a Virgo, one of the caretakers of the universe."

Pete knew nothing of astrology but felt that an intellectual waitress would add class to his establishment. Especially as a contrast to Violette's sloe-eyed sensuality.

Violette had kept quiet, but she was a Pisces, as Harriet knew from their former high school days, and therefore lazy. Also self-indulgent. And now that she was falling asleep everywhere, in the most ridiculous positions…

Harriet zoomed around the room in a righteous fervor. Swish of the sponge. Plop of the butts. Swish, plop, swish, plop! Her sponge swept across the piano and stopped at the pale blue envelope addressed to Earl, with a return address from Altadena, California. "Uh, oh. Better hide this before Vi sees it." She shoved the letter into her back pocket.

By the time Earl and Vi arrived, Harriet had worked herself into a titillating frenzy. First of all, Pete was clearly stunned into speechless admiration by her sexy appearance. But more important, she had decided Earl was a primary turd. Imagine, carrying on with other women by mail, when he was killing dear Vi with his nightly sexual activity. Why, they must do it all night long, and in every conceivable position. Probably in every room of that duplex.

Harriet could visualize Earl and Vi, like X-rated gymnasts, fucking in the bathroom, on the stairs, on the kitchen table, under the bed, even on the television set. Standing, sitting, bent, crumpled, legs and arms going every which way, a human alphabet of sexy Chinese characters. Unthinkable! Harriet thought, as she bumped into tables, served customers the wrong drinks and forgot to pick up her tips.

"Hey, Hair," Earl said. "What'sa matter? Cat got your tits?"

At the very best of times Earl's stupid humor annoyed Harriet. But now, when... Just look at dear Vi, sleeping behind the bar in a puddle of beer! Could there be an example of more perfectly naive devotion?

"If you speak to me again, I will be forced to assault you." Harriet gave Earl a ferocious sneer, while his blue love letter burned her ass.

Earl leered at her in the way men do, Harriet was convinced, when they want to charm you into thinking they take you seriously. "Ooo, ooo," Earl said, underlining his words with a few heavy chords, "old Hair's a wild one, in them fancy pants. Aren't you, Hair?" Loud guffaws from the three male customers mournfully nursing their beers.

Enough was enough. Harriet marched straight to the bar. "Gimme a beer, Pete."

"No drinking on duty." Pete loved it when he got a chance to be tough.

"It ain't for me."

"Well, okay then." Pete nestled his foot under one of Vi's soft buns while he filled a mug with cheap draft.

"Thanks." Harriet clutched the mug determinedly and headed for Earl at the piano.

He was ready for her, all right, oozing sweet talk. "Hey, hey, there's a girl, old honey-pie, bringin' me a beer on the house," Earl sang in his sappiest voice.

"Not on the house, you rat-faced nightingale. On your head!" Splat! Harriet aimed the beer right at Earl's astonished eyes.

Before he had time to respond by mugging her or, even more likely, publicly raping her, Harriet had fled to the door. Safe in the doorway, she turned to face the furor she had aroused. "And that goes for the rest of you puke-brains! Except," she amended, "you, Vi," for Vi was now sitting up and arranging her breasts in a dazed manner.

Hoping for a satisfying smash, Harriet threw the beer mug to the floor. It bounced, rolled up to a wooden chair by the door and stopped. "Oh, damn!" Harriet said. "Damn and piss!"

Violette began to cry in her endearing way, beautiful tears like rhinestones running down her cheeks, so of course all the men turned to console her. Forgetting entirely about Harriet and her trauma.

Demon energy drove Harriet to stamp on the disappointing beer mug. Snap! The four-inch heel of her new orange patent leather shoe broke right off. She picked up the mug and hurled it out into the evening.

There was a loud *thwonk*.

"Shit!" someone yelled, followed by a heavy thud.

Oh, no, she must have killed someone! Harriet limped outside to see, and yes, indeed there was a man, apparently dead, lying on the path to the bar. Harriet studied him in the blinking red neon light. A tall gaunt man, with graying hair and a handlebar mustache, he wore a white robe tied around the waist with a rope.

"Don't die!" she said, for he was the most handsome man

she had ever envisioned. She bent down to caress his bare feet.

"Aargh!" The man jerked his feet away from Harriet's hands and jacknifed into a fetal position. He moaned and felt his forehead, where a large lump was forming over his right eye.

Harriet knelt abjectly in the sand. "I did it."

The man opened his eyes. There were two red-headed women appearing and disappearing in the pulsing red light. Gradually the two women coalesced into one shimmering beauty. "An angel," he said. "My God, I've died and gone to Christian heaven, and I didn't even believe in it."

"Can you ever forgive me?" Harriet said.

"Angels don't apologize," the man said. "In every Theosophical tract I've read it's clear that…" He clutched his stomach. "I'm going to puke. Now that I wouldn't expect. What a joke." He vomited weakly into the sand.

"I'll get some ice," Harriet said. "Stay there."

"Oh, rest assured," the man muttered.

Armed with a mission, Harriet marched into the den of her enemies.

Violette, still surrounded by men, was now ensconced in a mammoth wooden chair, carved and painted to resemble a totem pole. She alternated between soft sobs and hiccups as she sipped a bright pink drink through a straw.

"There, there," the men murmured to her. "Buck up." "Life ain't so bad."

Earl was playing "Sweet Violets." "Sweeter than the roses," he bellowed, and Violette managed a smile.

"Pete, gimme some ice," Harriet said.

"Get it yourself." Pete was busy mopping Vi's tears.

When Harriet emerged from the bar with a bucket of ice and a towel, the man was stretched out in a crucified position.

"You look like Jesus."

The man grabbed her ankle. "Who knows? A little to the left, you would have opened my third eye and released the Christ in me."

"I'm Harriet." She knelt down again and covered his forehead with an ice pack.

"Clyde here," he said. "Here, there and everywhere. Could you give me a gentle kiss?"

"Sure," she said. "I could probably manage gentle. See, it's been a very long time since I…"

"Don't worry," Clyde said. "Love conquers everything."

By the time the local motorcycle gang known as the Prickly Pears had roared up to the bar, Clyde had managed to sweep away Harriet's inhibitions. His white robe was open, Harriet's overalls were unzipped, and the path was strewn with the Kleenex from Harriet's bra.

"Look at that," the three-hundred-pound gang leader known as Monster said. "Pete's bringing the entertainment outside."

Zit, the youngest gang member, inspected the lovers. "If you think that's entertainment, Monster, you got a big problem."

Monster smiled beatifically. "Everything about me is big. Let's go have some a Pete's cheap draft."

When Clyde and Harriet wandered in at ten p.m., the bar was raucous with laughter and music.

"Forty-three bottles of beer on the wall,

Forty-three bottles of beer.

If one of those bottles should happen to fall,

Forty-two bottles of beer on the wall."

Harriet and Clyde, their arms entwined, watched the smoky scene from the door. "I wonder," Harriet said, "how long it's taken them to get to forty-two from a hundred?"

Clyde gave her a squeeze. "Long enough."

"Willya look at that!" Monster shouted. "The outside entertainment's inside."

Wide awake for the first time in weeks, Vi was briskly serving customers. She turned to the door, shrieked, and dropped to her knees. "It's the Lord!"

"Oh, for Christ's sake!" Pete said. "The busiest night in a month, and he's got to show up!" He stomped over to Clyde and grabbed the front of his robe. "Now, get this," he said. "Lunch is bad enough without you havin' to ruin my business."

"Unhand me, toad," Clyde said.

"Yes, unhand him," Harriet said. "He's mine."

Still clutching Clyde's robe, Pete glared at Harriet. "I don't know how you get so familiar."

"You shoulda been outside, you really wanta know," Monster said.

"Forgive me, Master, for I am sin," Vi said, shielding her eyes from Clyde's holiness.

Earl slammed his hands on the piano keys, and the gang froze in mid-song, their mouths open like angels'. "Okay," he said, "I've had it! This is the dumbest joke in the universe. I'm gonna count to ten, and you better get your ass outta here, Jesus, because every intelligent body knows you don't exist!"

"Are you, by any chance," Harriet said, "addressing my husband-to-be, you peckerhead?"

Pete let go of Clyde's robe. "You're going to marry this crazy dame? Jesus, she ain't no virgin!"

"I was," Harriet said primly, "two hours ago."

Monster grinned. "There's a doll that learns fast."

"Where's your nail holes?" Pete said.

"Six, seven..." Earl was counting in slow motion.

Clyde stared at Pete's exotic eye patch. "My what?"

"You know. Nail holes. Didja just come down from the cross, or what?"

"Oh, beg your pardon." Clyde laughed politely. "You must think I'm Jesus. Well, don't be embarrassed. You're not the only one who's thought so."

Earl stopped counting. "Right. Just him and several billion other suckers."

"No, sorry to disappoint you, but my name is Clyde. Clyde Simmons." He held out his hand.

Pete inspected it closely. "Don't see no sign of 'em. So, if you ain't Jesus, how come you're runnin' around in a white Jesus dress?"

"Because he's a fump," Earl said.

Clyde looked at Earl with interest. "What's a fump?"

"Haw! He don't know what a fump is. Every red-blooded non-fump in this room who knows what a fump is, rise!"

All members of the Prickly Pears rose to their feet.

"Okay, Zit," Earl said, "tell that fump what a fump is."

"A fump," Zit said, "is a guy who goes into the bathroom and sticks his foot in the toilet and pees down his leg so nobody can't hear him."

Earl, Pete and the Prickly Pears applauded.

"Then it's clear to me," Clyde said, "that I'm not a fump. And that's all that matters. Although one day it will also be clear to Harriet, my beloved fiancée, when she has had a chance to hear me in the bathroom."

Vi was still on her knees. "Imagine!" she said. "Our Lord goes to the bathroom! The things they don't tell you!"

"What are you, then?" Pete said.

"A faith healer."

Pete was suddenly furious. "Okay. Mr. Faith Healer, you can dance right outta here in your fancy dress. And take your bride with you. We got no broken faiths here, just..." He eyed Vi tenderly. "... maybe a bent one."

"Sorry you feel that way." Clyde backed reluctantly out the door. "I sure would've liked a beer."

"Wait," Harriet said. "Lemme get my purse."

"Hold on, I got an idea." Earl strolled over to Clyde and pulled him back into the room. "Just whaddya mean when you say you're a faith healer?" He put his hands on his hips and leaned back to look up into Clyde's eyes.

"Well, I..." Clyde knew that whatever he said would be wrong. He was just too tall. "Perhaps if I could sit down for a minute?"

"Okay." Earl was all graciousness because he was now in command.

Clyde sat at the table. "A faith healer cures people's ailments."

"You mean like diseases? Broken bones?"

"Yes. But instead of using medicine, we use faith."

"So," Earl said, "you gotta believe in God, right?"

Clyde smiled indulgently, although his head was throbbing.

"Naturally. Or at least in some sort of Benevolent Intelligence. And don't think it's a hoax, either. Time after time, I've seen it work."

"Fine," Earl said. "Then how 'bout a demonstration? You cure somebody right here, and you get all the beer you can drink. Okay? Okay, Pete?"

"Sure," Pete said. This could be better than live music.

"All right," Clyde said. He wished he could cure his own headache. "Who among you needs to be cured?"

Everyone stared at Pete.

"Now, wait a minute," Pete said. "I've gotten kind of fond a this patch. Without it, I'd be just an ordinary guy."

Clyde sighed with relief. "I can't cure anyone who doesn't want it."

Earl turned menacing. "Sure you can. If you got faith. Now, Pete here lost an eye in a cockfight..."

"Lost it? You mean there's no eyeball behind that patch?"

"Nothin' but a hole." Pete said. "Wanna see?"

"No thanks."

Harriet laid her orange purse on the table and put her hands protectively on Clyde's shoulders. "I wouldn't mind."

"No, angel," Clyde said. "You see, it's not so difficult to cure an eyeball that's there, but it's very hard to make an eyeball grow back. I'm sure it would take several sessions."

Pete shrugged. "What the hell. I ain't had no eyeball for ten years, so I guess I can take it slow and kinda get used to the idea."

Clyde looked to Earl for approval.

"Okay, okay. Take as long as you want, up to two weeks. But we gotta get it clear: it's you and God against me and the

Atheist Society, Tucson Branch." He pulled a chair up to face Clyde, climbed on it and squatted casually. "Whaddya say?"

"I'll do it, if I can have a beer in advance."

"Me, too," Harriet said. She looked defiantly at Pete. "I'm no longer a working girl. I'm engaged."

Earl was ecstatic. "Right. Beers all around, on me." He found Violette asleep on her knees. "C'mon, Vi, wake up, you gotta serve. Harriet quit."

Violette stumbled to the bar where Pete was busy lining up beers. "Something happened tonight that sure was weird," she said. "Wish I could remember."

"Don't worry, honey," Pete said. "You will, soon as you get to that table over there. Just don't drop the beers."

Ta-dum, ta-dam! Back at the piano, Earl played a few smashingly dissonant chords to get everyone's attention. Then he jumped on the piano bench. "Place your bets! Lay your money on God or the Atheists! And I gotta warn you, God is a losing proposition!"

"Wait, now," Monster said. "You can't take bets. You're an involved party."

"You think he's a party?" Violette said. "Funny. I never would've thought so."

"I'll take the bets," Pete said. He put two beer cans on the bar. "The can on the right's for God, can on the left's for the Atheists."

"That ain't fair," Harriet said. "People are gonna get confused."

"Okay," Pete said, "label 'em, then."

"Well, even though I ain't working here, I'll do it, because I want God to have a fair chance. And..." She smiled coyly at

Clyde. "…my fiancé. Gimme some tape, paper and a pencil."

The bar hummed with activity. Harriet fixed up the cans and tore paper into neat little squares for the men to write their bets. Earl broke into a frenetic rendition of "Yes sir, That's My Baby." Violette circulated among the tables to hand out beers. The men lined up to write out their bets and stuff them in the cans while Pete called out the score: "God's ahead, two to three! Nope, now the Atheists are neck and neck. Wrong again, God's moving ahead! Guess you just can't hold Him back."

"Ahhhh! Jesus, now I remember!" Violette had reached Clyde's table. She slammed down the tray with its two remaining beers, which Clyde quickly grabbed. Violette fell to his feet. "Bless me."

Clyde guzzled one of the beers. Then he mopped his lips neatly with the sleeve of his robe and looked down at Violette's bent head. "Stand up, my child. You've made a mistake. I'm not the Lord; I'm Clyde."

"You're what?" Violette shouted over the music, which grew louder and faster by the moment.

"Clyde," he shouted back. "An ordinary man." He saw himself in Violette's trusting eyes. "Well, not really ordinary."

The music suddenly stopped. "Time for the healing," Earl said. He turned to Clyde. "How do you wanna set it up?"

"The important thing is…" A dramatic pause while Clyde started in on the second beer. "…silence. That is, everyone in the room must cooperate. And then I need…"

"Where do you want the victim?" Earl said.

"The patient must be near me, of course, so I…"

Pete stayed behind the bar. "I can't be a patient. This ain't no hospital."

Everyone stared at him. "Whaddya looking at me for? I can't stand too much attention, makes my brain fuzz over. Maybe we should call it off."

"Be a patient," Monster said. "We placed bets."

"This situation is larger than this bar," Earl said. "We're talking the triumph of *reason*. You gotta do it." He steered Pete over to Clyde, who was finishing his beer.

"I'll clear off this table," Clyde said, "so you can lie down and close your eyes."

"Eye," Earl said. "You forgot the point."

"Oh, yes. My mistake."

"You gotta be crazy!" Pete said. "I ain't lying down on no table."

"You heard the man. We all gotta *cooperate*." Monster picked Pete up and laid him across the table. "Close your eye."

Pete went limp, and Violette clasped his hand, which was hanging over the edge of the table. "The Lord can work miracles, Pete. You remember the story of Lazarus?"

"Vi, whose side are you on?" Earl said. "All those nights of Kant, and you still can't get it."

"Sure I can."

Oh, those purple eyes! Still kneeling, Vi looked like a plump madonna in opera stockings. Earl tried unsuccessfully to harden his heart. "Never mind. If Kant can't do it, maybe Spinoza can."

"Harriet, could you dim the lights?" Clyde said. "And could you perhaps light some candles?"

Harriet blushed with importance. "Why not? I like to help, it's part of my astrology."

"Wow!" Zit said, when the saloon was glowing with candlelight. "The place could be a whorehouse!"

"Now." Clyde waved his hands in figure eights over Pete's body. "Relax. Cleanse the mind of all distracting thoughts. Imagine yourself an empty vessel. You are going to receive a white light..."

"See how relaxed he is," Harriet said. "He's snoring. Isn't that sweet?"

"You wanna touch his eye hole?" Monster said. "I'll take off the patch."

"No, thanks. A healer doesn't need to make physical contact. The vibrations alone create a force field."

"Vibrations," Harriet said. "Isn't that sweet?"

Earl glowered at Clyde from the piano bench, where he was perched like a malevolent owl. "Right. *Vibrations.* Mumbo-jumbo."

"Be quiet," Harriet said.

Swaying back and forth, his eyes closed, Clyde conducted a silent symphony in the air. Within ten minutes everyone but Earl was swaying sympathetically.

At midnight Harry Leshner, the oldest cop on the force, arrived in a cloud of cigar smoke for his off-duty drink. He parked his bike neatly in line with the others, sauntered into the bar and stopped in surprise. "I didn't know there was a dance. Somebody mighta told me." He brandished his cigar. "Specially when you guys all get discount tickets to the policemen's ball, courtesy a yours truly."

"Amen," Clyde said.

"Hey, hang on," Harry said, "I just noticed a real peculiarity. There ain't no music."

Monster creaked to his feet and lumbered over to Harry. "We got this contest going. God against the Atheists." Draping his arm comfortably over Harry's shoulder, he led him toward the bar. "Why dontcha place a bet?"

As they passed the table where Pete lay, mouth gaping like a stunned fish, Harry bellowed, "Christ! Look at that! Pete, my old buddy, dead!" He lunged for Pete's body. At the same moment, Pete sat up and inadvertently rammed his head into Harry's belly.

"Umph!" Harry fell backward into Monster's arms.

"Sure is a lot going on tonight," Monster said, as he arranged Harry in the totem armchair and went to fetch him a beer.

"Do I got a new eye?" Pete felt underneath the patch. "Nope. But I think maybe I feel a little change. A small lump possibly."

"Round one is over." Earl strutted over to Clyde, who had collapsed into a chair and was allowing Harriet to massage his temples. "Lemme buy you a personal drink, none a that cheap draft. You worked almost as hard as an atheist."

Clyde gave Earl a glazed stare. "I always do."

"Yeah, I gotta hand it to you, you got so pale and sweaty I thought you'd pass out. Musta lost ten pounds, not that you need to."

"I think I'll have a sandwich," Clyde rolled his eyes upward. "Harriet? Could you get me a ham and cheese on rye, with maybe a thin layer of sauerkraut?"

By five in the morning Earl and Clyde were close friends. They had progressed from the bar to Earl's, from beer to Earl's homemade cactus brandy. Earl's living room was decorated with momentous volumes of Kant, Spinoza and Marx, delicate Theosophical tracts, stale cigar smoke and the sleeping bodies of Vi and Harriet.

"Well." Clyde balanced his brandy glass on a bust of Spinoza. "If I didn't know I was right, I'd certainly know *you* were right."

"I feel the same," Earl said. "Even if you do look like Jesus."

"No reason not to take advantage of my genes." Clyde smirked modestly. "But I forgot to ask. What made you decide there was no God?"

Earl gave an elaborate fake yawn. "I had the wrong kid."

"Are you making a joke? I have absolutely no sense of humor."

"Wish I was." Earl chewed morosely on an unlit cigar. "This kid, see, was sick all the time. Couldn't breathe, you know? How could I have a kid like that? I smoke ten cigars a day, minimum, and I'm healthy as a chimpanzee."

"Happens all the time," Clyde said. "Look at me. I'm thin and fragile, in terms of my psycho-physical balance, and I'd probably have a tough, insensitive child."

"I'd been thinking there wasn't no logic in the world anyway; otherwise, I'd never of gotten hooked up with Dena, his mom. That was a miserable woman. No good in bed, neither." Earl patted Vi's thigh. "Not like this one, if you can keep her awake long enough."

Clyde smiled. "For a newly awakened virgin, Harriet

is insatiable. Especially when I start whispering Universal Secrets. Drives her over the edge."

Earl was back in his past. "Stayed with Dena, her mom and my kid three years in that dark house. Like a morgue."

"Dena's an odd name. Think I met a woman named Dena once." Clyde chewed meditatively on his mustache. "Out here in the desert. But she was a hot number, if you know what I mean."

"That ain't my old Dena. She acts hot, with them big tits. But for down-home reality in the fucking end of things, you can't beat Vi."

Clyde got up and opened the door. "Look, Mr. Atheist." He coughed delicately. "The Santa Catalinas, purple against the rosy-fingered dawn. Can you imagine a sight more beautiful?"

Earl squinted at the mountains. "Oh, fer natural beauty they ain't bad. Not like the ocean though."

"Do you think beauty like this just happened?"

"Sure."

"I'm certainly not advocating Christianity, which I find unpleasantly Medieval, but you cannot deny a creative intelligence governing the universe."

"Don't see why not. Most a my life's been governed by stupid accident. And, hell, for sheer beauty and creative intelligence, you can't beat that atom bomb going off over the desert. Some mushroom cloud, even if it is evil!"

"Are you proposing an evil God?"

"We don't need no God to blame fer our evil. Lookit how hard them scientists musta worked to figure out that bomb. Can you imagine sittin' up nights tryin' to find the best way to destroy the most people? Amazing!"

"I agree. Our quarrel is not about human nature. Nor about what people do with the resources given to them."

"Not given, fer Christ's sake! Available." Earl joined Clyde in the doorway.

"But who made them available?"

"Nobody. Couple a rocks rolled along through no fault a their own. Maybe there was a big wind that day, blew some more rocks over, and after a dozen centuries, whaddya got?" Like a smug real estate salesman, Earl stretched out his arms. "The Santa Catalinas."

Clyde ignored Earl's drama. "That still doesn't explain the existence of you and me."

"That ain't hard. If anybody'd tried to plan either one a us, they could of done a much better job. Specially in my case."

"Don't be modest. You may be hard-headed, but you've got talent."

"Oh, sure. I play a mean piano in a rundown bar out in the goddamn desert."

In Earl's yard a desert tortoise breakfasted on the succulent pink fruit of a prickly pear. As he watched the prehistoric creature, methodically focused on its meal, Clyde felt an early-morning despair. The tortoise accepted its universe, didn't question the splendors of creation. Hell, the old wrinkled reptile didn't even question its shadow.

Suddenly woozy, Clyde sat down in the sand and began to bury his feet. "Do you keep in touch with your son?"

"Nah. I figure they're happier without me."

"Sounds like a convenient rationalization."

"You don't understand because you don't know Dena. She wanted a kid, that was why she married me. After the kid was born, I was just in the way. Kept trying to sweep me out with the dustballs, till finally I took the hint. After I was gone, I got so happy I couldn't figure out why I'd waited so long. Guess I had some crazy idea of trying to be a father."

Clyde's feet had now disappeared. "Why not? Your child might be missing you at this very moment."

"He was three when I left, and he must be..." Earl sat next to Clyde and scrunched up his face thoughtfully. "Fourteen now. Wouldn't even remember me. Dena probably told him he was a virgin birth."

"You'd be amazed what children remember. I had a child once, a girl, and when she was thirteen, she'd describe little incidents from when she was two and three years old."

"Wait a minute. You had a kid? So you left her, and you're laying guilt on me for leaving my kid?"

Clyde closed his eyes. "I didn't leave her. She died. She and her mother."

"Oh." Sliding back into the sand, Earl said, as gently as his curiosity would allow, "How'd they die?"

"Murdered."

Earl jerked upright. "What're you talking about?"

"I owned a bookstore in town, on Granada, and one afternoon I got a call from the police. An old lunatic, who had hidden away somewhere in the mountains, broke into our house and stabbed Laura, my wife, and Sonora, our daughter."

"Oh, Christ! Why?"

Clyde fixed Earl with an intense blue stare. "I told you, he was crazy."

"Unbelievable."

"Even I didn't believe it. Things like that just don't happen. But when I got home, there they were, in the kitchen where they'd been having lunch. And they were dead, all right. They..." Clyde closed his eyes. "It was a Sunday, right before Christmas, and I was keeping the shop open for the holiday. If I'd been home with them..."

"Don't think about it," Earl said. Then, to cover up his awkwardness, he asked, "Did they catch the old guy?"

"They found him dead at the back of our yard. Apparently, he ran screaming out of the house with the bloody kitchen knife and was seen by our neighbors just before he plunged the knife up under his own ribs." Clyde tortured himself with horrible details. "The story ends on a grimly humorous note: the man fell backwards into a giant saguaro, where the police found him. Crucified on a cactus."

"God!" Earl put a sympathetic hand on Clyde's shoulder, but Clyde shrugged it away, so Earl hoisted his tired body to a squat. "Lemme get some more brandy. It ain't good to run out at a time like this."

"Thank you." Clyde kicked his feet free and leaned back on his elbows. Although the morning was cool, he was drenched with sweat. Pain, blinding and violent. Twelve years since their deaths, and he had spoken his terrible secret to no one after the early days when he talked too much and finally turned away from the curious sympathy of the townspeople.

Now, prompted by cactus brandy, he had released his burden to Earl, a stranger whose cynicism was oddly nonjudgmental.

Earl returned with their glasses and the gallon jug of his special brew. He filled the glasses to the brim, handed one to Clyde, who noted with surprise that Earl's hand was trembling.

"So." Earl sank back into the sand and took a hefty swig. "How in hell did you become a faith healer? If something like that happened to me, I'd know there wasn't any creative intelligence running the show. In fact, I'm so pissed right now..." His eyes glowed fiercely as he punched the sand. "Accident, that's all there is, and the evil of man!"

Clyde drank the musty brandy like medicine. "That's how I felt too, at first. I sold the bookstore, moved out to the edge of town and started working in a gas station. Quit talking to anyone but our old dog. I lived on curses, guilt and cheap wine.

"Then one day my dog, half blind and deaf, wandered out on the highway, got hit by a speeding car. I brought her body back home, laid her on the couch and started crying like I hadn't let myself when my wife and daughter were killed. One more proof, that's all it was, of a godless universe. I shouted, 'Okay! I'm going to turn evil too! No point in trying to be a good man.'

"I went over to Margarita's, a Mexican café on the other side of town from here, near where I worked, got drunk on tequila so I could face going back to bury my dog. And that's when I met that woman whose name I think was Dena."

Earl leaned forward. "Dena? That was my wife's name."

Clyde sighed. "Well. This Dena was on the prowl. Just looking for sex. So we went out and rolled in the sand and fucked like I never fucked before. Angry, wild fucking, the kind I wouldn't do with Laura.

"Afterwards, just out of pure nastiness, I said, 'I knocked you up, baby.' She pretended not to know what I meant, just like she pretended she was a virgin. I laughed and told her I'd put a baby in her belly, and she'd have to deal with the consequences. When I left her, she was crying, and I never saw her again. But it's funny, you know, I think I wanted another child, always have, but I wouldn't trust myself not to lose it."

"You and Harriet can have one." Earl flinched at the idea of Harriet in bed.

Clyde sighed. "I suppose. In any event, I went home in a pretty hellish mood, and there was my old dog, sitting up on the couch and wagging her tail!"

"She hadn't died, after all."

"But she had. When I brought her in the house, she wasn't breathing. No heartbeat. By the time I was leaving for Margarita's, she was getting stiff." Twisting around on his side, Clyde watched Earl through his glass.

"Impossible."

"One would think. But there she was, lively as ever."

"What about her wounds?"

"They were all internal. I tell you, I was as disbelieving as you are, but I had the proof. Right in front of me. I took Concha, my dog, for a walk in the desert. She was fine. And as I walked, I thought about the meaning of all this. Gradually, one fact became clear: this was no accident. I was being given a message from God, or somebody out there, and I had to listen.

"So I quit work and took off with Concha in my old van. Drove all around the country and listened for messages. Certainly didn't find any in the churches, which I visited, but finally, in San Diego, I found a group of faith healers who were working miracles."

"Miracles!" Earl poured another round of brandy.

"I don't expect to convince you now, but you should come with me some time. The blind regained their sight, the lame walked again, and the deaf began to hear."

"Any resurrections from the dead?"

"No, but numerous healings. And what was even more amazing: I discovered the power in myself! Everyone had been urging me to try, so I touched the arthritic hands of a very old lady, and her crooked fingers straightened themselves as I watched!"

"So how come you couldn't cure Pete's eye?"

"I will. It doesn't often happen that fast."

"Maybe you should of touched the empty socket."

"Hey, where is everybody with the coffee?" Harriet called from within the house.

Clyde set down his brandy glass and smiled fondly. "Out here, angel." He made an effort to get up, but, finding his body cemented to the sand, he turned to Earl. "Got any coffee?"

"Just instant. Ran outta the good stuff last week, so I thought maybe I'd hit the old herb tea trail for a while."

"Oomph!"

"What was that?" Earl's face contorted with the effort to lift himself up. Impossible. No sleep and far too much brandy.

Harriet, her makeup streaked across her face like an angry finger painting, appeared in the doorway. "Poor Vi! I rolled over and smashed right into her."

"She all right?" Earl said.

"Oh, yeah. She ain't thin like me, so she got a solid layer of protection." Harriet smoothed her wrinkled overalls.

"Come here, you long-legged beauty," Clyde said, "and give me a kiss."

As Harriet knelt beside Clyde and embraced him, Earl watched with amazement. Gawky Harriet, her homeliness a painful joke, actually became lovely, graceful even, in the protective circle of Clyde's arms. For the first time Earl wondered whether Clyde's powers might be real.

Violette crawled out the door and plumped down on her stomach next to Earl. Arching blissfully into the sunshine, she lifted her breasts right out of her scanty costume. "I dreamed I got run over by a Mack truck. Thank God it was only Harriet."

"I ain't so sure I like being compared to machinery." Harriet interrupted a kiss to glare at Vi over Clyde's shoulder.

Clyde pulled her back. "You can be whatever you want."

Harriet giggled. "How 'bout Shirley Temple?"

"Why not choose someone more interesting? A queen, say, or a princess?" Clyde swept Harriet's fake orange curls to the top of her head. "Look!" he commanded Earl and Vi. Earl reluctantly pulled his head up from Vi's breasts. Sure enough, Harriet had become aristocratic, gilded by the desert sun.

"Stop! I hate being teased. You're hurting my feelings." Harriet knocked Clyde's hand away, jerked her wig off and tossed it into a clump of cacti. Her woeful face, half-hidden by lank, sweaty brown hair, made Earl want to cry. Never again would he kid around with her, he vowed.

But Clyde, unpredictable as always, was even more enamored. "Oh, yes." He ran his fingers through Harriet's hair, fluffing it out as he spoke. "Your real self. I wondered when you'd trust me enough. Now let's go inside and wash up. Then we'll make coffee for everyone."

"Maté tea for me," Earl said.

"All right," Harriet whimpered.

"But you'll have to lift me up," Clyde said. "The lower half of my body is remarkably uncooperative."

Earl felt a peculiar sting of jealousy. "Maybe you're finally worn out."

"I doubt it," Clyde said, as Harriet pulled him to his feet.

"Although I wouldn't mind a half-century of sleep, punctuated by some spicy cavorting." He fondled Harriet's ass as she helped him into the house.

"Wow," Vi said. "They really like each other."

"Just like you and me," Earl said.

"Yes," Vi said. "I think so."

Half an hour later Clyde emerged with a breakfast tray. "Here we are: huevos rancheros." He set the tray on the sand, and Vi held out her hands greedily.

"What are those?" Earl pointed to a greenish stack of pancakes.

"Banana cactus pancakes. Oh, don't worry," Clyde said when Earl shrank back as though the tray held a live rattler. "I used flour and baking soda, as well as a little honey. Try some; they couldn't be worse than your cactus brandy."

"I'll try some," Vi said. "And lots of eggs."

"Here comes the coffee; here comes the tea," Harriet sang in time to the wedding march. Her face and hair were freshly washed and shining. In a pair of Earl's boxer shorts and his Tucson Atheist Society tee shirt, she looked like a sweet young girl.

"When are you getting married?" Vi said.

"This afternoon," Clyde said. "After I've had a few hours' sleep."

Harriet knelt behind Clyde, eased his robe down and massaged his shoulders. "Wish I had a white wedding dress. With real lace and a veil."

"Well, don't rush then," Vi said. "We'll find you a beautiful dress and veil and have a big party at Pete's."

"Maybe we should wait a little. What do you think?" Harriet asked Clyde, whose head had fallen forward onto his chest.

"He's asleep," Vi said. "God, I can't imagine marrying someone who looks so much like Jesus. Don't you feel sinful when you're in bed? Like fucking the Lord?"

"Well," Harriet said modestly, "we've never been in a real bed together, but it sure was fun in the sand."

Earl felt all growly. "Being sinful's half the fun, Vi. Don'tcha realize that?"

Harriet started in on her breakfast. "Oh, I don't know. I think I'm too inexperienced to feel sinful. Aren't these pancakes terrific?"

"Yeah, if you don't snag the roof of your mouth on a pricker." Earl pointed to a pile of cactus needles on the side of his plate.

"They make good toothpicks," Vi said helpfully.

"Hey, I forgot!" Harriet said. "I got a letter for Earl. A suspicious letter."

"How in hell can a letter be suspicious?" Earl said. "Think it's got a bomb in it?"

Like a schoolteacher, Harriet admonished him with her fork. "It's in a blue envelope."

"Oh, blue! Now I know exactly what you mean. There's nothing worse than a blue envelope. 'Course, yellow can be pretty awful on a rainy day, but we don't see much rain out here right now, so..."

"Cut the crap," Harriet said. "I'll go get it."

While Harriet was inside, Vi finished her eggs. "Sure was a

nice breakfast."

Earl eyed her plate. "You didn't finish those pancakes."

"Well," Vi sighed. "The flavor was good. And I love the coffee."

"Instant." Revolted by his own churlishness, he was suddenly desperate for sleep. "Wanna take a nap with me, Vi?"

"I slept an awful lot," Vi said. "Isn't Harriet sweet?"

Earl did not want to answer that one. "I'm going inside. See ya in a couple a hours."

Harriet met him in the doorway. "I lost it. I'm sorry, but it was a busy night."

"I don't care. I hate blue letters."

After Earl had stumbled off to bed, Vi and Harriet helped Clyde in to the living room couch.

"So he won't get sunburned," Harriet said.

When they had finished cleaning up, they sat out behind the house in the shade of Earl's sun porch, a faded, green-and-orange-striped awning stretched over a makeshift wooden frame.

"You sure you want to get married?" Vi fanned her neck with her curls.

"Of course! It's what I've always wanted, but I never thought that I... Well, you know, I never was one of those girls like you that..." Embarrassed, Harriet poured two glasses of iced instant coffee. "Don't you? I mean, want to get married?"

"Oh, Vi, oh, Vi, oh, Vi," Violette's parrot croaked from Earl's bedroom. "Oh, baby, do it again."

"I don't know." Violette sipped her drink. "I think I've got a mission in life, only I'm not sure what it is. Maybe I'll be a singer."

"I didn't know you could sing."

"Well, I can't, yet. But I got this feeling the other day that pretty soon I'll sing. Although I would like some kids."

"I'd love kids! And Clyde'll be a perfect father, don't you think?"

"Sure. He ever been married?"

"I don't know. But he's old enough."

"How old is he?"

Harriet slid her glass across her toes to cool them down. "I don't know."

"You better get married right away, so you can find out a few things."

"Yes. I do think that's the best way to get to know a person. A male person."

"Probably." Vi watched a white-winged dove perch precariously on a prickly pear framed in a midday opalescent shimmer. "Nothing much doing out here. Maybe we should go wedding shopping."

"I wouldn't mind."

After Vi had changed into shorts and tee shirt, they left a note, climbed into Earl's truck and roared off.

Four hours later Earl woke up. "Christ!" he said. "What a dream!" The desert sun had turned his apartment into a dark little oven. Earl stumbled through waves of dry heat into the kitchen. There was a note, scrawled in eyebrow pencil, on the white formica table: "Gone wedding shoping. Back pretty soon. Love, Vi."

Earl smiled. Everything about Vi was irresistible, even her misspellings. He took a glass of lukewarm water into the living room and put some jazz on the record player. Brubeck riffed around the room and made even the heat seem fairly affable.

"What time or day is it?" Clyde tilted in through the doorway. With his bloodshot eyes and unshaven face, he looked less like Jesus now and more like the bad guy in a grade B Western.

"Dunno," Earl said. "Same day, I think, only later."

Clyde collapsed in slow motion onto the motel green couch. "Where are the women?"

"Out buying stuff for the wedding. You still want to go through with it?"

"Oh, yes," Clyde said. "May I have some of your water? It's difficult to talk." He took a few gentlemanly sips from Earl's glass. "I need Harriet."

"Why?"

"She adores me, for one thing."

"You musta had lots a women adore you. Great-looking broads."

"Yes. But not sweet. Not selfless and innocent. And loyal. Furthermore, I am going to turn Harriet into a beauty, and that, my friend, is powerful medicine."

"You can't do that."

"Not only can I do it, I have begun. Don't pretend you didn't notice."

Earl was silent, remembering the glimmer of grace that had fallen over Harriet as she knelt in the sand and embraced Clyde.

"Most important, she'll forgive me."

"For what?"

"For not preventing the murder. For not being there, where I should have been..."

"Hey," Earl said. "You give yourself too much credit. Who says you gotta be caretaker of the universe?"

Clyde slumped morosely back on the damp pillows. "You don't understand."

"Look. If you walk in the can and a rattler bites your foot, is it my fault because I should of known what was in my bathroom?" In spite of the heat and his hangover, Earl was getting excited.

"I don't want to talk about it. Yes, it's your fault."

"Things just happen, goddammit!"

"Apparently it pleases you to think you're not responsible. But you're wrong."

"Can't you see that's all ego? You gotta believe you got control so you can feel important."

"I have no desire for importance. But nobody is going to get hurt, not if I can help it."

"Good," Earl said. "You just agreed with me."

"I did not."

"Okay, here's a scene for you: Vi and Harriet are driving home, too fast and laughing about the wedding..."

"It will be a serious wedding."

"Yeah, but there they are, having a fine old time, going too fast, and they see an old turtle in the road. They swerve, the truck goes outta control..."

Clyde clutched the fuzzy, clover-patterned sofa cover. "My God! Are you having a vision?"

Instant guilt, that omnipresent bum, begged for Earl's attention. "No. Hell, I meant, lots of times you can't help what's happening, especially if you don't know about it."

"That was a stupid illustration."

"Sorry. Lemme get us a couple of cold beers. Hair of some hound."

While Earl was in the kitchen, Clyde tried to erase the vision of Harriet and Vi careening off a desert road. No use: the images tumbled about in his brain like a malevolent collage. Sometimes they hit the turtle; sometimes they didn't. Vi was driving, no, Harriet. The truck flipped over, smashed into a cliff or a giant cactus...

He took the frosty can and held it over his eyes. "Just bringing up images like that can cause them to happen."

Already the beer was mellowing Earl's brain. "Well, I discovered a great secret. If you finally accept the idea that everything's accidental and there's not much you can help, unless it rolls right across your path, you just let go. And life gets a hellava lot looser."

Solemnly, Clyde held his beer aloft like a blazing torch. "Everything has a meaning, a divine pattern, and we are here to find out what it is. And what we must do, as smaller pieces of the pattern."

"So you imagine a God who isn't pushy, right? He knows the way things oughta go, but he likes a little mystery. Likes to play games."

"What are you talking about?"

"Seems to me your God has fun watching you try to figure things out, so you can do the right thing, when it would be easy just to tell you. He could say, 'Lookit, Clyde, if you really wanna fit in, here's what you gotta do.'"

Clyde paused in mid-gulp to glare at Earl. "God is not some folksy guy who sits around chomping tobacco in the corner store. In fact, I don't envision a personal god at all. I would say, rather, a benevolent Intelligence."

"Hey. I don't care if your dog did come back to life. The

murder of your wife and kid was not rational, and no goddam benevolent Intelligence would of allowed it."

Earl's excitement propelled him to his feet and across the living room. He needed space to say what had to come next. "And I'm sorry if your way of thinking has been some kinda comfort, weird as it is. But there's a lot more comfort in dropping the whole idea of God. Oh, at first it's a little scary, because you kinda rattle around without your usual props. Aimless, y'know? Life feels like a random junkyard. But after a while, it's a real relief. Like growing up."

"Are you finished?"

"No, but I'll quit fer a while." He returned to the couch and drained his beer. "You pissed at me?"

"How absurd. But I just want to point out one thing: if I make Pete's eye grow back, you'll have to admit there's something going on that you haven't acknowledged."

"Oh, I hope fer Pete's sake, and yer own satisfaction, you can do it. But I ain't holding my breath."

"Good. Breathe normally. You'll live longer."

"Say, you musta told Harriet about your wife and kid."

"No."

"But you said she'll forgive you."

"She will. And she forgives me in advance. For the past and the future. A forgiving person, that woman."

A pleasantly melancholy silence. Clyde could feel the healing effects of the beer as it worked on his hangover. He imagined the beer, a tiny Florence Nightingale, whisking around the various ill areas of his body.

"Whaddya think of jazz?" Earl said.

"I don't know."

Earl turned over the record. "Listen to this. Dave Brubeck."

As he listened, Clyde began to smile. "How charming and intricate. That man understands something that I certainly don't."

"Yeah. He's got a sense of humor." Earl hummed alongside the music. Then he leaned his head over the side of the couch and rested it on the floor. "Helps the beer clear the brain. Try it."

"No, thanks. My head is happy to be upright."

"I had a peculiar dream just now."

"Ah. A waking dream. Those are usually visions."

Earl pulled himself back up. "No, a sleeping dream. I didn't mean just now now; I meant just now an hour ago."

"Oh."

"It was a dream about my kid. Remember that kid I told you about?"

"Of course. I don't forget children."

"Well, my kid was standing on this mountain and yelling at me. Real red-faced, like he was angry or upset. A funny- looking kid, y'know? Skinny, with big ears."

Though his increasing haze, Clyde inspected Earl's oversized ears and his small, but muscular, frame. "Nothing like you."

"Nah. So I'm down here in the desert, having myself a beer--just like I am--and I keep yelling back, `What? What?' Because I can't hear him."

"Why didn't you go up on the mountain to meet him?"

"I would've. But I couldn't move. I was glued to the sand. So I yelled, `C'mon down here and talk!"

"And did he?"

"Hell, I guess he couldn't hear me either. Then he got smaller and smaller. Looked to me like he was wearing a dress made outta green and white stripes. And he disappeared."

"That dream is distressingly obvious. Your conscience is telling you to go to your son."

"I told you: my son don't need a guy like me. Dena probably found him an educated guy, one with a real aptitude for being a father."

"You could learn. Don't be so hard on yourself."

"Forget it. Besides, I think being an atheist ain't so good if you're a father. A kid needs something to believe in."

"You could pretend."

Earl bared his teeth. "Hah! If there's one thing I am, it's honest. Especially to my kid, if I ever see him again."

"I don't understand." Clyde set down his beer and massaged his temples. "As an atheist you should be able to lie without any problem, since you have no god to answer to."

"Boy, for a smart guy you really are dumb. An atheist gotta have more integrity than anybody else because he ain't got the usual supports. He's gotta stand on his own."

"Morality in a random junkyard. Like a perfect Greek column in the center of Woolworth's. At first you don't see it; your eye refuses to take it in. You focus instead on pink plastic purses, nail polish, velvet flowers, a jumble of glittery trivia that titillates even while it irritates. Then, smack! You back into an anachronism."

"I ain't sure I know what you're talking about, but I like your intelligence."

"Thank you. That's quite a compliment from a thinking man." As Clyde curled and uncurled his feet, he studied this fiercely iconoclastic fellow, incandescent with curiosity. He could learn much from Earl, who had the courage to be vital.

Earl sighed. "You know what gets me about Vi? She don't think at all. She feels. She don't dislike intelligence, but it's all the same to her, know what I mean? A flower is as good as Spinoza."

"Better, probably. But that's what makes her so beautiful. She exists perfectly in each moment in a way you and I never will. She's not bound by ideas of the way things ought to be, so she has no anger, no self-righteousness."

"Yeah. No history, either. No sense of life going in a straight line. She'll tell me she's an atheist, and five minutes later she's kneeling to Jesus. Pardon me, I mean, you."

"Right," Clyde said. "And you can't have a conscience if you don't believe in linear sequence. Cause and effect. I made this mistake; here's the bad result, and now I'm sorry."

"Which means she could ride right outta here with that damn parrot on her handlebars and never even say good-bye. Just like she did to Pete. Hell, I don't even know if she remembers she lived with Pete for a while."

"Amazing. Her mind must be a crazy quilt of silks, calicos, velvets in the most brilliant colors. Each new experience contributes its own texture and delicious lack of meaning."

"She's gonna drive me crazy. I wanna marry her and have her stay with me forever."

"Like marrying a butterfly."

"Never knew a butterfly that sexy. Can you imagine sex without thinking? Vi does exactly what she feels without worrying about what do I think or when is breakfast coming. Every second kinda expands like it's looking at itself in a mirror. I even forget who I am, but at the same time I find myself somewhere beyond my name..."

Clyde drew in his breath quickly as though he had stepped on burning coals. "Never," he murmured. "Never have I lost my ego in that way. Always something in me wanted to control the moment. Even my sharing was a form of control, a facade covering the fear of failure. Or worse, the terror of invasion."

"Yeah. Usually I'm like a spider, spinning out my web onto everything. Vi detaches me all at once, just cuts the lines, and she don't even know it."

"If I could become silent somehow, do you think it would be possible with Harriet?"

"Hell, I don't know. I suppose anything is possible, like me being friends with a goddamned faith healer."

They chuckled at this charming irony; then Earl, disconcerted, jumped up. "We need more beer." From the kitchen he called out, "The trouble is, I got all this money I been saving up so Vi and I can get married. But she don't give a damn about money." Earl returned with two icy mugs.

Clyde took his gratefully. "Delicious. Oh, by the way. Do you have any money you'd like to invest in an interesting project?"

"Depends. How interesting?"

"Piggy banks."

"Go fall in a hole." Earl disdainfully crossed his legs and closed his eyes.

"No, no, this is serious. Pink and blue plastic pigs that tip their hats when you drop coins in. I got a brochure in the mail from a friend of mine."

"What kinda friend? What's he know about investments?"

"He's not trained, if that's what you mean. But he knows a great deal intuitively, because..." Clyde hesitated only a moment. "...he's a great faith healer. Rabbi Saltzman. One of the best."

"Oh, terrific. Just what I..."

A horrendous horn blast stopped Earl in mid-cynicism.

"The beauties are back." Clyde smiled fondly.

Sunburned and disheveled, Vi and Harriet rushed in, their arms laden with boxes and bags.

"Whew, it's hot!" Harriet dumped her packages on the couch next to Clyde. "Wait till we tell you what we've been doing."

"Wedding shopping," Earl said.

Clyde pulled Harriet down and kissed her. "Are you going to show me?"

"Not till the wedding." Harriet nestled into Clyde's arms. "But you're going to be so surprised. We found the most beautiful dresses in the world. At Levy's. First place we walked into, because Vi wanted to see Shoey Lou."

Earl reached out for Vi. "Who's Shoey Lou?"

"You know. The monkey in the shoe department. Everybody knows Shoey Lou." Vi plopped down into Earl's lap. "But even before that, we had a cherry phosphate at Catalina Drugstore, and then..." Vi's eyes shone. "We did something really wonderful. But I'd better not tell."

Earl played with Vi's curls. "That's not fair. You shouldn't tease people when it's so hot."

"Well..." Vi rested the tip of her nose against Earl's nose and stared soulfully into his eyes. "If you promise not to get mad?"

Oh, those purple eyes! Earl was helpless with adoration. "Anything you want, Vi."

Vi pulled back. "Okay. We went to the Garden of Gesthemane."

"What?"

"Those statues over on Congress Street by the Santa Cruz River. There's the Last Supper, the Crucifixion and the Holy Family. Really pretty, and I..."

Embarrassed, Vi turned away, so Harriet helped her out. "Vi knelt down and prayed."

"Jesus!" Earl said.

Vi looked at him accusingly. "You promised."

"Okay, okay. I didn't mean to say 'Jesus.' Just slipped outta my mouth. All right?" Earl pulled Vi close. "I erase it."

Clyde couldn't resist the chance to be portentous in front of Harriet. "Every word echoes throughout the universe."

Earl glowered at Clyde. "Wanna get punched out?"

"I forgive you," Vi said. "Because you get all red when you're mad." She squeezed his fingers. "Anyway. I was praying for the wedding. And then we..." She turned to Harriet. "You tell."

"We went to the Wishing Shrine."

"Ah," Clyde said. "El Terideto."

"What's that?" Earl said.

Clyde smiled grimly. "It means 'The Little Saint Thrown Down.' A shrine erected to honor a murder victim."

"That's right," Harriet said. "I forgot that."

"Only the murdered man wasn't a saint; he was apparently having an illicit affair with his mother-in-law or his sister-in-law or his daughter-in-law. There are several versions of the story."

Vi shuddered. "Imagine having an affair with your mother-in-law. Not that I've ever had one."

"You'd like my mother," Earl said.

"Some people believe," Clyde said, "if they light a candle at dusk, make a wish, and the candle burns until morning, the wish will come true."

"We did it," Harriet said, "even though it wasn't dusk yet. I wished for our marriage. And Vi made a wish too."

Earl's eyes lit up. "What'd you wish for, Vi?"

"I wished I'd find my destiny."

"Oh."

"And I wished you'd find yours too. I hope it's okay to make two wishes on one candle."

"Why not?" Harriet said.

"Ah," Clyde said, "you'll find your destiny whether or not you light a candle."

"Maybe we got the same destiny," Earl said hopefully.

"We might."

"But I think Earl's destiny involves his son," Clyde said.

"You've got a son," Vi said, "and you didn't even tell me?"

"Yeah, I've got a son. I guess I do."

On the afternoon of the wedding, Pete's was ablaze with activity. Monster and the Prickly Pears were hanging decorations, streamers of red, green and yellow crepe paper from the Sprouse Reitz, diminutive Mexican wedding dolls and pink and purple paper flowers from Woolworth's. Zit was strewing the bar and tables with Christmas tinsel he had found in the back room of Keller Drug. Pete was washing glasses and setting them out, two sets, one for drinking champagne and one for smashing when the bride and groom kissed.

"But not the first kiss," he said. "The one they do when they cut the cake."

Cranky, the gang member covered with tattoos (even, he claimed, on his "private parts," although no one believed him), looked down from the top of the ladder, where he was perched, gluing mirrors to the ceiling. "When they cut the cake, they eat it. They don't kiss."

"Sure they do," Monster said. "They kiss with their mouth full. Where'd you get all those mirrors, Crank?"

"Harriet bought 'em. She wanted to make the place look like a church."

"If it's a church, we gotta have a lotta candles. Anybody remember the candles?"

"Yeah," Zit said, "Harry's buying 'em."

As though he had been summoned, Harry Leshner strolled in with several bags of candles and a large cake box.

"Hey!" He removed the cigar from his lips and waved it in circles as he talked. "Place looks great. Looks like the inside of the Paramount."

"Nah," Zit said. "I think it looks like the Lyric."

"Either one," Harry said. "Harriet called and asked me to pick up the cake at the Bon Ton." He handed the box to Pete. "And I gotta go back later and get the ice cream from Georgette's."

"Kinda risky bringing that cake on your bike," Pete said.

"Yeah," Harry said. "I tied it down good, but I think I squished it a little. Not too bad. You can fix it up."

Pete carefully lifted the cake, a mountain of pink, white

and silver, from its box. "Yeah. Some of these flowers are mashed. I'll fluff 'em up with a toothpick."

Monster eyed the cake greedily. "Wonder what the flavor is."

Pete dug in under one of the flowers and pulled away a few crumbs, which he tasted with the air of a connoisseur. "Banana."

"Are you sure?" Harry said. "I thought it was supposed to be mocha chip."

"Definitely banana," Pete said.

Monster lumbered over to the bar. "You better let me taste it."

"No," Pete said, "you can't..."

"Look," Monster said, "just because I'm big don't mean I'm sloppy. Gimme a spoon." As he held out his giant paw, he flashed Pete a menacingly innocent smile.

Pete handed him a spoon. "Okay, Monster, you win. But if you wreck it, I swear I'm gonna call the cops."

"Don't bother to call; I'm here already." Harry was busy lining up candles in miniature cigar-store Indian candleholders. "And if you think I'm gonna tangle with Monster, your brain has disintegrated. I'd rather bake a new cake."

"I didn't know you cooked." With his two handfuls of tinsel, Zit looked like a troglodyte cheerleader awaiting the arrival of Santa.

"I'll tilt it a little," Monster said. "If I just hold on to this little bride and groom on top..." He began slowly to tip the cake. "Uh-oh." The plastic bride and groom proved to be less than reliable: already ankle-deep in frosting, they were sinking fast. "Now what?" Monster said, as he let the cake plop back onto the bar. The bride and groom sank to their knees.

Harry surveyed the cake. "Looks like they walked outta the church and into a snowbank."

"I know," Monster said, "I'll pull 'em out and clean 'em up."

"I give up," Pete said. "I'm not looking anymore. Who wants to help with the hors d'oeuvres?"

Panda, the self-proclaimed intellectual of the Prickly Pears, peered at Pete through his thick glasses. "What're we having?"

"Tortilla chips with hot bean dip and chocolate-covered pork and onions."

"Christ!" Panda put down his copy of *Hoofs 'n Horns* and waddled over to the bar.

"Watch out," Pete said. "You say his name, he's liable to show up, he's that self-centered."

"What was the source of such a hideous culinary inspiration?" Panda said.

Pete stared at him. "Smart guys gimme a stomachache."

"Who," Panda said patiently, "thought of chocolate- covered pork?"

Pete was pretending not to watch Monster lick the plastic cake ornament. "Harriet. Said she had chicken once in a chocolate sauce over at El Charro. I said if you could do it to chicken, you could do it to pork, which is a lot cheaper."

"Chicken mole," Panda said. "I hope you're doing the sauce with garlic, peanuts, sesame seeds and hot chiles."

"Nah," Pete said. "I'm just melting Hershey bars."

"Ook." Panda mopped his balding head with a bar towel. "Could I persuade you to..."

"Ferget it," Pete said. "Simple food is always better."

"Then at least let me make the bean dip."

Monster was delicately probing the center hole left by the bride and groom.

"Monster," Pete moaned, "I'm gonna feel so sad if you eat that damn cake."

"Okay," Monster said. "I didn't eat much. Got any marshmellows to fill up the hole?"

"No. Nothing but cocktail onions and maraschino cherries."

"Cherries'll be fine."

Zit had finished tinselling all available surfaces, including the toilet in the women's room. "Look at that!" He gestured grandly.

Everyone surveyed the room, glittering with hairy silver and throbbing with primary colors. A magnificent carnival, repeating parts of itself endlessly in the mirrors Cranky had fixed to the ceiling.

"Oh,"Vi said, when she and Earl arrived at seven p.m. "Oh, my. I think I'm going to cry. Except for my mascara."Vi was a pink candy confection, in a strapless satin dress with a bustled full skirt, festooned with dozens of fuchsia velvet bows. Her curls, pulled loosely up, were threaded and attached with pink and silver roses to match her silver heels, so high she tilted slightly forward.

"Stand up, Vi," Earl muttered. "You're spilling outta yer dress."

"I can't," Vi giggled. But she tugged her dress up a little to please Earl, radiant in his blue satin shirt embroidered, on cuffs and collar, with shiny white cowboys.

"Wow," Pete said. "Best-looking best man and woman I ever seen."

"And look at the cake! Oh, Harriet will be so surprised!"

Monster patted Vi's bustle in a patriarchal way. "Yep, she sure will. And don't let anybody tell you it's banana."

The mariachis, a bustling band of black and silver machismo, were fortifying themselves with Pete's punch, a deceptively fruity blend of tequila, rum and pineapple juice, through which he had swirled red grape concentrate. "Like marble ice cream," Pete said.

Vi teetered over to the punch bowl, and the leader of the mariachis, whose mustache reminded Vi of a longhaired black cat, handed her a drink. She batted her lavender eyes. "Would you play me a song?"

With his left hand he swept off his hat fringed with silver balls; then he adjusted his bullet-studded gun belt and bowed slightly. "Si, Senorita." His voice was fuzzy with lust.

Immediately Earl was at Vi's side, his arm draped possessively over her shoulder. "Play 'Sweet Violets,' wouldja?"

The man gave Earl a yellow, snaggle-toothed smile of apparent assent. He gathered his musicians together, and the band broke into a boisterous version of "Cielito Lindo."

"Hey!" Earl said. "That's not..."

Impulsively, Vi kissed him. "Wasn't it sweet of Harriet to ask me to sing?"

"That's right," Earl said. "What song are we doing?"

"How about 'Amazing Grace'?"

"I don't do church songs."

"All right, but the only other song I know is 'I Wonder Who's Kissing Her Now.'"

"It's a little odd for a wedding, but what the hell."

"Don't worry. Everyone will be too drunk to notice."

And, indeed, everyone was getting loopy on Pete's potent punch. The bar assumed a hallucinatory, underwater quality, a fruity, tequila haze. People moved in slow motion. Guests--former high school friends of Harriet's and Vi's, Harriet's elegant grandparents who had raised her after her mother had run off, two of Clyde's neighbors who had helped him after the murder of his wife and child, a fat priest Vi had snuck in along with her beaming parents--drifted in, had several glasses of punch and wandered about like bemused dreamers.

"I know I'm going to cry," Vi's mother said, sobbing. "Young people always make me cry."

Pete leaned on the bar and waved to everyone like a movie star. People waved back, at first because it seemed funny, but later because Pete seemed to have grown in stature somehow, and people were proud to know him. "That Pete!" Zit said. "What a guy!"

Monster dragged Cranky over to Pete. "Wouldja gimme yer autograph? Just write it anywhere on old Crank." Cranky lifted his shirt, and Pete squeezed in his name under a tattooed ad for Mexican beer.

At five minutes to nine Zit lit the candles and turned off the lights. The room glimmered with hundreds of real and reflected flames. Ever more rowdy, the mariachis bounced about the bar, bellowing out the bawdiest of Mexican songs and patting women and men alike on the ass.

Monster finally put a stop to the ass-patting. "It was okay fer the women, but you touch another man, I'll rip all yer arms off!"

"Well," Vi's mother said, "he's right of course, but it was fun!"

At exactly nine o'clock Clyde and Harriet appeared in the doorway. Swathed in white satin and lace dotted with silver sequins, Harriet was a queen with a rhinestone crown. Her face glowed with unusual beauty as she leaned ever so slightly on Clyde and clutched his arm with her lace-gloved hand. Clyde wore a new white robe, embroidered about the neck and sleeves, and a leather belt and sandals Harriet had given him. Greenish-pale, he smiled determinedly at the festive scene.

"Oh, look!" Vi cried. Everyone turned to the door.

"Jesus and His Holy Mother," Zit said, and the crowd murmured a melancholy assent.

Although it was time for Earl to play "Here Comes the Bride," the band forgot themselves and broke into "Ave Maria." Pete tried to quiet them, but it was no use. Earl waited through two verses, then, his patience evaporating, he pounded out "Here Comes the Bride."

The crowd parted, leaving an aisle among the tables. Swept along by the two conflicting songs, Clyde and Harriet passed the guests who lifted their glasses in a silent toast.

When they reached the piano, Vi handed Harriet a bouquet of cactus flowers streaming with ribbons. Pete, strangely dignified in a shiny black jacket, waited with an open book of sacred writings Clyde had prepared. Both songs stopped suddenly, and in the silence Pete cleared his throat.

But the priest was too quick for him. Wedging his rotund body through the crowd, he stepped in front of Pete and lifted his arms in benediction. "O Lord," he cried, "bless Your Son and His Mother on this holy day."

"I'm not his mother," Harriet said.

"Oh, excuse me."The priest dropped his arms in confusion.

"It's the punch," Monster said, as he led the priest away.

Vi whispered to Earl, who played a lilting melody to cover the awkwardness. Then she turned to the crowd. "I'll sing now, a song for Clyde and Harriet, one I've sung for years in my mind. It's called 'I Wonder Who's Kissing Her Now.'"

Several people in the crowd, among them Harriet's grandparents, rolled their eyes and tittered at the title, but when Vi drew herself up and began to sing, the room was quiet. Untrained and sometimes off-key, her voice was nonetheless rich and strong, a husky, siren voice luring men to their doom. Earl's mouth fell open and Pete's eyes glazed. Even Clyde snapped into alertness as a faint pink spread over his sallow face.

When Vi had finished singing, Pete cleared his throat again and with great dignity he read: "Who is this coming up from the wilderness, leaning on her beloved?" He handed Harriet his book.

Harriet beamed. "My beloved said to me," she read, "Rise up, my darling; my fairest, come away. For now the winter is past, the rains are over and gone; the flowers appear in the country-side; the time is coming when the birds will sing..."

She handed the book to Clyde, who swayed slightly and turned pale once again. Harriet helped him hold the book, and Monster stepped forward to put his huge arm around Clyde's waist for support. "C'mon," he whispered, "don't fink out."

Clyde straightened up and began to read. "Wear me as a seal upon your heart... for love is strong as death... Many waters cannot quench love, no flood can sweep it away...I have come to my garden, my sister and bride, and have plucked my myrrh with my spices…" His voice grew stronger. "I have eaten my honey and my syrup, I have drunk my wine and my milk. Eat, friends, and drink, until you also are drunk with love."

"Amen," Pete said.

"Amen," the crowd echoed.

Pete took back the book and closed it. "Okay. Now, kiss 'er, and let's make it a good one."

With a desperate passion, Clyde took Harriet in his arms and kissed her.

"Oh, how lovely!" Vi's mother said.

The kiss went on and on. "Heavens!" Harriet's grandmother said. The crowd grew restless.

"This is going a bit too far," said Harriet's grandfather.

Harriet finally pulled away. "Somebody help," she said softly. "I think he's fainted."

Clyde fell backwards, slowly, all in one piece, like a cardboard mannequin. "Watch out!" someone said to Harriet's grandmother, who was directly in Clyde's path, but Monster caught Clyde just in time. He and Earl carried Clyde to the bar, propped him up and sprayed him with champagne.

"Awg," Clyde gasped, coming to. "Ack." He sat up abruptly. "All right," he said belligerently, "tell me where I am."

"Congratulations," Monster said, kissing Clyde on his cheek, "you're married. And it's about time, too, because I can tell that sweet little bride of yours is pregnant."

"What?" Clyde said. "Don't be ridiculous. We've known each other less than two weeks."

But when they were ready to cut the cake, under cover of the mariachi music and the lively babble of the guests, Clyde said, "Do you think you're pregnant?"

"Probably." Harriet grinned mischievously. "Or if I'm not, I will be soon. My center of gravity is slipping."

"Oh," Clyde said. "I'm being given a chance to redeem myself."

When they cut the first piece, an avalanche of cherries surged out onto the tinselly table. "Good God," Harriet's grandmother said, "the cake is bleeding."

"A sign from the Lord," said the priest, who had crawled out from behind the bar, where he had been sleeping.

"Shut up," Earl growled.

The little plastic bride and groom dropped silently down the center hole in the cake. "Isn't that adorable?" Vi's mother said, "A cake with an elevator."

The Prickly Pears had been bustling about the room, filling people's glasses with champagne. "To the bride and groom," Pete said, holding his glass in the air. "Long may they wave!"

"Hurray!" people shouted.

Harriet and Clyde shoved their pieces of cake into each other's mouths. "Kiss!" Pete commanded, and when they did, laughing, he shrieked and smashed his glass on the floor.

"Isn't it interesting," Vi's mother said, staring at Pete's painted black patch, "what happens when you hire a pirate priest?"

"C'mon," Pete exhorted the crowd, "it's your turn."

A few of the Prickly Pears threw their glasses against the far wall, and the mariachis dropped their glasses and stamped on them. The rest of the crowd smiled appreciatively and continued drinking. "HEY!" Pete said. "Why do you think I bought two sets of glasses? These break real easy. Try it."

Vi put her hand on Pete's arm. "Pete, I think we should forget it. People might get hurt."

"Okay," Pete said, but he slumped sulkily.

Monster and Vi served cake, adding a cherry to each piece. "Line up over here," Harry called, "if you want chocolate ice cream on top."

The cake was a great success, as the bean dip had been and, to a lesser extent, the chocolate-covered pork. While people were still eating, Clyde turned to Harriet. "May I have this dance?"

Harriet wiped cake from her face. "Do you know how?"

"Madam," he said, "my sister and my bride, I was once an Arthur Murray instructor."

Clyde whirled her around and around to a spicy waltz, making great dips and fancy flourishes. Harriet laughed and the crowd applauded madly. When the music turned to a cha-cha-cha, Vi led Earl to the dance floor, and other guests followed. Soon everyone, even Pete and the priest, was bouncing up and down enthusiastically.

"I've never had so much fun at a wedding," said Harriet's grandmother, as her husband snapped her out to the end of his arm and pulled her back. She giggled at her usually dignified spouse, now flushed and beaming, his hair falling into his eyes.

"Pardon me," Panda said, "but I've been eyeing you from afar." He took Harriet's grandmother's hand, bowed, and swung her away from her astonished husband. "I like older women," he said. "Especially women with class."

"Well," Harriet's grandmother said. "My goodness!"

"Do you think I can make it?" Vi asked Earl as they were bumped and jostled by the lively crowd. "As a singer?"

"Absolutely," Earl said. "I was amazed, Vi, I really was. But you gotta have lessons, which I'd love to pay for. Why don't we write to this guy out in Hollywood I read about who trains singers? If he says okay, we'll go on out there for a while."

"Could we? Oh, I'd be so happy. Because sometimes you just know what's right, although you don't know why, but if you don't do it, your whole self aches."

They were in the center of the room when they stopped dancing. Vi threw her arms around Earl's neck, and they kissed. Around them the room spun like a carousel on high speed.

Monster interrupted their kiss. "Earl!" he shouted in their ears with a voice so booming it knocked Earl backward. "I forgot!" He caught Earl and set him upright. "I got a letter addressed to you that I found on the floor. Here." He shoved the pale blue envelope into Earl's back pocket.

"Open it," Vi said. "Maybe it's from a long-lost friend."

"Nah, I don't think so." Earl kissed her again. "I'll open it later."

Bam! Bam! Bam! Monster pounded on a table to silence the crowd.

"Harriet got a few words to say." As though he were picking up a doll, Monster held Harriet aloft and set her gently on the table. Never had she looked prettier. She had removed her veil, but her crown still glittered on her head. Her hairdo, so carefully arranged and sprayed by Vi, was descending in limp tendrils, her eye makeup was slightly streaked, her dress drooped off one shoulder, but she looked open and complete in herself.

"I'm going to throw this," she said, lifting the cactus flower bouquet over the heads of the crowd. "And I hope whoever catches it will be as happy as I am." She smiled down at

Clyde, who was holding her foot in its white satin slipper. "Anybody can try, men too, because even they might get married someday."

The tittering crowd rearranged itself as the unmarried ones moved closer to the table. Monster, who for the past hour had suffered an unbearable longing for a tiny blonde cherub named Cindy Lou, shoved past the crowd until he was next to Clyde. He raised his arms in the air.

"That's not fair," Zit said. "Nobody should hold their arms in the air, especially not a tall person, although I ain't mentioning any names."

"Don't worry." Harriet closed her eyes. "What will be will be."

"Isn't that the truth!" Vi's mother said.

Harriet, who knew exactly where Vi was standing, pitched the bouquet, which sailed just past Monster's outstretched arms. All the Prickly Pears jumped for it, even Panda, who usually pretended to be above such bourgeois rituals. But the bouquet calmly, single-mindedly, headed towards Vi. For a moment it hovered sassily in the air over Vi's head; then, with a smug sigh, it descended.

Distracted by the letter she was discreetly trying to remove from Earl's back pocket, Vi was taken by surprise. "Oh, look! I guess I caught it."

Earl rode the waves of applause like a triumphant sailor. "Shall we set a date?" he said huskily.

"For what?"

"To get married."

Vi smiled vaguely as she held the letter behind her back. "Oh, I don't know. We already live together."

With much guitar-thumping and occasional shrieks, the mariachis broke into a zealous version of "La Bamba." Pete began a sort of samba, and people lined up behind him. Bopping and kicking, they wound around the room, a laughing, drunken, human snake.

"Where are we going?" Harriet's arms were draped around Clyde's neck as he carried her out the door.

"Tonight we'll stay at the Pioneer Hotel, in the bridal suite, and tomorrow we're going to confront my dreams."

"That's nice." Harriet trembled happily and rubbed her cheek on Clyde's robe like a contented, pregnant cat.

"Who's Danny?" Stretched out naked on the rumpled sheets, Vi was reading Earl's letter in the bright desert moonlight.

Earl snored in response.

Vi stared thoughtfully at the shifting satin shadows, those night secrets hidden in the folds of their clothes strewn about the floor. Then she leaned over and bit Earl's bare ass.

"Aargh!" Earl yelled, as he contracted into a self- protective ball.

"Just say 'Damn it,'" the parrot squawked, "or 'Fuck you!' Keep it simple."

"What the hell are you doing?"

"Who do you know named Danny?"

Earl was now wide awake. "I don't know. Why do you ask me something like that? I only know one Danny, and that's my kid."

"Well." Vi waved the letter, which looked to Earl like a

blue, moonlit dove. "I hate to tell you this, but your son is dying. Although..." She inspected the upper right corner of the letter, where the date was inscribed in Esther's ornate script. "...this letter's pretty old. He might already be dead."

Part Three

Pasadena, 1952

F*riday, May 13,* Danny wrote in his journal. *This is a lucky day, which would surprise me if I were superstitious. I'm better after another week with the Positive Pressure Breathing Therapy Unit and Isuprel, Streptokinase and Streptodormase. Not well enough to go home, but I've lived so much of my life in hospitals, I almost don't mind. That would be an interesting project: to count up all the hours of my life, then the hours I've spent in hospitals, which I would subtract, of course, from my living total. That could get confusing, because the living total will continue to grow. I hope.*

I wonder if I will die soon, and if it will be in the hospital. No one tells me much because they don't want to upset me. But now that I know I have cystic fibrosis, I've begun to read about it. "The Children's Disease" it's called, because no one who gets it ever grows up. Also "The White Death," because of the way your lungs fill up with mucus.

This is a disgusting disease. Farting, sweating, spitting. And what's worse is I get used to it when I'm at home or in the hospital, and I think that's the way the world is. One big smelly sickroom, with everybody trying not to cough, like a bad game show. If you cough too much, you lose. And everybody's playing, the patients and the doctors. Only nobody has the answers. So I suppose if you win, it's really an accident.

Now where does God fit in? I guess he would be the game show host. Smiling in his long white Santa Claus beard and a blue satin suit. He'd introduce people and medicines. "Dr. Cohen is going to try Isuprel on Danny Norman. Will this work? The lines are open now, so call in and place your bets."

Most of the time I don't believe in God. Certainly not God the Creator and Cause of everything, because then I would have to hate him. If I had the energy, which I usually don't. And if God isn't the creator and cause, what good is he? Who wants to believe in a sad, Hollywood-type god who can't control or fix anything? A god who just shrugs his shoulders when people pray to him about their problems. "Oh, I'm sorry, Mrs. Norman, but I really can't do anything." Pause. "Yes, I know your son has cystic fibrosis, but that really isn't my fault." Pause. "No, I don't know whose fault it is. I just work here because it seemed to be as good a job as any."

I suppose God could be a creator without being evil, although if he allowed evil into the world (and it's certainly here), then it must be part of his nature. Unless there were two creators, a good one and a bad one.

But let's suppose everything isn't accidental. If there's only one God and he's not evil, then he's got to be.... absentminded. Careless. When he's molding men, he slips. "Oops! Mashed that batch." As he's making up the laws of the universe, he forgets a couple of important formulas, which he only realizes later when Hitler has wiped out six million Jews. "My, my! How did that happen?"

No, this thinking doesn't work, because if God were just careless, he would correct the situation. Bring the Jews back to life. Stop wars, heal diseases. So either he's evil, or he doesn't exist.

If I die, it will be an accident, just as my living is. Jessamyn's health has no more meaning than my sickness, and I wonder if it makes her any happier. It ought to. I would be happier if I were healthy, if I could go to school all the time and be an athlete, but not a dumb one. Imagine having muscles and being able to run and jump!

Gram says I should be happy that I have a good mind and talent in music and writing. This is what she calls bravery, accepting the goodness in yourself and others. Seeing the sunrise and not the darkness. "But the darkness comes," I said. She reached over to my bedside lamp and pressed the switch. "Then turn on the light."

So I'm making a list of light, and not just my talents, but the people I love, like Mother, Gram, Jessamyn, Melissa, Uncle David, Aunt

Kathleen and some of my doctors, especially Dr. Gettleman, who talks to me every morning.When I grow up, I might want to be a psychiatrist like Dr. Gettleman.

Oh, no, I said it, even though I promised myself I never would. "When I grow up." It doesn't seem fair to be a kid and not be able to say that.

I guess I've lost the light, just like I lost my father.

Danny closed his journal, turned out the light and settled into the familiar darkness of his hospital room.

Every day Esther checked the mailbox, but there was no letter from Earl. Ah, well, perhaps they didn't need him, because Danny seemed to be improving, although she sensed the doctors had little hope. And what, really, could Earl have done? He never had much sense of being a father, of having any connection to Danny. So there must be something deep in the blood, life passing through the bloodline like a universal current.

Esther wondered if Danny's real father felt a sense of loss, an emptiness, without knowing why. Perhaps Danny was missing his own father and not Earl. Would it have been wrong of her then to have brought Earl here because she listened only to Danny's words and not the message pulsing underneath?

Danny had said he did not believe in God, and he had told only Esther, who was the ostensible bastion of faith in their family. Dena had what Esther considered silly spiritual quirks, which annoyed her but were not, somehow, serious. She, on the other hand, represented Judaism: the Torah, the Sabbath, the Chosen People. Tradition in all its purity.

But Danny knew her somehow in a way that only Benjamin ever had. Not even her dear David, who never suspected her doubts and her questioning. What would they think, her family, if they knew she visited a psychic? Why was she not content with prayer?

Something was changing in Esther, she sensed it; something was opening, and she was not at all sure she liked it. At her age, shouldn't life be predictable? Shouldn't her beliefs be as clear and solid as her jewels in the vault? Ah, but she could feel them slipping away. She had given her beliefs away, just as she had given away her jewels, and what had she have received in return?

Certainly not the reliable universe she had wished for, one with straight paths through green landscapes under glass. The longer Danny's suffering continued, the less able she was to ask him to put on a prayer shawl and follow her. The paths were crooked and dangerous, she knew now, the grass and trees withered. She could speak of goodness with a faint voice, never of God.

And Kathleen as well. Esther must not be afraid to look at this: she was beginning to care for Kathleen in a way that she had never cared for Dena, her own child. This caring had crept up on her, insidiously, even while she was rejecting a Christian woman with her Christian children. Kathleen had a sweetness and a strength which Esther could not help but admire. Her children were Esther's grandchildren. They loved her, even though they knew she did not approve of them. Kathleen tried to cook like a Russian Jew, she brought Esther See's candy with soft centers, and she sang when Danny played the piano. She learned his songs.

Not because of the money, Esther knew, that was not why Kathleen loved her, and not even because of her husband. If Esther were to ask her, she would not know, as Esther herself did not know but was too proud to ask.

Benjamin would have loved these grandchildren, Esther knew. Jessamyn fierce and fearless as a hawk, so protective of Danny that she almost killed him. In Esther's first days of fear when Danny was in the emergency room, she was angry, but now she understood. And little Melissa like a tumbling, giggling baby bear. They brought sunlight into Esther's shadowy house, a rush of energy she needed more than she had ever acknowledged.

Dena could tell that Esther was changing her attitude toward Kathleen and her children, and Dena didn't like it. She said, "Mother, David was wrong to marry a shiksa, and just look at the result. No boy at all, just two wild girls, one of which almost killed Danny."

"Yes, Dena," Esther said, "that's true."

That way of talking made Dena furious. She knew her mother always did it to put Dena in her place, as though she wasn't worthy of any real interaction. So this time Dena said, "Mother, why don't we have a discussion for once, like two intelligent adults?"

"What would you like to talk about, Dena?" Esther said in that slow, deliberate way she had that drove Dena crazy. She put on her little wire glasses and looked at Dena, but not as though she was her equal. More like Dena was an odd animal who had gotten into her house by mistake.

"I told you," Dena said as her face got hot and she began to sweat at the roots of her hair. "I want to talk about that invader, that idiot Kathleen, and her destructive children."

"All right," Esther said. "Then talk, and I'll listen."

"No, no, no! Both of us! I want an exchange."

"Fine," she said in a patient voice, but Dena saw her begin to tap her foot in her little black shoes, and her fingers play an impatient rhythm on the arms of her chair.

"We should keep them away from our house."

"I can't do that, Dena," Esther said.

"Why not? Just tell them we want to live in peace, a nice, quiet, respectable Jewish family. They can live their Gentile lives somewhere else."

"What about David?" Esther said. "He is your brother."

"David has chosen!" Dena said in a voice that began to rise and frazzle with frustration. "He wants to rub shoulders with Christians, and I'm not surprised. I remember him even as a child staring at those awful pictures of Jesus hanging on the cross in Woolworth's."

"It is unfortunate," Esther said, "that Kathleen is not Jewish, and in that sense David has, I suppose, made an unwise choice. I was convinced of it for a long time. But now I am beginning, even at my age, to look past my prejudices, and I see how lovely Kathleen is. I understand why David loves her. I, too, would love her in that way if I were a man."

"Oh!" Dena shrieked. "Mother, I can't believe it! Your old age is getting to you, if you think an Irish whore in a tight red dress is lovely!"

Then Esther did something not at all like herself. She stood up out of her chair, and her voice got strong, the way

Benjamin's was. She even started to look like Dena's father, all stern, even in her usually soft cheeks. "Dena," she said. "I am going to say something, and I want you to remember it. I will say it only once. You have no right to call anyone a whore, unless you openly acknowledge that quality in yourself."

"What?" Dena heard her voice twisting up like the tin around an opened can of Spam.

"Be quiet!" Esther said. "All these years I have been an accomplice in your deception. I have known who Danny's father was, but for the sake of the child I have not spoken. What would have been the point? But a woman who gets pregnant by a man she has never met before and will never see again, a woman who has always worn the tightest and most alluring clothing she can get away with and still pretend respectability, this woman cannot call her sister-in-law a whore!"

Dena's eyes began to itch, and suddenly she was sobbing in a way that embarrassed her. "You've never loved me, and this is the proof."

Like a balloon deflating all at once, Esther collapsed in her chair. "You may be right," she said, "but I do try, Dena. Even though you make it very difficult for me. And yet, I cannot blame you for what you are. I think Benjamin and I neglected you."

"You did!" Dena cried. "You loved Leah and took her to Paris. I had to stay home with Father, who was always at work, and those damn boys, who hated me! Nobody ever curled my hair the whole time you were gone; it hung straight down my back like a wet stocking. And speaking of which, my stockings got so dirty they could walk all over the house by themselves, and who would care? Not you, who was having a good time in

Paris with Leah."

"I know," Esther said. "It was wrong. But you whined all the time, and Leah was beautiful and easy to love."

"Mothers and fathers should love all their children the same," Dena said, although she knew they never did.

"Yes," Esther said. She pulled a shawl of silence over her head.

"So?" Dena said.

Esther stared at Dena blankly, and gradually Dena saw a little light at the back of her eyes. "Ah, well, you know, after Leah's death, I became crystallized with grief. Her death was my fault..."

"It was not!" Dena said. "This is a crazy idea of yours that I wish you'd drop. There is no connection between Leah's interest in hats, which you apparently encouraged, and the fact that she lost her head. None!"

"You think not?" Esther said. "But a mother influences her child, as even scientists agree, and on deeper levels than we would imagine."

"If that was true, then Danny would know that Earl was not his father. Because never, in my heart of hearts, have I lied to myself about this, even though I know you think I do. And Danny doesn't even suspect!" Dena snapped her fingers, which were trembling because she had never talked about this to her mother. "So much," she said, "for a mother's deep influence!"

"This is not the same," Esther said.

"We are talking," Dena said, "about things which are not talked about but which have an effect anyway."

"I talked about hats," Esther said.

"But you did not talk about losing someone's head! Did

you? Did you ever say to Leah, 'Now, Leah, I want you to think about losing your head?' No, you didn't say that! And don't look at me like I'm a dragon. You never even said, 'Be careful about losing your head, because people do sometimes.' You never spoke about it at all, and you never even thought it in your deepest self, because that sort of thing just doesn't happen! People don't lose their heads. So you did not make Leah take that fatal car ride. It was an accident in every possible sense!"

All of a sudden Dena heard herself shouting, which she had never done to her mother, but she didn't care. This was something they needed to say.

Esther opened her eyes very wide, and spotlights went on inside. "I wonder if you could be right."

Dena's whole self rose up and clapped its hands with joy, too soon, of course, because as soon as Esther said that, the light turned off. "After Leah's death," she said, "I became rigid through fear. I had been innocent too long, protected by Benjamin, and now that he was no longer there, I had to cling to the familiar customs, rituals, beliefs, because the unknown terrified me. Without realizing, I became a bigot."

Dena's skin began to crawl. "Mother," she said, "Father was still alive when Leah was killed."

"Oh, was he?" Esther said, as though she couldn't be less interested.

"Yes," Dena said, "he was. He brought Leah's body back and arranged everything, don't you remember?"

"But Nathan and Samuel..." Esther said vaguely.

"Did nothing! They were helpless, just as we all were. Father did it; he was our strength."

Esther smiled. "Yes, he has always been our strength."

"I can see there are some things we can't discuss, so perhaps we should get back to Kathleen and her corrupting Gentile influence."

Esther arched her eyebrows and looked at Dena slyly over the top of her glasses. "Why don't you admit your jealousy? You've always been fascinated by Gentiles."

Dena bolted out of her chair.

"Rose sat on a tack," Esther murmured. "Rose rose."

"No," Dena cried, "don't do this to me. Don't let your mind go all to pieces, not now, when we..."

"What?" Esther said.

But Dena didn't answer, because she realized, as though she had been knocked over by a thunderbolt, that she and her mother were having an honest conversation. Like equals. Which meant, no matter what Esther said, that she loved her!

At last Jessamyn felt justified. Now everyone knew she loved Danny and he loved her, which they should've known all along, but they were too stupid. He was getting better, so they were letting him have visitors, and who was the first person he asked for? Jessamyn!

She went out and spent all her allowance on a huge card with Bugs Bunny on the front. He was chewing a carrot and saying, "What's up, Doc?" Then inside he said, "I ear you're getting better." Danny had the card propped up on the table right beside his bed.

Every day after school Jessamyn rode her bike to the hospital, and the nurses let her in even if it wasn't visiting hours. This afternoon she and Danny played a game called "What Would You Give Someone?" Jessamyn made it up. You had to think of a person and the one thing you could give him. First she said Gram, and she picked a bouquet of white roses. Danny said he would give her Grandpa. "But he's dead!" Jessamyn said.

Danny folded his arms and looked at her like a schoolteacher. "You didn't set any limits."

"A thing is not a person, whether he's alive or dead," she said, "but okay. Now, let's take my father. I would give him money."

"He has money," Danny said, "from his novel."

"No, I guess he spent it all on the piggy bank factory, and now he needs more."

"Well, I think what he needs is to write another novel and not waste his time with piggy banks."

"You sound like my mother. What would you give her?"

"Oh, something soft and silky, I suppose. A shawl in bright colors."

"I'd give her a box of happiness."

"She is happy. She's got you and Melissa and Uncle David..."

"No, she's not. She wants Daddy to write and not spend his money in crazy ways, and she wants..." Jessamyn quit talking before she said Mother wants Aunt Dena and Gram to like her.

"What would you give my mother?" Danny said.

Just after Jessamyn had been so good about holding her tongue, a devil popped out and said, "Kindness."

Danny and Jessamyn stared at each other while the hospital machinery hummed away. Then he looked out the window at the palm trees. "I'd give her a healthy child."

"You will be healthy," Jessamyn said.

"Thanks," he said. "Would you like some lemonade?"

Jessamyn said sure, so Danny poured some from his pitcher. When he handed her the cup, she saw how skinny his arms were, like chicken bones. And his skin was so white you could almost see through it.

"You're looking at death," he said.

"Danny, don't talk like that! You're getting better. Everyone says."

"I'm sorry. That's called being morbid." He pushed back his covers. "Why don't you take a walk with me?"

"Last time I took you for a walk, we got in big trouble."

They laughed; then Jessamyn helped him out of bed and he leaned on her a little while they walked around the shiny beige hospital corridors. She noticed that everyone seemed to like Danny. People would wave, and if they could get up, they'd come to their room door and talk. In Danny's wing there were mostly children with the same sickness, cystic fibrosis. So there was a lot of coughing and spitting going on, but it didn't stop anyone from being glad to see them.

There was a little Southern girl with wispy red braids tied with yarn. She was skinny and pale like Danny but with freckles. "Hey," she said, holding her hand out like a grownup, "I'm Roseanne. What's your name?"

"Jessamyn."

Roseanne shook her hand for about five minutes, while she smiled and smiled. "You sure are lucky to have a cousin like Danny," she said. "He reads books and knows arithmetic, and sometimes he tells stories in the nicest way. Here." She handed them two pieces of bubble gum. "I saved these for you."

"But you don't know me," Jessamyn said.

"Maybe I will now."

Chewing their bubble gum they walked into another wing with old people. A man who looked as though he was a hundred years old, with white eyebrows and scraggly white hair, came out to talk. "Hi, Danny." He pushed up the sleeves of his blue flannel bathrobe. "Wanna see my new muscles?" When he flexed his arms, little bumps appeared. "Wouldja like to touch?" he said to Jessamyn.

She didn't really want to, because he was so pale and wrinkled with big tan spots like melted moles. But she said to herself, what if I was sick and funny-looking, would I want people to be afraid of me? So she felt his muscle and said, "Wow!" He seemed to feel better, and Jessamyn really didn't mind doing it.

"Introduce me to your cute little girlfriend," he said.

Danny blushed and said, "Jessamyn, this is Mr. Mulvaney."

They shook hands, and Jessamyn started to say, I'm not his girlfriend; I'm his cousin, but she didn't because Danny didn't. He must've had a reason, Jessamyn realized. Finally, this voice inside her head, like a radio announcer, said, Danny wants a girlfriend! That's silly, Jessamyn thought, he's too young and sick. But she knew it must be true, even though it was hard to imagine. Would Danny ever kiss a girl? Send her a valentine? Drink a soda with her in a drugstore? She had known Danny all her life, and he probably was her best friend as well as her cousin, so why didn't she see that he might want a girlfriend? She had a picture of him always sitting with his books and coins and stamps in his dark house. And maybe the reason she thought he needed his cousins to pull him out into the world was that she had heard her father say that so often. Now she saw Danny in the hospital talking and laughing with people, and she was surprised that she could know someone really well and not know him at all.

They walked much more slowly back through the hallways because Danny was tired. When they passed Roseanne's room, she didn't come to the door, so Jessamyn looked in. There was a curtain around her bed, and Jessamyn could hear her coughing.

Then a doctor came out. "Roseanne can't have visitors right now," he said. Danny pulled Jessamyn away. She blew a huge pink bubble, because she thought Roseanne might like that, and when she turned around, she saw the doctor closing the door to Roseanne's room.

Ever since Benjamin died, Esther had been talking to him, telling him her secret thoughts she had never been able to do when he was alive. After her conversation with Dena, she left the house, closing the screen door gently behind her, and walked slowly across their front lawn. The night was cool, and a full moon was hanging from the top branches of their live oak tree.

"Benjamin," Esther said, "we need to talk. All our lives we have closed the door to Dena, who is our child, whether we like her or not. Just as we closed the door to Kathleen, when David brought home his new bride. When I was younger, I felt good about this. I liked being in an inner room with you, a room cozy with pride. No one allowed in without our approval, and, oh, our standards were high!

"Family members generally, although I think only

successful ones. Wealthy people, cultured people, and never the unwashed, uncircumcised goyim, their bellies rotten with pork and shellfish.

"There were our golden boys, Nathan and Samuel, who knew money and loved it, as you did, my dearest, so wealth came easily to all of you. Then David the poet and story teller, also like you. Leah was mine, with my dark beauty, you often said, of a slender kind that made men want to protect us.

"But Dena, the runt of the litter. No one cared about her or noticed her until she whined, so her stunted little spirit, which we never helped to grow, wandered away from us. At thirty, it flowered into full rebellion in a way that made me very unhappy, Benjamin.

"If it had not been for Danny, I might have sent her away, this vulgar aberration with her tight dresses and common language. But she stayed with me, she and Danny, and now I see that she cannot help what she is, and furthermore, she is not stupid. She has an honesty and a surprising earthy intelligence which sometimes shines out past her petty possessiveness.

"Let me tell you one thing she said: I did not cause Leah's death. Is that possible, Benjamin? Could I die without this terrible burden on my heart?

"There is something I need to do, and I think you could help me, because Leah is gone in a way that you are not. I need to learn to love Dena. If I could do that, if we could, then, with your permission, I could take Kathleen into my house, into our inner room. She could be the daughter I lost.

"My feet are wet, Benjamin, out here in the grass, silver with moonlit dew. What a comfort it is to have you here beside me! When we go back into the house, will you take off my shoes and massage my feet with your warm hands?

"Listen to the applause of the leaves! Those trees are old too, so they appreciate the time of our love. Imagine, we have been married sixty-six years! If I am eighty-two, then you must be ninety now, Benjamin. So old and so handsome.

"I've been meaning to ask you whether God exists. You won't tell? No, please, don't move away from me. It's a simple question, but if you prefer not to answer, I withdraw it. Come, let's walk down the street together, and be sure to use your cane, these sidewalks are so cracked. What are those tiny purple flowers? Could they be violets, like the ones I wore on my pink silk honeymoon dress?"

Dena was upset, because her mother was wandering around outside again, the sixth night in a row. She wrote "MW" on each square of the kitchen calendar when Esther went out for another evening ramble, so she could keep a clear record of her trials.

Each night Dena went out after Esther, partly because she felt guilty that she spent so much time at the Temple of Health, and with Danny still in the hospital, Esther was alone quite a bit. Then there were the neighbors, who were nosy as hell, which was no surprise to Dena.

"Wasn't that your mother?" old Mrs. Watts had asked her yesterday, "I saw walking down the street talking to herself?"

"What made you think so?" Dena asked, as snotty as she could be without causing a neighborhood uproar. "I thought it was *your* mother." Mrs. Watts, whom Dena privately called "Mrs. Wart," harrumphed and limped back into her house.

But Dena would have liked not to say anything at all, and she knew her mother wouldn't like to think the neighbors were spying and gossiping behind their Venetian blinds.

"Besides," she said to Rabbi Saltzman, "Mother could get hurt. She could walk right into the traffic without seeing the red light, and who would there be besides me to help her? Certainly not David who is frittering away his time on Gentiles and plastic piggy banks."

"This walking outside is a dangerous business," Rabbi Saltzman agreed.

"Oh," Dena said, "how could it be that Mother would get senile just when we are beginning to talk to each other? It's hardly fair. And Danny needs her too; she has been such a comfort to him, reading to him every morning to give me some time to myself. Which means," she said sweetly, "time with you, dear Daniel."

"Yes." He stroked her hair. "Time for us both to prepare for the Great Healing."

Dena and Rabbi Saltzman had been spending every morning and most evenings together for an hour or so at the temple, but Thursday night she persuaded Daniel to come home with her. "I need help with Mother," she said. "It's too much for me alone, she needs a man's vibrations to center her, and I'm not asking David."

When they arrived, the house was empty, with the door wide open, "like an engraved invitation," Dena said, "to every thief in the area." She ran inside quickly to see if her mother was there, although Dena knew she wouldn't be, and she checked to see if anything was missing. But the house looked just the same, with the radio and lights on, and the jewelry still in her mother's underwear drawer.

Dena locked the house and dragged Rabbi Saltzman down the street, because she knew the exact route her mother took, after following her for five nights. She knew her mother was heading for the big palm tree on the other side of Huntington Drive, the one with the tinsel from last Christmas dripping down from its highest fans.

"Why does she want to go to a tree?" Rabbi Saltzman was huffing along behind Dena and trying to maintain his dignity.

"She says Father told her Leah's soul is caught in the top somewhere, and she thinks the tinsel is the soul's tears."

"Oh, my," Rabbi Saltzman said, and Dena knew he was thinking her mother was a total loony. But she wasn't, of course, not total, except on recent evenings.

They found her right at the foot of the tree, looking up and muttering. "Mother," Dena said, "this is Rabbi Daniel Saltzman, and he's come to take you home."

"Hello, Mrs. Sherman," Rabbi Saltzman said, as he put his hand on Esther's arm. Esther gave a horrified shriek.

"Mother," Dena said, "how can you shriek like that? Daniel is a rabbi."

"I'll have none of it," she said. "Unless you can get Leah's soul out of that tree."

"Leah is not in that tree, Mother," Dena said.

"Not Leah," Esther said. "Are you deaf? Did you hear me say 'Leah'? No, I said quite clearly her soul is in the tree, and obviously caught. Look up, you can see the tears."

"Mrs. Sherman, those are not tears but Christmas tinsel," Rabbi Saltzman said.

"If ever a rabbi lacked some basic comprehension, you are

he." Esther gave Rabbi Saltzman one of her shriveling looks. Then she focused back on the top of the tree. "Leah's soul," she said quietly, "come down, now. I implore you in front of strangers. You are not caught, you only think you are, which is a common human condition as well."

Rabbi Saltzman gave Dena a look down to the very depths of her feet; then he began to climb slowly up the palm tree.

"What is he doing?" Esther said.

"He is bringing down that bunch of tinsel, Mother, so you can see Leah's tears for what they are not."

Esther watched Rabbi Saltzman crawling and making little umphing noises.

"Climbing a palm tree is not easy, in case anyone ever said it was, with all those prickers and little knives," Dena said. "And Daniel in white pants, but at least in tennis shoes."

She was sure her mother would be impressed, but after a few minutes Esther said, "I don't like seeing men climb palm trees. Such vulgar exhibitionism, and if you said this man is a rabbi, then I am certain you are lying."

"Mother, you will do anything to be contrary." Dena hoped Daniel hadn't heard her, because he was fairly high up by then. All they could see was his feet and legs.

"It will do him no good, in any event," Esther said. "Leah's soul will be frightened and will simply move away."

"I'm almost there," Daniel called down to them.

Just then a police car pulled up, with two very young policemen. One leaned out and said, "What's going on here? You two ladies need help?'

"No, thank you," Dena said. "But it was nice of you to offer."

"We certainly do." Esther pointed to the top of the palm

tree. "Do you see that wild man up there?"

The policeman craned his neck around and said, "Oh, Jesus, Frank, look at this!"

Esther went over and patted him on the shoulder. "I'm glad you see it the way I do, young man. Furthermore, that is a so-called rabbi."

The policemen got out of the car and stared up into the tree. "Call the fire department, Frank," the first one said.

"Please don't bother," Dena said. "You're making a big mistake. Rabbi Saltzman is perfectly capable..."

They didn't listen to her, of course. While the second policeman went to the car to call for the fire department, Esther said confidentially to the first one, "Such unbecoming behavior, don't you think?" She held her head high, like a queen, and raised her eyebrows.

"What's he doing in the tree?"

"He's rescuing a young girl's soul. Or he thinks he is, although clearly that is impossible."

"God damn!" the first policeman said to the second. Then he turned to Esther and apologized. Esther said that was fine, she didn't mind a little swearing, and she moved forward so the streetlight would hit her pearls.

"I got transferred to the Pasadena area to get away from all those L.A. kooks," the second one said.

"Rabbi Saltzman is not a kook," Dena said, but she could have been speaking in pantomime, for all the good it did her.

"Not only is he being ridiculous," Esther said, "but also foolhardy. Climbing a palm tree, especially so high, is dangerous, and I would think someone would have tried to stop him!"

Esther tried to nail Dena with a look, but she wasn't

accepting. "He's doing it for you, Mother!"

"Did I ask him to climb that tree?"

"Not in so many words, but he understood..."

"Nothing," Esther said.

That drove Dena wild, because everyone always used to finish her sentences, and Leah and her mother were the worst. As though they couldn't stand to hear the rest of her thought, in case it might be different from theirs. And why was poor Daniel in that tree if not for her mother? Could she tell the policemen her mother was not in her right mind and cause a public scandal? No, she could not.

"I've got it!" Daniel shouted. They saw him leaning out to dislodge the ball of tinsel.

"Be careful, Daniel!" Dena yelled.

"Daniel?" the first policeman said. "You married to this nut?"

Dena could feel herself blushing, and she said quietly, just to hear the sound of the words, "Someday I may be."

"He'd better be careful," Esther said, "because he's likely to slip."

"Don't say that!" Dena cried, as a fire siren began to wail. The bundle of tinsel descended right down into her arms, and she held it out. "Look, Mother. Do you see what this is?"

"Do you think I'm a lunatic?" Esther said. "That is a ball of tinsel."

Dena was relieved. "At last, you admit it: these are not the tears of Leah's soul?"

"Of course not," Esther said.

"Who's Leah?" the first policeman said.

"The dead girl whose soul that idiot was trying to rescue,"

Esther said, looking disdainful.

The fire truck screeched up, and the firemen scrambled out with a big net.

"Go away," Dena said, waving her arms at them. Then she turned to her mother. "I will not have you maligning Rabbi Saltzman..."

She was cut off by a hideous howl.

"It doesn't matter," Esther said. "Look, he's falling."

Indeed, Rabbi Saltzman was plummeting down. "And if the firemen hadn't been there with the net," Dena said later, "I do hate to think!"

He landed with a thump that wrenched Dena's heart out of her body, and he lay bouncing a little in the center of the net. His eyes were closed, his pants and shirt torn, his hands and face bleeding.

"Quick!" Dena shouted. "Call the ambulance! Give him oxygen!" She tried to climb into the net, but the firemen pushed her back. They lowered Rabbi Saltzman to the ground.

"I think I'll go now," Esther said. "This is more excitement than I am accustomed to." She turned away.

"Would you like us to press charges, Ma'am?" the policeman named Frank said.

"No, thank you," Esther said. "Why bother?"

"Charges?" Dena cried. "Wouldn't it make more sense to find out if he's alive?"

Hearing her voice, Rabbi Saltzman sat up and swayed in little circles. "I'm all right, but I would like a handkerchief."

Dena was outraged, because no one responded, just stood there staring like cast iron lawn statues. She supposed they thought they'd get contaminated if they touched a rabbi they thought was a crazy man but who was really the sanest person around. She wiped Rabbi Saltzman's face with some Kleenex she had in her purse; then she straightened up and glared at the firemen. "If someone would help me get Rabbi Saltzman back to the house, instead of gawking like idiots, then people in this town might realize for the first time that firemen are human beings." No one moved, so Dena said, "Perhaps gestures like these will help you to raise money for the fire department."

Suddenly their eyes unglazed. This short, fat fireman came over and said, "I'll help you, Ma'am." He and another fellow who wore his fire hat down over his eyes lifted Daniel into the fire truck and invited Dena to join them.

Even though she was worried about Rabbi Saltzman, who was crumpled against her shoulder, she did love the ride. Way up high like that, whizzing through the warm night streets!

After the firemen had laid Rabbi Saltzman on the couch and said goodnight to Esther, who was listening to the radio with a glass of milk as though nothing at all had happened, Dena walked them to the door.

"Tell that rabbi," the short one said, "if he keeps doing kooky stuff like climbing palm trees on Huntington Drive, he's gonna give his religion a bad reputation."

Dena didn't even bother to answer.

Her mother went to bed without so much as a yawn in their direction. Dena bathed Rabbi Saltzman's wounds; then she led him in to her bedroom.

"Oh, no," he said, "I can't spend the night here, Dena. Not in your mother's house."

"Don't worry," she said. "Everything will be fine. Mother doesn't even seem to notice you're here."

He was so tired he didn't argue any more. Dena helped him undress, took her own clothes off, and they got into bed.

Miraculously, Rabbi Saltzman seemed to revive, with the most huge and beautiful erection she had ever seen or felt. They couldn't keep their hands away from each other. Never had Dena felt her juices flowing like that, and they made delirious love for hours. "Oh, Daniel," she whispered, "you have amazing energy. I mean, you'd think one time would be all for a while, but no, after about ten minutes, back again?" Naturally, for her mother's sake, they stifled their groans and cries.

Some time near dawn they fell asleep. At about nine a.m. Esther walked in without even a knock to tell Dena she was taking the bus to the hospital. She looked at Rabbi Saltzman asleep next to Dena, humphed a little, and said, "I knew you were desperate." And that was all.

Last week I won three pairs of Owl Drug Store nylon stockings from "Quiz Down" on KMPC, Danny wrote. *Also a canary in a gold-colored cage. The canary's name was Chopper, which I thought was silly, so I changed it to Bobbie because you can never tell the sex of a bird. Bobbie is hanging here in my hospital room, and I think he or she is very unhappy, which I could understand. Who wants to be caged up all the time? I told Gram if the bird looks too desperate, I'm going to set it free.*

"Just make sure you let it go outside the hospital," Esther said. "If it gets loose in here, you know how the doctors will react."

Danny knew she was right, but it would be funny to see their faces, especially since most of them knew him. His doctors now were Dr. Gregg, Dr. Hyman, Dr. Bloom, Dr. Ware, Dr. Boyd, Dr. Housepian, Dr. Bernstein, Dr. Cohen, Dr. Schaffer and Dr. Shoor. Danny liked them all except for Dr. Shoor, who was too serious and scary when he came around. The doctors never agreed on anything. Dr. Boyd and Dr. Bernstein thought Danny could go home, as long as he rested and continued his breathing exercises. Dr. Gregg, Dr. Ware and Dr. Houspian wanted Danny to stay in the hospital. Dr. Shoor wanted to transfer him to a sanatorium.

Clearly what Danny wanted didn't matter, especially since he didn't want any of their choices. He wanted to live outside, in a sunny garden, and have only his favorite people come and visit. Then, when he got healthier, he wanted to walk all over the country with his father and see what people were like. They would visit people on farms in the Midwest, real cowboys on ranches in places like Wyoming, city people in New York and Southerners. He always imagined Southerners sitting among magnolias and sipping mint juleps. His father would give piano concerts everywhere, and sometimes they would even play duets. Everyone would love them; at least, Danny hoped they would.

Why didn't his father come back?

In his journal he had made a list of birthdays, and he'd noticed interesting correspondences: Jessamyn, his Uncle Nathan and Aunt Kathleen's youngest sister were all born on September 2, Aunt Leah on September 6. Uncle Samuel, Uncle David and his father all were born in March. Melissa was born on December 17 and his cousin Bernie on December 15. The only odd ones were Gram, born in May, Aunt Kathleen, born in July, and Danny, a January child.

Danny would have liked not to be odd, although if Gram was odd too that made it better. Every morning Gram came to read to him. They were on the twelfth chapter of his world history book, and he loved to lie with his eyes closed and listen to her soft voice with its faint, husky accent. Such stories of ancient people roaming the earth, building great cities, fighting battles with invaders and then dying out! He worried that Gram might get tired, but she said she was getting educated herself.

One thing that bothered both of them: how, exactly, could a whole civilization die out? "Just because people conquer your country doesn't mean your whole way of life, your beliefs, your language changes, does it?" Danny asked. "Suppose I were an Egyptian, worshipping certain gods and goddesses, and some barbarians took over. Could they make me change to their gods? Or my language; how could they make me speak in a whole different way? I know it must happen slowly, but I'd like to imagine how. History books never tell you the details."

"I know," Gram said. She was a better teacher than Miss Jacobs, his latest home teacher, because Gram talked with him about how things might have been and why things happened. Miss Jacobs liked facts, and she was quite good at math.

This morning when Gram came, Danny was a little depressed, but Gram was flushed and excited. She said his grandfather, who had been dead a long time now, had been coming and taking her for walks every night. That sort of worried Danny, but he knew Gram wasn't crazy, just very deep and sensitive, so he thought maybe it could be true. After all, Danny felt a sort of mystical connection to his father, who hadn't come back yet. Why shouldn't people continue to exist even after their bodies die? Danny intended to.

"Well, at least if I were dead, I could get out of this hospital and travel around a little," he said.

His grandmother frowned at him and then reminded him of the trip they took to Chicago three years ago on the Golden State Limited. They went to Riverview Aquarium, Chinatown, two museums and two zoos.

He didn't remind Gram that he was also in the hospital for a week during that trip having X-rays, cardiograms, blood counts, allergy tests, vitamin A tests and stool and urine tests.

They took the Grand Canyon Limited back, though, and saw a lot of the country both ways. Danny loved eating on the train, the white tablecloths and napkins, the red roses in thin crystal vases, and the nice waiters. Sometimes when his mother took a nap, Gram and Danny would sneak back into the dining car to have an extra chocolate pudding. Even the endless wheat fields looked beautiful outside the windows of a dining car.

Danny had been saving money and now he knew how he was going to spend it: He was going to take another train trip with his mother and grandmother in the summer. Maybe they'd go across the desert, to see the sun setting on the mountains, red and gold glittering sand.

"I dream about the desert so often that I think my father must be there," he said, and his grandmother gave him a funny look. They didn't usually talk about his father, because the subject made everyone feel bad.

Gram gave Danny fifty cents a week allowance and his mother gave him eighty-five cents. So far he had managed to save seventy dollars and twenty cents. He also had two hundred dollars in savings bonds, so he could pay for his mother's and grandmother's tickets, as well as his own.

Danny told Jessamyn he was going to take a train trip in the summer, so she asked if she could come along. He said no.

"Why not?" Jessamyn said. She hated it when people didn't take her along, especially if it was because they thought she was too young. Fortunately for Danny, he didn't say that.

"I'm just going with Gram and my mother," he said, looking out the window. He was propped up in a chair with four or five pillows.

"Oh," Jessamyn said, "that's okay. I'll just ask Gram if she minds." She didn't say she'd ask Aunt Dena, because she knew her aunt didn't like her or Melissa or her mother. Jessamyn wasn't sure why she didn't like them. She heard her mother tell her father it was because they weren't Jewish, which would be a weird reason, in Jessamyn's opinion. She didn't care if people didn't go to her church. But her Aunt Dena was hard to figure out. Jessamyn thought maybe her aunt didn't like her because she was a hard person to like once you got to know her.

"I don't want you to talk to Gram," Danny said.

Jessamyn rolled her eyes the way she had seen her mother do when her father talked about piggy banks. "Why not?"

"I just don't," Danny said.

"Damn it," she said, raising her voice almost to a shout, "it's not fair! She's my grandmother, too, and don't think she isn't, just because she lives with you."

"I didn't mean that," he said. Jessamyn could tell she hurt

his feelings, which wasn't surprising. She hurt everybody's feelings all the time. Especially the people she really loved, like Danny and Melissa.

So she told him she was sorry, and he said okay and let her take Bobbie out of the cage and hold the bird on her finger. Danny said Bobbie wasn't necessarily a girl, which Jessamyn said was silly because Bobbie looked like a girl bird. Very delicate, with a high little voice.

"Then all canaries look like girls," he said, but he was laughing.

Then he started to cough, deep and loud, so the nurse came in and told Jessamyn to leave. While the nurse was getting Danny back in bed and giving him oxygen, Jessamyn put Bobbie in the cage and tiptoed out into the hall.

It was four-thirty and Jessamyn knew her grandmother would be coming any minute, because Danny had said she was bringing him a package that had come in the mail. She decided to talk to her grandmother about the train trip, even if Danny didn't want her to. She always liked to do things people told her not to do. Usually it turned out they were right, but not always.

For a few minutes she just stood there listening to the murmur of television sets and people talking in other rooms, but she got bored, which she often did. She walked down the hall to see if Roseanne was around. Her door was closed though, with a "No Visitors" sign on it. "Phooey," she said, which her mother claimed was a much better word than "dammit." All the way back to Danny's room she took giant steps, saying "Phooey, dammit, phooey, dammit," until she ran right into her grandmother and almost knocked her over.

"Oh!" Esther dropped her package and grabbed Jessamyn's shoulders, while she grabbed her grandmother's legs to keep her standing up, because she knew old people's bones were very delicate.

"Which is it," Esther said, "phooey or dammit?"

"I'm sorry." Jessamyn kept holding her grandmother's legs and looking down at her black little-old-lady shoes.

"Jessamyn," she said. "I am not angry." There was something in her voice that let Jessamyn know she wasn't just pretending the way grownups usually did, so they could really let you have it later.

"Okay." Jessamyn picked up the package and they started to go into Danny's room, but the nurse came out and said he needed to rest.

"Ah, well," Esther sighed. "Would you please give him this package?" The nurse took the package and closed Danny's door.

"So, uh, good-bye," Jessamyn said, because it seemed like the wrong time to ask about the train trip.

"Would you like to take a walk," Esther said, "while Danny rests?"

Jessamyn's face brightened. "Sure."

They went down the elevator to the first floor and out into a small park in front of the hospital. They strolled around slowly, looking at the roses, the birds-of-paradise and big, puffy yellow and white chrysanthemums. "Like pompons," Jessamyn said. Esther laughed and took her hand, for the very first time.

"That's a pretty dress," Jessamyn said. It was pale blue silk with tiny pink daisies on it.

"Thank you," Esther said. "Benjamin gave it to me."

"Who's Benjamin?"

"Your grandfather."

"Oh. I never met him."

"He's a wonderful man. How odd it is that you haven't met."

Jessamyn got a creepy feeling, like fuzzy caterpillars crawling up the back of her neck. "When did he give you that dress? It looks new."

"Just the other day. I found it in my closet. Benjamin often does such things to surprise me."

"But he's dead."

"Yes, but lately he's been coming to visit me."

"Like a ghost?" They sat down on a wrought iron bench to rest.

"Well, I suppose, but he seems almost alive. He always wears a white suit and a Panama hat, and he carries a cane. There is not the slightest bit of gray in his hair or mustache. 'Benjamin,' I asked him, 'weren't you silvery gray when you died?' 'Yes,' he said, 'but now I have the power to change things.' 'Can you change me too?' I said. He smiled and touched my hair. 'Not yet.'"

"When he touches you, can you feel it, like a person?"

"Of course. His touch is very real. Above all..." Esther blushed, "...when he kisses me goodnight."

"I saw a fox once, all dressed up in a green jacket and hat and holding a cane. He was standing up at the foot of my bed, staring at me. But he didn't touch me."

"Sometimes it is better not to be touched."

"Yeah," Jessamyn said. "By some people."

Esther adjusted the combs in her white hair; then she folded her hands in her lap. Jessamyn thought she looked really pretty in the blue dress and pearls, with her eyes sparkling. She could imagine her being a young bride.

"I told Benjamin it wasn't fair for me to remain white-haired while he was getting younger. And do you know what he said? 'You always look like my bride.'"

"I wish I could see him," Jessamyn said, because she'd read a lot of books about ghosts and knew they were possible.

"Perhaps sometime he will come to you and to Danny."

"And to Aunt Dena?"

"No," Esther said. "Never to Aunt Dena." She stood up. "Come. Let us continue walking and try to name the flowers."

Jessamyn took a huge breath and whapped it out like a snort. "Gram, do you like me?"

"Yes, I do. I must have been very unkind, if you need to ask."

"No," Jessamyn said, "most people have a hard time liking me. Like Aunt Dena."

"Aunt Dena has a difficult time liking most people."

Jessamyn thought that was one of the nicest things she had ever heard her grandmother say. She looked down at the flowers and smiled, then pointed. "Snapdragons."

"Yes," Esther said. They were walking again on the curving paths covered with sparkling marble chips.

"We used to make them talk by opening their mouths. And what are those?"

"Delphiniums."

"Is it because I'm not Jewish that Aunt Dena doesn't like me? That's what Mother says."

Esther was so startled her hand jerked and she stopped walking. "Aunt Dena would probably say so. And even think so. But I suspect she is jealous of you and your mother and Melissa. As she is of most people."

"Why?"

"Because she lacks a center in herself, a center that comes from love. You will not understand this, Jessamyn, because you love and are loved. You have a center."

"Oh. But I wouldn't mind being Jewish, if that would help. Only Danny says I can't be, because my mother isn't."

"We are moving beyond those limits," Esther said. Then she bent down and kissed Jessamyn on the cheek. "Now," she said, "that kiss made you as Jewish as you'll ever be." She straightened up very slowly and held her back. "Ooh, I do not bend the way I used to, and I will be glad when this infirmity is past."

"Are you going to take some medicine?" Jessamyn said.

"No. I am going to change."

Twilight was purpling into night when Esther realized she had gone farther than usual. Ah, well. She shrugged and leaned a bit more heavily on Benjamin, who was walking beside her. "Do not judge us, Benjamin, for you walk in the light and we are sealed in darkness," she murmured. "Transform us, instead, bring fire to our inner lives. Make me once again a white rose."

Benjamin dropped her arm, and she stumbled. "Oh, Benjamin, do not play tricks on me the way you did last week!" she cried. "Remember, we mortals don't understand humor the way you do, we've been caught so long in logic and conventions. I'm sure it amused you to convince me Leah's soul was hiding in that tree, because you wanted the rabbi to make a fool of himself. Were you hiding somewhere, laughing at the scene? Oh, how foolish of me not to have seen it before: this is your message to me that I should no longer be limited by ideas of the Chosen People. That pitiful rabbi was a sign that you've opened the door of our inner room so David's family may enter."

Benjamin took her arm once again. "What do you think of little Jessamyn, Benjamin?" He remained silent, as always, but he smiled. "Ah, I thought so," Esther said. "Well, I would suggest in that case that you visit both Jessamyn and Danny. It's not right for children never to know their grandfather. You have much to teach them, and they're both bright children who will learn quickly."

Then Benjamin gave her a look so imploring that her heart froze. "No, Benjamin, that's impossible. I cannot come to you yet, although I wish I could. You see, Danny still needs me, and I've just begun to accept Dena, which is only the first step toward love."

Esther's feet began to resist the pull of Benjamin's arm. "Where are we going? To Mount Wilson? Don't be silly, my darling, that's much too far. You forget how old I am, you really do, and I don't like the snow, it burns my feet.

Let's sit down here by the side of the road first. I'm so very tired, and I have many questions."

She lowered herself painfully down on the grass in front of a yellow stucco house, and Benjamin bent over her. "No, don't take off your jacket," she protested. "You'll catch a chill. For me to sit on? How sweet of you! And look, you're wearing a vest, just as you did in the old days, and your gold watch on a chain. Now, isn't that odd? I thought that watch was still in my shoe box at the back of my closet, with the last of my jewels."

She saw Benjamin raise one eyebrow in the teasing way he had. "No, of course I didn't pawn it. How could you think of such a thing?" she asked. "Darling, those jewels in my underwear drawer aren't real. I thought you knew that. All costume jewelry, pretty rhinestones and colored glass. Why would I let the children play with them?"

Esther closed her eyes and leaned back into Benjamin's arms. "Do you remember when you took us to Florida when the children were small? We made a castle in the sand, a huge one, and for once the children weren't fighting. You and Nathan and Samuel built up the walls, very thick and solid. David and Leah made windows and doors, decorated the walls with shells and shining wet rocks. You dug a moat, to keep the dragons away. Dena was only a baby then, perhaps two years old. I carried her down to the ocean so we could fill our pails with water, which we poured into the moat.

"We stopped for lunch, I remember, cold blintzes and fruit, and lemonade a touch too sour but made from real lemons, not like today. How hungry the children were! As I watched them sitting on the blanket, I worried about their sunburned skin, but they didn't care; they were too busy with happiness.

"Then, while the children were working once again on their castle, you scooped me up in your arms and ran with me down to the water. Can you imagine it, being that young and strong?"

Benjamin kissed her hair lightly. "Do you think that can ever happen again?" she said. "That I'll be young when I have left this body?"

There was a silence whiter than the drifting of clouds.

"I remember the waves rising up and crashing into us, the

taste of salt as we fell, laughing, and that night the tracings of salt like lace on our skin. What lovely, firm skin we had then!" Esther trembled and felt a blush rising up from her heart.

"Do you remember our first apartment in Chicago, down in the basement? Do you remember our big brass bed?"

"This is getting to be the absolute last of the last straws!" Dena shrieked. Rabbi Saltzman had driven her home on Friday from their session at the Temple of Health. They arrived by eight, or perhaps eight-thirty, which was her mother's usual time to wander. "Look," Dena said. "The house is lit up like a Ringling Brothers' Barnum and Bailey Circus." When she saw David's Studebaker parked in front of the house, her heart sank to her very knees.

"You don't think…?" she said to Rabbi Saltzman. Dena never finished her sentences when she was extremely moved.

"Have faith, little Dena," he said. "Your mother would not leave you before the love between you is firmly established."

"Maybe she had no choice." This sort of babbling was something she always did when she was nervous. They were hurrying up the front walk.

"We always have a choice," Rabbi Saltzman said. Yes, Dena thought, this is one reason I adore him: he says the most profound things, whether it's the right or the wrong moment.

When they went inside, she fully expected to see her mother lying on the couch motionless with her eyes closed. But no, there she was, lively and giggling, having tea and cookies at the dining room table with David, Kathleen and their unpleasant little girls.

"And what is the occasion," Dena said, "for all this merriment at such a late hour?" She took a cookie and handed one to Rabbi Saltzman, even though they were just those silly Oreos you could get at Safeway. And none too fresh, either.

Jessamyn and Melissa were playing with their Oreos in a way Dena always detested when she was their age, partly because it was always the popular girls who seemed to do it and partly because it was so messy. Sliding the cookies apart, so the white filling was smeared across each half. Oh, she knew those tricks, and now a third reason for hating them occurred to her: such bad manners!

"Isn't it," she said in a way she hoped would restore the situation to its proper gravity, "a little late for a party? After all, Danny is sick in the hospital, Mother has not been at all well, and the little girls should no doubt get their sleep!"

Jessamyn and Melissa rolled their eyes at each other, dropped their chins on the table and laughed in a way that made Dena forget all the charitable impulses Daniel had been helping her to develop.

"This is a Friday night, Dena," Kathleen said in a firm way. "The girls can stay up later, and Mother is--as you yourself can see--doing quite well."

Dena could not believe the tone of that woman's voice! What had she ever done to Kathleen, that she should speak in that way or look so challengingly right into Dena's eyes? "You have not answered my statement about Danny," she said, just to have the last word.

But then Esther herself spoke to Dena as though she were a child. "Dena, Danny is asleep now, and he would be very happy to see us having such a lovely time. Please, introduce your crazy rabbi friend and join us at the table."

"How do you know Danny is asleep?" Dena said, ignoring her mother's slur against Rabbi Saltzman.

"We just came from the hospital," David said, "and we decided to stop off to visit Mother." Then he stood up and held out his hand. "I am David Singer."

Rabbi Saltzman shook David's hand. "Daniel Saltzman," he said, "and I must confess I am a former rabbi, not a present one, a fact which Dena often forgets."

"It is not easy to shed the trappings of religion," Esther said ominously.

"Trappings?" Dena said, "and you so religious, Mother, and by the way, where did you get that man's white jacket you're wearing?"

"Benjamin gave it to me," Esther said.

"I thought we had given away all of Father's clothes to David and the boys. Did you keep that jacket hidden in your closet?"

"I did not," Esther said. "If you would learn to listen, you would hear me say Benjamin gave it to me, and I mean tonight."

David pulled up chairs for Dena and Rabbi Saltzman, who sat down, but Dena was not going to give in so easily. "Mother, you know Father is dead. It would be healthier for you to accept this fact at such a late moment in your life."

"Ah, Dena," Esther said. "If you could keep your mouth shut, I wonder if your mind could be more open."

Just as Dena was about to answer, David pushed her gently into a chair, as though she, and not her mother, was the old lady. "We found Mother sitting on this jacket right on the curb a couple of blocks away. I'm sure it's Father's jacket; it even has a Marshall Fields label."

"Does this mean, David," Esther asked, "that you believe me or not?"

"I believe you," Kathleen said, which made Dena understand why Cain would murder Abel.

"We believe you, Gram," Melissa and Jessamyn said, like a chorus of detestable children in Dena's worst nightmares.

"Thank you," Esther said, in a voice fraught with apparent sincerity. "I appreciate that. And now, I would like to know: does my son believe me when I say his father gave me the jacket this very night?"

There was a long pause while David weighed his words. Dena could see the little scale in his mind, and she thought, hah! now he's caught!

But he looked at Esther solemnly, without a trace of ridicule, and said, "Yes, Mother, I believe you."

"Let us find out what the rabbi thinks." Esther focused all her attention on Rabbi Saltzman, who was appreciatively eating Oreos. "Do you recognize the fineness of the line between what we mortals call 'life' and what we call 'death'?"

He choked a little, covering it with a cough, but when he realized the whole table was staring at him, he pulled himself together and spoke in the mellifluous tones Dena adored. "When I was a rabbi, I would have said a man lives on only in the memory of others. Now, however, I would have to say life is a continuum, and death is no more than an illusion."

"Well," Esther said. "You are not as crazy as I thought." Then she leaned forward and whispered, loud enough for everyone to hear, "But you should control your erratic, tree-climbing behavior."

"Thank you for your advice, Mrs. Singer," Rabbi Saltzman said with a straight face.

So now Dena knew she was the only bad person at the table! Everyone else, including her beloved Daniel--who was only being considerate of an older person's age, and she really couldn't blame him--was willing to humor her mother in her fantasies.

"All right," Dena said, "suppose I agree that Father's spirit could still exist and that he could come to visit Mother's mind. Even then, how could he hand a jacket, which is real and feel-able in this world, through to Mother from the world of the spirit?"

Now Esther became very sweet and calm. "Dena, dear, you must realize how little we know. When I see us through Benjamin's eyes, I realize how pathetically we mortals cling to apparent logic and conventions of the material world."

"A poet knows through intuition that this too, too solid flesh is merely a handful of shadows," David said with a smile that made Dena want to knock his teeth out.

"Fine," she said. "Fine. I give in. Father can hand all the clothes he wants right through from the realm of the spirit, and I do hope he keeps on handing out good quality merchandise."

Jessamyn and Melissa snickered until they spat their milk all over the table, which made Dena so furious she said something she hoped she would not someday regret.

"Why," she snarled at Esther, "don't you request women's clothes instead of men's?"

Esther touched her hand, again as though Dena was only a child. "This is the second dress Benjamin has given me, Dena." She was wearing a lilac silk dress with thin white stripes, which

Dena didn't remember seeing before. But, of course, Dena knew her mother had money of her own and was perfectly capable of taking the bus to the stores in Pasadena.

"Oh," Dena said, mimicking Esther's tone, "how very nice for you, Mother. Perhaps he could go beyond clothes and give us some money or--if he doesn't mind heavy objects--a new stove."

Esther didn't even get angry, which made Dena sizzle with fury. "Your father left us money, and Danny won you a new stove only this year, so let's not be too silly, Dena."

"I have an idea," Rabbi Saltzman said. "Why don't we all take hands and observe a period of silence?"

Everyone looked a little awkward and embarrassed, but slowly--and Dena wouldn't have believed it if she hadn't seen it --they took each other's hands. So what could Dena do, but hold out her own hands, until there they all were, one big, happy-looking silent circle.

But she wasn't happy, only amazed and uncomfortable. Especially because Melissa's sticky little hand was clutching Dena's right hand, and if her dear Daniel hadn't been holding her left one, she might have screamed.

Just then the phone rang. Saved by the bell, Dena thought as she went to answer it. But it was Dr. Gregg, calling from the hospital to tell her Danny's right lung had collapsed.

"Unhh!" Danny cried, though none of the doctors and nurses heard him. "Don't hit me! Not in the chest. Falling, back, down, backwards down stairs into my mind.

"Where did the air go? Is this Death in here, darkness,

down so deep, what a small room. No breezes? Then I can't move along, swept by wind.

"No god, I knew it, only four walls, and who is that sitting on my chest? Off, off, get away! Sign here says No Trespassing, Hunters Will Be Shot. And this means you, pointing at you, a long, bony finger.

"A game show? A contest, here in the velvet dark, burning so hot, this cannot be, the absence of light is cool. Blazing darkness, and you want to play? To whom am I speaking?

"All right, I'll fight, I'm a good opponent. Contestant with words, numbers, even a song. Want to fight with music? You name the tune, I'll put up a closetful of soap, the kind for sweethearts. You'll like it, whoever you are.

"You're putting up a Helbros wrist watch, seven jewels, sells for $22.50? But I can find that in the S & H green stamp book, and that's nothing compared to my side. Enough soap to wash the whole world clean.

"But you've got the time, and I don't? Okay, okay, wise guy, I always knew Death would be some comedian crouching in a black corner. Listen to this melody, you'll never guess it, so let it sweep right on by. Each note perfect and heavy, like Gram's lead crystal. Glasses shining in the dark.

"When you're dancing and you're dangerously near me, I get ideas. I get ideas… No, no, no, that is not it! You lose, it was a song of my very own. One I wrote for my father to play, and if you were smart, you would've guessed.

"Makes perfect sense: Death is stupid, just like Life was. Is, is, you lost, and now I've got the time!

"What is that rush of air, too much, I can't take it! Not fair, I'm going to explode! Poor loser! Don't give me that watch, don't watch me, just take some air!

"Oooooh, such pain! Who punctured my heart?

"Light, light at last. Fine, I'll take it. Oh, such a crummy room, and who is that boy lying there? Look, they're putting needles in his heart.

"Well, well, well, now there's something I can rely on. A series of numbers, solid as a walkway, and see, they stretch out to infinity. Put one foot down, then another. Careful, it's a little slippery, depending on the way you look at it. And up above, another number line. But you can't hang on to that, those are numbers in a mirror, with some pieces missing.

"For me to guess? I'd be delighted, but right now I'm sliding down this tunnel. What paintings on the walls! There's Rascal and the guppies, so many, and Bobbie flying away, and, oh, there's Mother naked, so many ways, with her arms reaching right out from the walls.

"Ah, ha! Who is this in a white suit and Panama hat, sitting so cool in the center of the lake? Grandfather? I can't come to you. All right, hold out your cane, I'll hold it, I'll walk on the water.

"Easy, easy, I should've known, like Easy Sloman's Contest. Win when you least expect it.

"Two chairs and a table in the middle of the lake, just like a painting, tea cups and a vase of flowers. Thank you, Grandfather. Oh, so much sugar, which I don't, usually, or can't, you know. But then, why not? In these circumstances.

"Benjamin? No, I don't mind. Face-to-face you look just like your pictures, a little serious, such a heavy mustache. But if I turn my head, a trick of the light, lake light, you grow younger, almost my age.

"Tell me, Benjamin, two things I want to know. First, about God and fairness. Why are you laughing? Don't you think, if there is a God, he...Yes, of course, I can just drink my tea. It is so nice to be with you, you must be an angel.

"But about my father: will I see him again? Yes? Oh, thank you, Benjamin, you have made me truly happy!

"No, not your watch! Such heavy gold, even the chain, and the delicate engravings. See, Gram gave it to you, don't you remember? Here is her name, signed with love. You really must keep it.

"All right, I'd be glad to bring it to her.

"Now, light the candles, Benjamin, it's growing dark. A wind is coming up, blowing the flames. How they dance on the lake! A flame above, a flame below, and I'm moving.

"Good-bye, Benjamin, I'm going down fast, this is a non-stop elevator. See you soon!"

Before he opened his eyes, Danny heard applause. Then he saw his doctors and nurses laughing like a bunch of lunatic white angels, and one tiny nurse said, "Hallelujuh!"

"Yes," Danny mumbled. "I guess I'm back."

Kathleen explained to Jessamyn that Danny had had two spontaneous pneumothoraxes, which meant, she said, that his lungs got full of too much air or gas, and they had to stick needles in to get the air out. Jessamyn thought it was a little confusing, because the doctor had told Aunt Dena that Danny's lung had collapsed.

Nobody but Aunt Dena and her grandmother had been allowed to see Danny until today, so Jessamyn went to the hospital right after school. When she came to the open door of his room, she thought he was sleeping. She tiptoed in, careful not to wake him up. But when she came near his bed, she saw Danny had his eyes open, staring at the wall.

"Hi, Danny," she whispered.

Danny looked at her in a startled way and put his hand on his chest, just below where a tube was coming out.

"How do you feel?" she said, although she knew the question was stupid.

"Jessamyn, I've been seeing our grandfather."

"What do you mean?" She tried to sound nice, but she hated it whenever kids got freaky. It was okay for Gram because she was old, and her mother said that happened sometimes to old people.

"At first it was just a dream," Danny said. "Or maybe when I was almost dying. But now, when no one else is around, I can see him sometimes with my eyes open."

"Oh, Danny!" Jessamyn's voice spiraled up in a fearful whine. "You know he's dead!"

"That's true," Danny said. "Never mind."

"I'm sorry," she said, because Danny looked so sad.

"I'll probably see him again," Danny said. "He's very nice, and he looks just like Gram says he does. She sees him all the time now."

"I know," Jessamyn tried to sound like a grownup. "Does he talk to you?"

"Oh, yes. But just when I'm asleep. He's very busy, and he really hates to explain himself. He's an angel now, and they have a tremendous amount of work overseeing things. Which is something I didn't learn in Hebrew school."

"I never learned it either, in catechism."

The nurse stuck her head in the door. "Visiting hours are over."

"I just got here," Jessamyn said, but Danny's eyes began to close. He looked very, very tired. "Good-bye, Danny," she said, "see you tomorrow."

Danny smiled, with his eyes shut, and then she saw this big gold watch in his left hand.

"Where'd you get the watch?"

"From Benjamin," Danny whispered. "It's for Gram, but she's letting me keep it till I get better. Benjamin doesn't mind."

As she rode her bike home, she kept thinking, Danny saw a ghost, a real ghost, and he was her own grandfather. No, she told herself, don't be stupid. It's just those medicines they're giving him in the hospital. So where'd he get the gold watch? From Gram, of course, when he was in a coma. She felt better about figuring it out but also a little sad, because she realized she'd like to believe in ghosts. The friendly ones.

That night she dreamed she was riding her bike home from the hospital again. Suddenly this man dropped down right in front of her out of a palm tree. She screeched to a stop. It was her grandfather, only much younger and without the cane he had in the gold-framed photo Gram kept on her dresser.

He swept his hat off his head the way Jessamyn had seen movie stars do and made a deep bow.

"Hello, Grandfather," she said, as naturally as she could, although her heart was bamming away in her chest so loudly she was sure he could hear it. He straightened up and gave her one of those small smiles men with mustaches sometimes do, when the corners go up just a bit.

Then he said, "Good afternoon, Granddaughter."

"You must be a ghost," Jessamyn said, "and I've never seen one before."

"Yes," he said, "my form is somewhat different from yours. Is that what frightens you, or do you find it difficult speaking to an old man?"

"We're not really speaking," she said.

Just then a lady all in red with high heels clicked up behind them. "Careful!" Jessamyn said. Her grandfather moved out of the lady's path, which was too bad, because Jessamyn wondered if she would have walked right through him. Then the lady turned around and looked at Jessamyn in a disapproving way. "You're talking in your sleep," she said.

"Let me try some other form," her grandfather said, "to make our communication easier." And suddenly he turned into a boy about her age with funny brown pants to his knees and a little brown cap.

"No!" Jessamyn said. "Don't do that. I never had a grandfather before, and I know lots of boys. Except for Danny, they're very stupid."

Her grandfather became himself again, without any gray hair, but still old enough to be her grandfather. "May I accompany you part of the way home?"

"Sure," she said, "only I'm riding my bike. Can you keep up with me?"

"Of course," he said, and suddenly he was riding one of those old-time bicycles with one big wheel. "I never had the opportunity to ride your sort of bicycle."

They rode along quietly, and it was nice, because Jessamyn always felt riding a bicycle with someone was a good way to get to know him. She decided to stick to the side streets as much as they could, but when they came to Colorado Boulevard, she got nervous. "I don't mean to be rude, Grandfather, but I wonder..."

"No one else can see me," he said, "and, if you like, we can talk in your mind. Try it. Just think at me."

So she did, and it was really easy. She asked him all kinds of questions, like why it was important to be Jewish.

"It doesn't matter at all," he said.

"Well, what's God? Is he Jewish or Christian or what?"

He never really answered her about God, but he said religions were made up by people to make themselves feel better. Only, he said, sometimes religions made people feel worse, and many times they used their religions to do evil things to each other. Jessamyn had been wondering about that ever since Danny had read to her about the Crusades from his world history book.

She was so interested in what they were thinking about that she almost ran into a bus. Her grandfather reached out his hand and snapped his fingers in front of her eyes, and the bus disappeared.

"Oh!" she said. "Thank you. That was a close call."

"You're welcome," he said. "What else would you like to know?"

"Could you tell me about the Devil? Does he really have a tail and horns and a pitchfork?"

"There is no Devil," her grandfather said. "The Devil was an idea people invented to make them feel comfortable about God. Depending on their concept of evil, people see the Devil in different forms, some quite silly. The idea of evil is as necessary to the idea of good as the Devil is to God."

"I don't understand."

"No," he said. "But someday you will." By this time they were near her street. "Could we stop a moment, Jessamyn?" he said. "I'd like to tell you something which requires stillness, absolute attention."

"Sure," she said. She got really cold then, even though she knew it was May and the sun was hot on her arms and legs. They rode into a little corner park on El Molino, got off their bikes, leaned them against a tree and sat down on a green park bench with scrolly iron legs.

Her grandfather took off his hat and put it beside him on the bench. Then he folded his hands in his lap, just the way her grandmother did. "Danny's body is very tired," he said. "Always a delicate body, as you know, it is now nearly worn out. Soon he will leave it behind and come to be with me."

"Oh, hell," she said, forgetting as usual to be polite to older people. "Why don't you just fix his body and let him be a normal kid for once?"

"I don't fix things," her grandfather said, but he didn't look happy about it.

She could feel what her mother called her "ugly side" coming up. "What am I supposed to do?"

"I'm not expecting this to be easy for you. Particularly because, soon after Danny leaves his body, your grandmother will let go of hers."

"You know something?" Jessamyn said. "I don't want to hear this. You're nothing but a dream ghost, and I bet they lie to people all the time."

"Jessamyn," he said, "you will have to be the strong one in

the family."

"Forget it. I'm just a kid."

"I know," he said. "Use pine boughs when you can. The pine tree is both honest and healthy."

"What's that supposed to mean?" She bared her teeth like an angry dog.

Poof! Her grandfather vanished, just the way ghosts did in the movies, when they weren't fading away.

Jessamyn flopped down on her stomach on the bench and scrutinized the ground, which was thick with pine needles. Then she turned over and stared up at the pine branches criss-crossing the sunny sky.

When she woke up, she was looking at the ceiling where she'd pasted a burst of gold stars over her bed.

"Something must be done about that child of yours," Dena said.

"Which one?" David asked.

"Jessamyn," Dena said. "As if you didn't know."

"Did you come over here to complain?" David closed his study door, which Dena had flung open.

"I told Daniel about it, and he said talk to her father, so I'm trying," Dena said. "But I should have remembered how difficult you are. If ever there was a father who believes his children are perfect, you are that man."

"I wouldn't say perfect." David retreated behind his desk. "Jessamyn is difficult, because she says what she thinks, but I admire her honesty."

Dena plumped down into a leather armchair. "Daniel says

because you're an artist, you see the world without judgment."

"In a way, I suppose that's true."

"But I said, without common sense," Dena said. "If you think those pine boughs…"

"What's the matter with pine boughs?" David asked.

"You have the absolute lack of understanding of a two-year-old. Pine boughs are just fine on pine trees," Dena said. "But not in hospital rooms, where the atmosphere needs to be sterile."

"Sterilized," David said, laughing.

Dena gritted her teeth. "Clean and pure, then."

"But Dena, people bring plants into hospital rooms," he said.

"Yes, plants," she said. "But first of all, people buy them from a florist, which is cleaner than a tree growing in nature, where there are bugs, and dirt blows around…"

"Ah, yes," David said. "Dirty old Mother Nature."

"And secondly, people don't put plants everywhere, on the floors and the walls and on Danny's very bed. Do they?"

Dena was sure she had him there, but David was very slippery, which she knew was the essential nature of a writer.

"A wonderful idea," David said. "A room carpeted and wallpapered with roses! No, perhaps that would be overpowering. How about chrysanthemums?"

"Joke until you croak," she said. "The fact is, Jessamyn literally littered Danny's whole room with those damn pine boughs."

He smiled. "Danny thought it was funny. And so did Mother."

"Danny has always had a bizarre sense of humor, which is the curse of being a genius. And Mother is positively perverted with increasing senility."

"Mother is fine," David said. "Just because she takes walks at night and thinks she sees Father.... Dena, that sort of thing often happens to older people."

"If you were taking care of her the way I am, instead of waltzing in when it pleases you, after you've been playing with piggy banks all day..."

"I am not playing!" David said. "I'm working in a business all day so I can pay Mother back..."

"What are you talking about? Has Mother been giving you money?"

He ignored her question. "And then I write all night. I've got my second novel completely outlined..."

"Never mind," she said. "Back to the point, which is Mother, who is not well, no matter what you say, and Danny, who is worse, and should not wake up with pine trees all over his hospital room."

"Boughs," he said. "And there weren't that many, Dena. You're exaggerating as usual, although I like the image."

"This is life, not literature!" she said. "You drive me absolutely around the bend and down the hill. And how did she manage to sneak them in, in the first place? Why wasn't Kathleen, at least, watching her?"

"She brought them in a bag on her bicycle, when she came to visit Danny after school. As she always does. Said it was to heal him, because pine trees have this special property. Something like that."

"I won't have my son being used for a child's biology experiment! And if you think I'm upset, you should have seen the nurse who had to clean up. Or poor Danny, who can't even walk to the bathroom without getting pine needles stuck in his feet!"

"I'll talk to her again," David said. "She'll have to understand further vegetation is out."

"What you should do is punish her, not talk, but you won't, because you never take anything seriously. Least of all, your own sister."

When Dena returned to the house, she asked her mother about giving David money, but Esther talked in circles, as usual, and Dena couldn't find out anything. Finally, because she was up a wall with tension over Danny and that lunatic child Jessamyn and her mother's money no doubt going to David, who was a grownup man and should make his own, she started to beg. In a pitiful way, which she hated to even remember. "Please, Mother, love me!"

"I am learning to, Dena," Esther said. "Benjamin is helping me."

That afternoon when Dena went to the Temple of Health, she was a tear-streaked wreck. "My whole family is against me," she said, "with Danny sick unto the very point of death."

Rabbi Saltzman was working on the Healing Table, which had to be placed in the exact center of the Healing Circle, under the Holy Rose Window Skylight, but he dropped everything and took Dena in his arms. "Most extraordinary people are not accepted by their own families. And don't worry about Danny: the summer solstice will be here in less than two weeks."

As he held Dena, she rested her head on his chest and

stroked his furry arms. His presence was so comforting, and she knew when he said the summer solstice, he was referring to the Grand Healing.

"Five West Coast healers have accepted our invitations," Rabbi Saltzman said. "We have, let's see, Madame Olivia, who's right here in South Pasadena, Reverend Jarvis Bing from Eugene, Oregon, His Holiness Omar from Seattle, Tamara from San Diego, and Saint Simeon from Tijuana, who works more with herbs than faith, but still, he's necessary. Now, the only healer we need to hear from is Clyde from Tucson. Even though he's not West Coast, he was given the gift in San Diego, and he's important."

"I wish we didn't have to wait," Dena said. "Everything is gravitating toward this healing, and what if Clyde didn't get the invitation? Do we have to wait for the summer solstice? If he doesn't respond, we won't cancel or postpone, will we?"

"No, my dear," Rabbi Saltzman said, massaging her kundalini energy, which always got balled up at the base of her spine, "we won't cancel or postpone. But we need seven healers to surround Danny, and most of all, we do need Clyde."

Part Four

The Journey, 1952

When Harriet returned from town with warm chiles rellenos and enchiladas from El Merendero, she found Clyde kneeling on the orange and blue Navajo rug she had spread in front of the door to their small adobe house. Although they had only been married five days, Harriet was already bringing bright hues into Clyde's ascetic atmosphere. Now there were red towels in his beige bathroom, turquoise plates and cups in his white kitchen, as well as a yellow rag rug covering his chipped, gray linoleum. And most wonderful of all, Harriet thought, was the purple, blue and red Navajo blanket covering their mattress on the bedroom floor.

The rug on which Clyde knelt was an improvised porch, Harriet's effort to make some civilized separation between their home and the vastly barbarous desert. As she passed Clyde, who was looking inward although he faced the mountains, she noticed an opened letter by his knees. She set the food on the kitchen table, left her sandals by the door and returned to sit next to him. An afternoon breeze, unusual for May, ruffled her fine hair, which was beginning to curl naturally from the excitement of her love.

One thing Clyde was certainly giving her, Harriet thought, was the gift of silence. Never before had she been able to sit quietly without experiencing an inner agitation, an impatience to be up once again and on the move, away from herself. Now she crossed her legs and stared up at the giant Ponderosa pines and Douglas firs at Mt. Lemmon, less than forty miles away, at the top of the Santa Catalinas.

How cool it must be up there by the mountain lake that Harriet and Vi had visited last summer in a rented jeep. They had fished for rainbow trout in the icy blue water; then, after they had caught nothing, they had drifted off to sleep on the soft pine needles.

Perhaps she and Clyde could rent a cabin up there for their honeymoon. Clyde needed the healing effect of pine trees and mountain waters, Harriet thought, now that she understood the source of his sadness. On the morning after their wedding night, after they had made love for the first time on a real bed, they had sat up with room service coffee and recounted their private histories. At dawn they had crept back into bed. Clyde had immediately fallen asleep, but Harriet had lain awake imagining the minute details of Laura's and Sonora's murders.

Sonora, her two sandy braids twined with pink ribbons, sat at the round wooden table with her peanut butter and strawberry jam sandwich. Whole wheat bread. Milk in a glass with black and white cows painted on it. A blue, woven place-mat. The table itself scarred oak, and four unmatched wooden chairs, one with tracings of green paint.

Laura stood at the counter when the lunatic entered. She was making a fresh pot of coffee, so there would be some for Clyde when he returned from work. Barefoot, in a red house dress which was not red enough to hide the blood, she scooped coffee into the tin perk pot. Her thick black braid hung down her back and swayed a little as she hummed a Spanish song she had learned from her mother.

Neither one saw the old man until it was too late. He came in like a beggar, his left hand outstretched, his right holding the knife behind his back. "Could I have some food?" he whined.

Startled, they both turned to the intruder. "What are you doing in my kitchen?" Laura said. "Why didn't you knock?"

"I'm hungry." The grizzled old man shuffled closer to Laura.

Repelled by his filthy clothes and fecal smell, Laura raised her voice. "Get out of here!" Then, because she had lived her life in a simple goodness which had often nourished Clyde through his complex crises, she added, "If you wait in the yard, my daughter will bring you a sandwich."

"I don't want to wait." As the man shoved his suddenly menacing face at Laura, Sonora saw the knife.

"Look out, Mommy!" Her cry tipped the precarious balance in the man's brain; the violence that ensued was hideously inevitable.

Harriet saw the slashing, the blood everywhere, on floor, counter and table, where Sonora's sandwich soaked it up like a sponge. She saw the two innocent faces, surprised by unfamiliar terror. Then the phone call ripping open the sweet holiday atmosphere of Clyde's bookstore and exposing the darkness which always waited patiently for its turn to triumph. The Christmas carol record Clyde smashed on the floor in disbelief, the confused faces of his customers as he ordered them to get out. His wild drive through the streets of Tucson while his mind reverberated with denials.

Then the unmistakable signs of disaster: police cars everywhere, the front door wide open and neighbors bordering the yard like curious children.

As Clyde stepped into his house, the air was thick with ugliness, a hell he knew he would carry with him forever. And that was before he saw the carnage in the kitchen.

Although the scene before Clyde arrived may have been slightly different from Harriet's imaginings, she knew exactly what happened from that moment until Clyde sold the house and moved away from the terrible sympathy of his neighbors.

Clyde had spared her nothing, not his screams, his desperate fights with the police and reporters who were making notes and taking pictures, as though such violence were routine, somehow, and not the impossible ending of his world. Nor Sonora's bloody ribbon he carried for months in his back pocket like a talisman, a reminder of evil.

Harriet understood why Clyde hated the old man for killing himself before Clyde could kill him and the bitterness Clyde felt at the lunatic's mad parody of the Crucifixion. "Come to save what?" he repeated like a mantra of pain.

When he appeared at the borders of Pascua Village and offered himself to the Yaquis, she understood his desolation at the Indians' rejection. In fact, there was only one element in the whole tale that Harriet could not completely understand: why Clyde waited so long, until the death of his dog, to cry.

Someday I will ask him, she thought. As she turned to watch him, Clyde emerged from his inner sanctuary.

"Hello, my love," Clyde said, caressing her cheek. "Have you been here long?"

"I don't know," Harriet said. "Are you hungry?"

"Immensely. Hungry enough to devour the whole desert and you along with it."

"Good." She went into the kitchen and returned with the bag from El Menendero. "Mexican food."

Clyde helped her spread their midday feast. "Ah." He pulled the Dos Equis out of the bag. "Perfect."

"I'm afraid the dinners got cold and the beers got warm."

"Better for the digestion."

"I hope I can learn to cook someday."

"I'm sure you will," Clyde said, "and if you don't, I will."

"Are you always so accepting?" Harriet said.

Clyde's face tightened with pain. "Not always."

"I'm sorry. I could kick myself."

"Never mind."

Harriet stopped eating. "How could I say something so stupid?"

"We all say stupid things. Don't think about it another minute."

"But you said every word reverberates throughout the universe."

"Ah." Clyde tried to smile. "That's because I'm such a pompous bastard." He reached for her and knocked over one of the beers. "Clumsy, too."

"Don't be silly."

"Silly," Clyde said. "Harriet, will you ever understand how much I need you?" He pushed aside the food and pulled her on top of him.

"Oh," Harriet said, "we can't lie like this. We're both so thin our bones are crunching."

"We are," Clyde said solemnly, "just thin enough for you to feel my love growing."

Harriet giggled. "This is like the first time I met you, after I knocked you out. You weren't as holy as you looked."

"What could be more holy than lovemaking?" Clyde massaged her back. "Will you love me forever?"

"Of course I will. How could I help it?"

"I don't know," Clyde said, "and I don't ever want to find out."

"Let's make babies, just in case I'm not pregnant."

They pulled off their clothes and began to make love slowly

and blissfully in the waning desert light.

"I like being on top," Harriet said. "Do you like what I'm doing now? This sliding?"

"Almost unbearable." Clyde held her suspended for a second and then let go. "Don't stop."

"Oh, I won't. I can't. I'm.... coming."

"Yes, yes," Clyde said. "This is what's happening."

"Oh!" Harriet cried. "You're shaking the whole earth!"

But it was Monster and Zit, roaring up on their motorcycles.

"Did it again," Zit said, as they blasted to a stop. "Came at the wrong time."

"I don't think so," Monster said. "They're getting better at it."

"Don't stare, Monster; it's rude," Zit said.

They parked their bikes at the side of the house and waited discreetly for the lovers to finish. Then, when the last bit of movement had died down, Monster flicked away Zit's restraining hand and strolled over to the rug. "Hi," he said. "We came to visit."

Zit trotted after him. "Sorry to interrupt," he said, as Clyde groped for his robe to cover Harriet's bare ass. "We could come back another time."

"No, we couldn't, because we're here now." Monster squatted down and took a gulp of Clyde's beer. "Y'know, you really oughta cover Harriet's ass. She's gonna catch cold."

"What a good idea," Clyde said. "Could you hand me my robe?"

"Sure. Guess you weren't hungry, eh? Mind if I finish your dinner?" Before Clyde could reply, Monster had wolfed down the remaining chiles rellenos and was starting on the enchiladas. "Just cheese? You guys really oughta eat meat if you're gonna go at it all the time like that."

Under cover of Clyde's robe, Harriet carefully disengaged herself. She sat up, wrapping the robe around her body like a sarong, and reached for her sundress which she draped across Clyde's pelvis. "Didn't you guys ever hear of using telephones to make sure people are not otherwise occupied?"

"Nah." The last enchilada disappeared down Monster's throat. "We like to be spontaneous."

"We brought you a present." Zit held out a flat box like a peace offering.

Clutching Clyde's robe, Harriet inspected the dancing teddy bears and pink birthday cakes on the wrapping. "Whose birthday did you think it was?"

"It's a wedding present," Monster said. "But we didn't have no wedding paper. Got anything else to drink?"

Clyde wound Harriet's sundress around his hips and stood up. "We've got some Cokes in the house. Why don't you go in and..."

"Did you guys know you're wearing the wrong clothes?" Zit said.

"Yes, we know," Clyde said. "And if you'd go in the house, we might have a chance to change."

"Don't be modest," Zit said. "It's only us guys."

"I beg your pardon?" Harriet said.

"Oh," Zit said. "Right. C'mon, Monster."

By the time Clyde and Harriet entered the house, Monster and Zit had made themselves at home. On the yellow Formica kitchen table were four glasses of Coke and a bowl of pretzels. Tilting precariously back in his chair, Monster waved at them like a genial host. "Hi. Didja know your pretzels are a little stale?"

"But good anyway," Zit added apologetically.

"Oh, thank goodness!" Harriet said. "Now, if I'd known you were dropping by, I would've arranged to have other stale snacks waiting for you."

"That's okay," Monster said. "Whyncha open your present?"

Clyde sat down and Harriet sat on his lap. "Why not?" She tore open the paper and Monster, bursting with impatience, lifted the lid. In the box lay a sampler that read "Home Sweet Home" in wobbly pink and blue letters on a burlap background.

"Oh," Harriet said, "look at this."

"Do you like it?" Zit said. "Monster did all the cross- stitching, and I made the frame. Real balsa wood."

"Well," Harriet said, "it's certainly interesting."

"Unusual," Clyde said.

"Yah, ain't it?" Zit said. "And the cross-stitch was real hard for Monster 'cause he's got such big hands."

"I'm big all over." Monster beamed at Harriet. "But I like small things."

"Somehow, Monster," Harriet said, "I can't picture you embroidering."

"Well..." Monster was feeling the pretzels. "I like it 'cause it relaxes the mind, y'know? After a hard day of thinking."

"You have a thinking job?" Harriet said.

"Sure. I fix bikes."

"How would you like to go to California for our honeymoon?" Clyde said. They were stretched out on Clyde's mattress, their bodies glistening with moonlit sweat.

"Sure," Harriet said. "I've never been there."

"I've been asked to participate in a healing. Got a letter today from Daniel Saltzman, a former rabbi and one of the best healers I ever met. He did some amazing demonstrations in San Diego, where I found the power, and we've kept in touch ever since."

"How can we get there? Do you think your Packard can make it?"

In spite of his exhaustion, Clyde's hand was sliding down Harriet's torso to the softness between her legs. "I doubt it."

"We could ask Monster to fix it."

"Don't be silly. Bikes are not the same as cars."

"Then," Harriet said, pulling Clyde on top, "we could ask Earl and Vi to go, because Earl's got a truck."

"You've gotta be crazy." Earl leaned back and knocked a Mexican hat off the wall of the Aztec Café, where they were having breakfast.

Flora, the Aztec's tough, grandmotherly waitress, stopped pouring refills to glare at Earl. "You break the decorations, you pay for 'em."

"C'mon, Flora. How can you break a hat?" Harriet said.

"It's been done, is all I can say. So tell Earl he better be careful, because..." Flora rested the coffee pot on the table and gave Harriet an imposing stare. "...we know it's the women who gotta keep men from breaking things up. Just like kids, they never think of the consequences."

"Isn't that the truth!" Vi patted Earl's shoulder consolingly.

"Women create, and men destroy," Flora said as she moved away. "Unless you educate 'em."

Earl nibbled Vi's fingers. "Educate me, honey."

"Oh." Vi withdrew her hand. "Not here."

"Look," Clyde said, "I'm offering you a chance to test your atheism on a real level. This child is dying of cystic fibrosis. All the doctors say there's no hope at all. Now, if we can cure him..."

"You can't." Earl took a smug sip of coffee.

"Is that a true scientific attitude? Making up your mind before any evidence comes in that might disprove your hypothesis?"

"Atheism is not a hypothesis; it's a truth!"

"Don't confuse you with possible facts, when you can live a peaceful, a priori life, " Clyde murmured. "You're a real poet."

Earl slammed down his cup. "Nobody ever called me a poet and got away with it!"

Vi looked at Harriet. "Flora was right. See how fast men get violent?"

Earl jumped up. "Whaddya mean, violent?"

"Give it up, honey." Flora leaned on Earl's shoulders and forced him back into his seat. "Thinking too much makes men boring and wild."

"Wildly boring," Vi said sweetly.

"Okay, okay," Earl said. "I'll go. Wanna come, Vi? Maybe we can find you that singing teacher."

Vi scooped up egg yolk with her blue corn tortilla. "Sure, why not? I guess so."

"I'll put my piano in the back of the truck."

"Wait a minute," Harriet said. "That's where Clyde and I'll be."

"I don't go nowhere without my piano," Earl said. "The maitre d' at Woody 'n Eddy's gave it to me twelve years ago, and I ain't letting it outta my sight."

"We'll share the space," Clyde said. "This is Thursday. Can we leave tomorrow?"

"How can we do that? Vi and I gotta give Pete a little notice."

"The child is dying, and they need me to complete the Healing Circle."

"Which is more important," Harriet said. "A job or a sick kid?"

Although Earl could feel the pressure, he hated to give in too easily. He got up and pretended to study the large framed photograph of the Silver and Turquoise Ball. The caption under the photo read: "The True Festival Spirit Dominates Happy Tucsonians At The Magnificent Affair The Tucson Festival Society Held At the Arizona Inn, May 10, 1952."

After an appropriate time had elapsed, he turned back to the expectant faces at the table. "If I say yes, does this mean you're giving up on Pete's eyeball?"

"Not at all," Clyde said. "I'll do another healing before we leave."

"Okay, I give in. It'll be an interesting experiment."

"Oh, good," Vi said. "And we've got to take Maria Callas."

"Vi, we can't take that damn parrot."

"She can ride in front with me."

By sunset of the next afternoon Earl's truck was packed with blankets, pillows, four satchels of clothing and toilet articles, Earl's worn volumes of Spinoza and Kant, Clyde's book of theosophical poetry, a stack of movie magazines for Vi, a *Joy of Cooking* for Harriet, one box of canned beans and tomatoes, coffee, a can opener, knives and forks, several bottles of water and two bags of hot sauce and tortilla chips.

"Just in case we can't get any in California," Vi said, although Earl insisted they could. "Well," Vi said mysteriously, "sometimes you never know."

"Unnnh," Monster said. "I guess I'm outta shape."

The Prickly Pears were hoisting Earl's piano onto his truck, which was parked in front of Pete's.

"A little to the left!" Pete shouted from the doorway.

"Watch it!" Earl said, "You're scratching the varnish."

Panda stopped to breathe deeply and wipe the sweat from his eyes. "If you get fussy, we'll drop it."

"Yeah," Zit gasped from somewhere under the piano. "You're only paying us in cheap beer."

"Okay," Earl said. "I'll throw in a bottle of good tequila. Just be careful."

"Anyway," Monster said genially, as he leaned his shoulder against the piano that was tilting into the truck, "if we drop it, we squish Zit."

"Very funny," Zit said.

"Right," Monster said, "let's get serious. I'm thirsty. I'm gonna give one big shove, and..."

"Hang on!" Earl said. "I need Cranky up here on the truck with me, so it won't tip over."

Cranky leaped onto the truck, just in time to help Earl stop the piano from slamming right into the cab. The piano rocked back and forth precariously, until Monster stopped it with a hammy hand. "Good," he said. "Time for a drink."

"Don't go," Earl said. "Who's gonna help me tie it in place?"

"Not me," Panda said, "I've done more than my year's share of physical labor."

"I can't." Zit was curled up like a shrimp on the sand. "I'll never walk again."

"Sure you will." Monster picked Zit up in his arms. "All you need's a coupla shots a tequila."

Everyone but Cranky and Earl disappeared into the gloom of the bar.

"Sure isn't any fun losing my favorite pianist and my favorite waitress," Pete said.

"Thanks." Harriet gave Pete the evil eye.

"I lost you already, Harriet. Now I've had time to adjust."

Vi took the first of the beers Pete was lining up on the bar. "You're not losing us. We're just leaving for a while, and probably not forever."

"I hope this healing wasn't too rushed," Clyde said.

Pete felt around under his eye patch. "Who knows? It was an intense ten minutes."

"I find," Clyde said, "that even though there's noise going on outside, I can often work in a focused way under pressure."

"Yeah. Also, it was dark in here. I hate to turn lights on during the day." Pete looked out at the shadows of his friends milling about in the murky room. "Whaddya say we have a song from Vi, and then I'll open the tequila?"

"I can't sing without the piano."

"Sure you can, Vi," Pete said. "Do it a capella."

"She's not Italian," Monster said from somewhere in the gloom. "Whyncha let 'er sing in English?"

"All right," Vi said. "One song." As she rested one plump arm on the bar and arched her back like a cat, Pete turned on the single overhead bar light, which bathed Vi in a golden glow.

Earl and Cranky, who had finished tying down the piano, entered the bar just as Vi began to sing. "I Wonder Who's Kissing Her Now," she crooned in her wobbly, husky voice.

Harriet threw her arms around Clyde's neck. "Oh, our wedding song!"

"Shhhhh!" everyone said, and the bar lapsed into a profoundly admiring silence.

After Vi's song Pete broke open his best bottle of tequila, "aged seventeen years in a Mexican cave." Everyone agreed it was the most magical tequila they had ever tasted.

"It captures the essence of something." Clyde swirled the clear liquid around in his glass. "I wonder what it is."

"Desert sunsets," Vi said.

"Mountain streams in the morning," Harriet said.

"Dirty socks," Monster said. "But your favorite pair." And that put an end to the guessing.

They called in the twilight with toasts. "To Earl and Vi," Pete said. "My most special musicians, not to mention waitress and atheist supreme."

"To the best faith healer in Tucson and his beautiful bride," Zit said.

"He's the only faith healer in Tucson," Earl said. "But what the hell."

Clyde raised his glass. "Thank you, Earl and Zit. A generous toast."

"And now," Monster said, "as our friends go away and leave us here in the desert to rot of boredom, only I'm sure they don't mean too much harm, I'd like to make the final toast." As everyone waited expectantly, Monster hoisted his glass into the bar spotlight. "To toasts!"

Everyone applauded, finished their drinks, and it was time for good-byes. Clyde and Harriet climbed into the back of the truck and wedged themselves in between the piano and the various bags and boxes. Monster arranged pillows behind their backs and covered their feet with the Navajo blanket. Earl and Vi got into the cab, where Vi's parrot was waiting.

"So long!" "See you!" "Be careful!" the gang shouted, as the truck chuffed off into the darkening desert.

"Eat your hearts out!" Vi's parrot squawked cheerily.

Monster stood in the road for a long time, squinting after the vanished truck. Then he shuffled back into the bar, where Pete and the Prickly Pears were morosely finishing off the tequila. "I wish I was going to California for a honeymoon," he said. "Only girls don't seem to like me."

"Maybe it's your direct approach," Panda said. "Girls don't like to be told to dance with you or else. Not even if you say it with a smile. Given someone of your size, the 'or else' can be pretty intimidating."

"I notice you don't have a girlfriend," Zit said, "so don't throw stones at other people's glass houses."

"I wonder," Cranky said, "if Clyde really is a good faith healer. How's your eye, Pete?"

"Think it's coming along." Pete was slumped on the floor by the bar. "Clyde gave me the address of this Temple of Health place, so I can write and let him know. But I gotta think positive thoughts, which ain't always easy in the heat."

Cranky was flexing and unflexing his right arm to make his tattooed snake come out of its basket. "Well, I've got this funny feeling that he's real, know what I mean? In spite of the fact that he looks like Jesus, which makes him a very suspicious character. I think he's got the power."

Stretched out on the floor like a beached whale and already half asleep, Monster mumbled, "Amen."

"Amen," the group responded, and their woozy blessing lingered in the spring evening. "Amen."

"Look at that!" Vi wriggled free of their blanket and sat up. "Over there on the mountain."

Clyde, Harriet and Earl, their serene faces painted pink by the desert sunrise, slept in a tangle of blankets on the sand. Flat on his back, Clyde lay with one arm across Harriet's chest, the other across Earl's.

"Somebody wake up!" Vi took her pillow and puffed it down briefly on each sleeper's face. "Before it's too late, because you never know, when something like this happens, how long it'll last."

Clyde lifted his head. "Who calls?"

"I do," Vi said. "Do you see those people over there, right on top of the nearest mountain?"

"How interesting," Clyde said. "A mirage."

"Not a mirage," Vi said. "A man and a little girl. Or maybe it's just clouds."

"How could they have gotten up there?" Because the morning air was cool, Clyde pulled the blanket around his bare chest and sat up.

"Hey!" Wearing Clyde's striped pajama top and naked from the waist down, Harriet groped for the covers. "I'm freezing!"

"Wake up, my love, and look. The gods are dancing."

"Where?" Harriet crawled into Clyde's embrace, and he snuggled the blanket around her.

"See the man in the suit and hat?" Vi said. "Dancing up there with the little girl?"

"No," Harriet said. "I don't see anything but rocks. Sometimes, when the sun hits them at different angles, you think you see things. Or people." She patted Clyde's foot.

"Quite a stately dance," Clyde said. "Perhaps it's a minuet."

"Or a dulcimer." Vi played thoughtfully with her dark curls. In her white lacy cotton nightie she was elegantly voluptuous, a Renoir model plucked out of her rumpled boudoir and dropped into the austere desert.

"Okay!" Earl sprang into wakefulness. "Who's playing my piano?"

"No one is," Vi said. "But there sure are a couple of people dancing. They could use a little piano."

Earl got up and looked in his truck. "Nope. Nobody there. That sure is weird. Maybe there's a piano bar around the corner."

"One thing about the desert you can always depend on," Harriet said. "It doesn't have corners."

"Well, where the hell is that music coming from?"

"What music?" Vi said.

"Whaddya mean, what music? It couldn't be any louder if somebody was playing right under your elbow."

Clyde swiveled around to give Earl a strange look. "I don't hear any music."

"Cut it out." Earl strode to the edge of the blankets and glowered at Clyde.

"I don't either," Harriet said.

Vi gave a helpless shrug, her shoulders glinting gold in the morning. "Me too. I can't hear a thing. But what do you think of those little people dancing up there?"

"What people?"

"Up there on the mountain." Vi waved her plump arm in exasperation. "Right in front of you."

"Oh, I get it. You guys are razzing me. Well, I don't like to laugh this early in the morning."

"Wait a minute," Clyde said. "I think I understand. Vi and I can see the dancers, and Earl can hear their music. That's all. As different types, we are sensitive to different sorts of vibrations. No reason to get upset."

"I'm not upset," Vi said. "I'm hungry."

"Well," Harriet said. "I don't see or hear anything."

Clyde turned to Earl. "You hear piano music?"

Earl didn't know what to make of all this. "Right." He grabbed a black sweater out of the truck and pulled it on over his orange and white pajamas. "A little tinkly piano, kinda delicate, with ripples."

"Perhaps it's a harpsichord."

"Oh, hell!" Earl said. "It's a hallucination. I've heard of things like that happening in the desert."

"Oh!" Vi said. "They're waving good-bye! Wave back at them."

While Vi waved at the mountains, glowing in morning sun, Earl busied himself with making coffee on their camp stove. Ping! Clank! They could hear his irritable preparations.

"Has the music stopped?" Clyde said.

"Yes! It's stopped!"

Vi joined Earl at the truck. "What do we have for breakfast?"

"Beans and tortilla chips."

"Good," Harriet said. "With lots of hot sauce."

"You know what they reminded me of?" Vi sipped her steaming coffee as they lounged on the blankets. "Little people in a cuckoo clock."

Warmed by the rising sun, Earl removed his sweater. "Cuckoo is the exact word, and I hope nothing like that ever happens to me again."

"The atheist has a brush with the supernatural," Clyde said, "and it was a close call."

"Okay, wise guy, you wanna know the reason I'm going out to California with you nuts? The real reason?"

"Of course."

"Remember my kid I told you about? Well, he's real sick..."

"Dying," Vi said.

"Right. Maybe even dying, and I wanna see him."

"He might even be..."

"Don't say it, Vi! So. I decided to come along with you guys, because you're my best friends."

"Awww!" Harriet said, "That's so sweet."

And Vi because I love her. But I don't want no more supernatural trouble, and I hope if anybody's out there, they can hear me."

"Listen!" Vi said. "Somebody's giggling."

"No," Harriet said. "It's just the wind."

Clyde set his half-eaten breakfast down on the blanket. "What's the matter with your child?"

"I dunno." Earl swallowed the last of his beans. "He coughed all the time. And spit."

"Because," Clyde said, "I was thinking perhaps we could include your child in the healing." He traced a meditative pathway through his beans with his fork. "I don't see why not, since both children live in Southern California. Although I would have to get the permission of the other healers, particularly Daniel Saltzman, who has organized the event."

"I appreciate the offer," Earl said, "but forget it."

His longish gray-brown hair hanging over his eyes, Clyde hunched over his beans as though they held a secret message. "Where, exactly, does your child live?"

"Altadena. But I don't want to get my own kid involved in something like that. Somebody else's kid, okay, I can take a scientifically curious attitude. But my own kid, no."

Clyde straightened up and pushed the hair out of his eyes. "What is your child's name?" He watched Earl closely.

"Danny. Norman, of course."

"I knew that," Vi said. "I read that letter on the blue paper, remember? The one from his grandmother?"

Harriet had been sunbathing in shorts and Clyde's pajama top tied across her breasts like a sarong. She propped herself up on her elbows and looked at Vi. "You mean that letter wasn't from a girlfriend?"

"I'm afraid," Clyde said, "that your child is involved. He is the child we're healing."

"That's not funny."

"No, I should have figured it out. I should have put it together. There were clues, but because I didn't realize there was a mystery here, I didn't think..."

"Good," Vi said. "I love mysteries."

"No. Impossible." Earl paced back and forth on the sand like a trapped animal. "My kid couldn't be involved in a kooky thing like this."

"Earl." Clyde's voice took on a commanding tone. "Your son is fourteen, and you have not seen or attempted to communicate with him for eleven years. You know nothing about him, in fact, not who he is or what he does. Not even that he has cystic fibrosis. You have had no influence over his life at all. None. So he could be involved in anything at all, and you have nothing to say about it. You abdicated responsibility."

"Maybe so," Earl said, "but now I realize there's a bond between a kid and his dad that can't be broken so easily."

"Bullshit," Clyde said. "The first break was very easy. You just walked out. And how about the eleven years you stayed away? Was it easy to keep feeding yourself those rationalizations?"

"I don't want a friend who lectures me like he's so superior. What kind of friend are you?"

"A good friend," Harriet said.

"Well, he doesn't know anything about the kind of life I've had for eleven years, feeling like Dena didn't want me and Danny didn't need me."

Clyde stood up, faced Earl, crossed his arms over his chest and spoke deliberately. "You walked out because it was unpleasant. I heard you. And you stayed away to avoid further unpleasantness."

"So?"

"So, if your son is dying of cystic fibrosis, and his mother has arranged a faith healing as a last-ditch attempt to save him, then you have no voice in the matter. You may as well go along with it gracefully."

"Never!" Earl's voice was sharp-edged with anger and sorrow, like a child who is about to cry. "It's not fair."

Vi got up and held Earl. "There, there."

"I don't know," Clyde said. "It seems fair to me. Why should you be granted instant forgiveness, and authority, just because you've decided to return? And for how long? Have you thought about that? Suppose your son survives and he doesn't like you? Or you don't like him? Will you stick around?"

"Leave me alone." Earl's voice was muffled by Vi's chest. "I've decided to go back, damn it. That's worth something."

"Yes," Clyde said. "It is."

Harriet grabbed Clyde's ankle. "Why don't you let up on him, darling? See how upset he is?"

Suddenly Clyde was yelling; his sallow cheeks were streaked with red. "Because being a father is a privilege! And when you toss that away lightly, you have to earn the right to take it up again."

"How?" Earl pulled away from Vi. "Just tell me."

"Don't worry," Harriet said. "He will."

"Honesty is the most important, and painful, way. Why did you do it? What do you want now? What are you capable of? What effect will your actions have on your son? You have to know what questions to ask and then answer them without excuses." The impassioned tone drained away from his voice. "Now, I've said enough. I'm going for a walk in the desert, and I need to be alone."

In silence they watched his lean silhouette, fists clenched, stalk across the sand.

"I think I'm seeing something funny," Vi said after a few minutes. "That little girl and the man with the hat just started walking next to Clyde."

"I don't think so," Harriet said, shielding her eyes from the sun's glare. "It's a mirage."

Earl lay face down on the blanket. "Eat your heart out!" Vi's parrot squawked from somewhere under the truck.

"It's very important that Danny be in the exact center, right under the middle of the rose." Rabbi Saltzman, holding one end of a tape measure, squatted in a corner of the In-Depth Room and stared at the Rose Window skylight. "So don't let your end slip, Dena. Madame Olivia says we can't be off by more than a quarter of an inch."

"What else would I be, if not careful?"

Rabbi Saltzman looked at Dena, sitting on the Healing Table and clutching her end of the tape measure. How lovely she was, in her low-cut, hot pink dress with the wide black belt! Just then the sun emerged, bathing Dena's face and arms in a rosy radiance.

"I know what you want." Dena spread her knees just a little and arched her back suggestively.

"Not in here, my little one. This is one place which must be kept free from physical desires." Fine words, Daniel Saltzman thought. He was afraid to stand up and reveal the bulge in his pants, tighter now that he was eating so many take-out meals with Dena.

"You're right." Dena bit her lip remorsefully. "I just get carried away around you." She swung her feet back and forth like a child. "You make me so crazy I forget what I'm doing."

I want her, he thought, every second, even though she's entirely wrong for me. For years now he had been searching for the right woman to be his mate and partner in the healing enterprise. He had inspected and rejected a number of women, had had disappointing affairs with several devotees who had, at first, seemed to be the perfect type: elegant blonde women, gentle and soulful. What class they would add to his establishment, he would think at the beginning of his infatuation. But each one had turned out to be too pale, too passively ordinary in their devotion. He had given up, finally, and decided to be celibate.

Now, here was Dena, short, dark and plump. Aggressively forthright and often crude, she reeked of sex and was unbelievably wild in bed. He adored her.

"Don't forget," Dena said. "Today is the day." She looked at her watch. "In half an hour."

Dena's words wiped away all traces of his desire. "Do you think Danny will like me?"

"How could he help it?"

Daniel stood up slowly and adjusted his white tunic. "I'm not so sure. I don't seem to have a way with children. Look at your nieces; they laugh at me whenever I speak to them."

"Those little girls are absolute devils!" Dena hopped off the Healing Table. "When you see Danny, you'll know the difference. No matter how sick he is, Danny is always a gentleman."

"Well, your mother seems to like me a little more than she used to." Daniel sighed and put his hand over his heart, which was thumping painfully. Why should Dena's family matter so much to him?

"Yes," Dena said, "especially because you encourage her when she talks about Father's 'visits.'"

"It would be inconsistent," Daniel said, "to be a faith healer and not believe souls can cross over from the Beyond. I can't tell you how many times I've felt a strong contact with spirits on the Other Shore, helping me to heal someone."

"I hope they're all here on Friday for the Great Healing."

"They will be." Daniel held out his hands. "Come. The table is as close to the center as it'll ever be. Let's check the mail and then go to the hospital."

While Dena went through the pile of letters the postman had left in the foyer of the Healing Center, Daniel watched the angel fish dart through the murky waters of the Holy Fish Tank. "The problem was," he said pensively, "that tree climbing. I never should have done it."

"Mmmmmnn." Dena was arranging mail in various piles on her blond wood desk. "It was a dangerous sacrifice, and Mother should have appreciated it."

"I frightened her," Daniel said. "She was in an other worldly place, and the fear snapped her connection. So she got angry."

"Oh, here's a letter from Tucson. Shall I open it?"

"By all means." As Dena slit open the envelope with her crystal paper knife, Daniel looked over her shoulder.

"It's from Clyde, the last of the healers! See, he says he's coming. With his new wife and two friends."

"Good. Could they stay at your house? We have so many staying here, we're already crowded."

"I suppose, if Mother doesn't mind. Perhaps if you ask her?"

"No," Daniel said. "I think you should."

"All right. Just think, only three more days to finish the preparations. I have to write out the menus for the cook, call the florist to make sure the white roses arrive in time, and those musicians haven't given me a definite yes or no. Which is my usual experience with musicians, so wishy-washy, just like Earl, except when they're playing."

"Yes, and now I think we..."

"Oh, Daniel, how are we ever going to get Danny out of the hospital and over here? His doctors will never allow it!"

"Where there's a will, there is always a way. First, Danny has got to meet me and trust me. Shall we go?"

"Jessamyn dreamed Grandfather was riding a bicycle," Danny said to Esther, who was sitting at the edge of the bed.

"He used to." Esther adjusted a pink rose tucked into the bun at the back of her head. "Your grandfather was always athletic. I was the one who never learned to ride, although I was once rather a good dancer. Benjamin always said so. I wish you could have seen me."

"I can imagine." Danny experienced a pure, tingling bliss that carried him beyond his physical condition. He spent much of his time in an oxygen tent now, and he was being fed intravenously.

"I wish you could eat," Esther said. "Does that needle bother you?"

"I don't feel it." Indeed, he seemed almost to have passed beyond his wretched body. Struggling to breathe and to swallow, it weighed less than eighty pounds and could no longer walk.

"Benjamin said when we leave our bodies, we will be like snakes wriggling out of our old skins."

"I hope so. But I would like to see my father."

Esther rested her worn hand on Danny's long, limp fingers.

"Who knows? It may yet happen. Benjamin says it will, and he ought to know."

Danny's eyelids were getting heavy. "I want to hear him play.... the song I wrote for him."

Esther stroked Danny's sleeping face. "What a blessed child he is, Benjamin. Such a shame he won't have the time to use his talent. And yet...think of the happiness he has given to his family, his teachers, doctors and nurses. He will leave behind his music to be played, not by everyone, but by those who love him."

She smiled, her eyes glowing. "You will take care of him, won't you, after he leaves? Until I can join you. And I do hope it won't be long. I have been feeling so young and healthy, so alive, since you have been visiting me."

She leaned over Danny's body, her face lifted as though for a kiss, when Jessamyn hurtled into the room. Her hair was wild, her face stained with tears.

"Gram! Didn't they tell you? Roseanne died yesterday!"

Esther turned around. "Who, darling?"

"Danny's friend with the pigtails who lived down the hall. She gave me bubble gum!"

"Oh, yes. A lovely little girl." Esther stretched out her arms consolingly. "No, I didn't know."

"Dammit!" Jessamyn threw herself onto Esther's lap. "That kid was too young to die. She was my friend." She lifted her head. "Did they tell Danny?"

"Probably not," Esther said. "And lower your voice a bit, darling. Danny's sleeping."

"Didn't God ever hear of being fair?"

"Jessamyn," Esther said, handing her a Kleenex from the

box by Danny's bed, "there are many things about this earthly life we cannot understand."

Jessamyn blew her nose and stuffed the Kleenex into her pocket. "Gram, I'm not trying to be mean, especially since you're just starting to like me."

"Oh, my dear..." Esther's eyes glistened so with shame that she could no longer see through her wire-rimmed glasses. "I didn't know..." Removing her glasses, she dabbed at her eyes.

"But I hate it when grownups tell kids they can't understand. And you know what I think? I think kids understand better than grownups, because grownups always try to explain everything. Kids know it's not fair when a kid dies, and God ought to do something about it."

How admirable the child's spirit was, Esther thought. But she knew that Danny's death, and her own, would be impossible for Jessamyn to accept. What if her anger turned to a bitterness that warped her soul? That would indeed be unfair.

"Mother! I can't believe it!" Dena stood in the doorway, with Daniel hiding nervously behind her. "Why did you let that child in here?"

When Jessamyn saw her aunt and the man Gram called "the crazy rabbi," she had no desire to stay, not even to wait for Danny to wake up. Her aunt's disapproving presence radiated tension like poison gas. "Good-bye, Gram."

As Dena marched into the room, Jessamyn darted out past Daniel, who was still hovering by the open door.

"Dena," Esther said, "don't you see Danny is asleep?"

"Oh." Dena spoke more quietly now. "I'm sorry, Mother. It's just that child... Never mind. Rabbi Saltzman has been wanting to meet Danny."

"Hello, Mrs. Singer." Hesitantly, Daniel approached Esther. Although he had stretched out his arm to shake her hand, he looked, Esther thought, like someone warding off a possible blow. "I hope you don't mind."

"I am not the person in question here." She ignored his hand, so he let it drop.

"Well, Dena, it might be better if I came another day."

As he began to back toward the door, Dena grabbed his arm. "Daniel! You stay right here! Just because Mother is cranky is no reason to..."

"I apologize," Esther said. She did feel sorry for this man, so stupidly vain and yet well-intended. Even sincere, in a bumbling way. I suppose, Esther thought, I should admire him for being able to love Dena, showing off her breasts in that silly pink dress, entirely inappropriate for a visit to her dying son.

"Oh, please, Mrs. Singer, there is no need to..."

Danny opened his eyes. "Hello, Mama."

"Hello, darling."

When Dena bent over to kiss Danny, Esther averted her eyes. How embarrassing for Danny to see his mother dressed like this! She wished she could protect Danny, although the poor child seemed to notice nothing.

"Look." Dena took hold of Daniel's sleeve and pulled him to the bed. "I've brought you a visitor. A good friend of mine. His name is Rabbi Saltzman, but you could call him Daniel. I'm sure you'll be good friends, because you have the same name."

When Danny saw Daniel, he broke into a broad, mischievous grin. "Hi. Are you really going to try to heal me?"

"What?" Daniel reeled back as though Danny had punched him.

"What made you say that, darling?" Dena said.

"I had a dream."

Dena's whole body was on fire. "What sort of dream?"

"I was in this big building, with all these people around me. My father was there." He looked at Daniel. "And so were you."

"You see?" Dena said to Daniel. "This is a sign from God."

"Yes," Daniel said. "It must be."

"What is a sign from God?" Esther said. "I dislike being left out of conversations."

"Mother, we are going to have a healing ceremony for Danny."

"Go right ahead," Esther said. "It can't hurt."

"Oh, I knew you'd understand, Mother! The ceremony will be Friday, at Daniel's temple."

Esther inspected Daniel curiously. "A Jewish healing?"

"No, no," Daniel said. "I am no longer a rabbi, and my temple is not a real temple."

"Why have one then?" Esther murmured.

"Not in the Jewish sense. It is a healing center."

"Ah," Esther said. "Why not?"

"So you see, Mother, we are going to have to get Danny released from the hospital on Friday."

"Are you insane?" Esther said. "You cannot move this child! Look at him."

They all looked at Danny, who was now laughing faintly at some obscure joke. "It's all right, Gram," he whispered. "I have to go."

"You have to do nothing of the kind!" Esther stood like a sentinel by Danny's bed.

Daniel took a tentative step forward. "You see, Mrs. Singer..."

Esther turned away and addressed the wall. "But Benjamin, I should think I have an obligation which you, of all people, would recognize..."

Dena threw up her hands. "Mother! This is a serious conversation! Please don't start talking to Father again."

"I am being quite serious." Esther glared at Dena, who was not in the least intimidated. "Your father and I are discussing the fate of my grandson."

"My son!"

"Please!" Daniel massaged the air like a frenetic window-washer. "I didn't mean to cause a fuss!"

"You haven't!" Dena shouted.

"What do you mean, he must go?" Esther said to the wall.

"Mother!"

Esther sank into her bedside chair. "All right. Let him go."

"Here you are." Earl pulled up to the curb in front of an ornate pink stucco building. Except for its incongruous bronze Byzantine tower, the structure was all free-flowing curves, like a sand castle washed down by the sea. The windows, placed irregularly, were stained glass ovals and circles. The front door was carved wood, inlaid with brass mystical symbols.

Vi stuck her curly head out of the truck window. "Oh, it looks like a piece of salt water taffy that's been chewed a little. How cute!"

Harriet dislodged her weary body, stood and rubbed her ass, sore from sitting for three hours on the piano pedals. "No, I think it looks like our wedding cake."

"Happy birthday!" the parrot squawked.

Clyde climbed out of the truck and went to inspect the huge, hand-painted sign like a billboard in an antique brass frame. "Temple of Health Healing Center, Pasadena Branch," he read aloud. "Dr. Daniel Saltzman, D.H."

"What's 'D.H.'?" Vi said.

"Oh." Clyde chuckled. "It's a title invented by the group in San Diego. Means 'Doctor of Healing'."

"Well," Vi said. "Isn't that something?" With her parrot on her shoulder, she got out of the truck and smoothed the wrinkles in her purple cotton dress.

"Clyde," Harriet said, tossing a satchel onto the lawn, "would you help me out?"

"Of course, my love." He lifted Harriet out of the truck, set her on the grass and dusted the soot and pollen off the back of her white blouse.

"I know. I'm a mess." She patted her windblown hair and adjusted her green shorts.

"Not at all." Ruefully he surveyed his stained robe and dusty feet. "If anyone is a mess, it's me. But since we're several hours early, I'm sure Daniel will give us a place to clean up."

"I wish we hadn't broken down in Needles," Harriet said, "and had gotten here earlier. For one thing, I'm starving."

"Me too," Vi said. "I don't think the chicken salad was good in that truck-stop café."

The white parrot rubbed its beak back and forth on Vi's purple shoulder. "I liked it."

"Oh, Maria," Vi said. "You'll eat anything."

"Well, come on," Clyde said. "Earl, why don't you pull the truck into that driveway over there by those sculptured hedges?"

"Nah," Earl said. "I'm not coming in."

"What?" They all turned to him in surprise.

"I'm going over to Woody 'n Eddy's," Earl said. "It's just a few blocks away. I wanna see if any of the old gang's left."

"You can't do that," Vi said. "You wanted to see your son!"

Clyde strode purposefully to the driver's side of the truck and opened Earl's door. "I'm sorry. I should've kept quiet. If my words prevent you from seeing your son, I'll never be able to live with myself."

"No," Earl said. "You were right. I can't see Danny until I'm clear I could stay with him forever."

"I have enough guilt," Clyde said, "without this."

"Look," Earl said, "I've been thinking and thinking. And I still don't know what I want. All I do know is I wish I could say I'm not gonna pull another disappearing act."

"Earl." Vi came to the other window. "Don't be silly. This is your kid."

"Let me go!" Earl cried, his face crumpled with anguish. "If I show up, it means I'm ready to be Danny's father. If I don't, you can find me at Woody 'n Eddy's on Colorado."

"Hell!" Clyde said.

Earl jerked the door closed and started the truck. "Don't worry about me. You just get on with the healing and see if you can save my son."

As they watched the battered truck take off in a cloud of black exhaust, Clyde put his arm around Vi's waist. "He'll be back."

"Do you think so?"

"Yes," Clyde said. "He's having a profound experience."

"Well, let's get on with it." Harriet swung the satchel over her shoulder and started down the winding pink and blue slate path.

"Oh, no!" Dena said. "I forgot to take the jewels to the jeweler. Do we have enough money to pay everyone?"

"I took them this morning," Daniel said. "The jeweler will appraise them and have a check for us by four o'clock."

"Are you sure you can trust him not to cheat?"

Daniel lifted Dena's chin with his forefinger so he could gaze into her brown eyes. "He is absolutely reliable, my dear. How beautiful you look!"

Dena lowered her mascaraed lashes. In her long robe, silvery-white to match Daniel's, she was a buxom angel from a Christmas pageant. Daniel caressed her once-graying hair, which had grown progressively darker since their first meeting.

"Listen," Dena said. "The musicians are tuning up. I asked them to play quiet music, so Danny will be in an open state. Thank goodness, Mother agreed to come!"

"Yes. I don't know why she changed, but suddenly she has become a great help."

"I think she finally realizes you have the power."

Daniel looked over Dena's head at his handsome reflection in the pink-tinted dressing room mirror. "Do you think so?"

"How could she help it? Such confidence radiates from you, Daniel, it would be impossible not to feel it."

Because he had been struggling with his own insecurities lately, Daniel was somewhat relieved by Dena's reassurances. Of course, she was biased. Could it really be that his doubts did not show, like a giant stain on the back of his pants? What did the other healers think of his abilities?

He heard Tamara's shrill laugh from the Healing Center kitchen, where she sat with the healers having coffee. Were they laughing about him? Come to think of it, Saint Simeon hadn't been overly friendly when he arrived with Tamara an hour ago. And His Holiness Omar had the gall to appear in saffron robes and turban, when Daniel had asked them all to wear white.

"Come," Daniel said, "let me introduce you to the healers. You haven't met them all."

He may as well face them, he thought, since they were all going to work together. Fervently, he prayed this time would be different from the last Great Healing, when the very air had reeked of dissension. Instead of focusing on the patient, a girl with polio, they had focused on their own power struggles. Idiocies, like who was going to touch the child first, or say the last prayer, had dominated the session. Yet he needed them, he knew, because a group has more potential power than an individual.

"Well?" Dena waited by the door. "If we're going to do it, let's get going. Although I can't imagine they'd want to meet me, since I'm not a healer."

"They'll be charmed." Oh, let them be, Daniel thought, as he led the way down the pink, flower-lined hallway to the kitchen.

"The only one I met," Dena whispered at his back, "is that Reverend Jarvis Bing. And let me tell you, he's one scary character."

"Jarvis?" Daniel chuckled. "What could Jarvis have done to frighten you? Did he wiggle his whiskers?"

"Don't be ridiculous. You know how he looks."

Daniel thought he did know, but when they entered the huge, pink-tiled kitchen, he saw his old friend Jarvis, the backwoods, tobacco-spitting healer, had undergone an unsettling transformation. In his white robes with silver sequins sprinkled about in constellation patterns, Jarvis now had long, silky blond hair that contrasted oddly with his bushy eyebrows and fierce dark eyes. Furthermore, he seemed no longer folksy but cold and disdainful.

Although Jarvis ignored her, Tamara was hanging onto his arm as she told stories in her fake Russian accent. Paler than Daniel had ever seen her, her greenish-white skin blended right into her long white hair which she wore in thick braids down the front of her low-cut white robes. Which might have been designed by Dior, Daniel thought, to show off her figure, if she had had one. She batted her snowy eyelashes at the group clustered about the pink Formica table with its black border of Egyptian hieroglyphs.

"Allo, darling," she said to Daniel. "At last you arrive. But who, I say who, is thees small friend of yours? Have you surprise us with an unknown healer?"

"No, no," Daniel said. "Tamara, this is Dena, my invaluable secretary."

Dena could not help staring at Tamara's silver lips. "Hello," she said to Tamara's mouth. "Glad to meet all of you."

"You see," Tamara said to the others, "Daniel has now a new one."

"A new what?" Dena said, but Tamara laughed with an exaggerated air of mystery.

"He must to tell you sometime." She raised her pink cup.

"To you, Daniel, who have done it again."

"Please, Tamara," Daniel said. Clearly, this could be even worse than last time.

"That's right, Tammy. Cut the crap, unless you're trying to earn us an award for total failure." A diminutive gypsy slammed her hand down on the table. She sparkled with strands of rhinestones, her coarse black hair covered with a paisley shawl of the same reds and blues as the shawls draped over her shoulders and around her hips. Then she turned to Dena. "At last! I've been wanting to meet you. Did you know I met your mother not long ago?"

"You did? Well, I really can't imagine..." Where could they have met, Dena wondered. On one of Mother's nightly wanderings?

"I'm Madame Olivia." The woman rose. Less than five feet tall, her presence was electric. "Basically a psychic, but Daniel wanted my energy for the healing."

Oh, bless Olivia, Daniel thought. She would help them get through this without a major battle. "Is anyone hungry?" he said. "We have fruit and sandwiches."

"What sort of sandwiches?" said Saint Simeon. "I'm on a diet. Did anyone remember that?" Short and fat, his white robe bundled about his body like bedclothes over pillows, he was in a bilious mood. With his orange curls and flat, freckled moon face, he looked more like Little Orphan Annie than a saint.

Dena stifled a laugh. "We have turkey, ham and cheese, egg salad, tuna..."

"All with mayonnaise, I suppose. Exactly what I expected. Although I did write down lean roast beef and watercress."

"Daniel, dear," Tamara said. "Ees the egg salad separate

from the other sandwich? My system ees too delicate for the vibration of meat."

"I don't know." Damn her, Daniel thought.

Dena was determined to play hostess. "I think they're on the same plate as the tuna. Let me see."

Tamara ignored her. "You see, Daniel, thees fish ees as bad as thees meat."

When Dena and the hired cook placed platters of sandwiches and bowls of fruit on the table, everyone but Saint Simeon found something they could eat. "Never mind," he said petulantly, "I'll take a walk in the garden, so I won't have to watch."

A precarious peace settled over the group, so Daniel excused himself. He needed some quiet time to prepare for the healing, to allow the power to infiltrate his whole self. When he was in the correct state of being, he would become a channel for healing energies to flow through his body. Then all he would have to do would be to touch the child... Of course, there were the others. Always unpredictable, they could by their very nature block the process. And where was Clyde?

As he glided meditatively down the corridor, he paused by the closed door to the Preparation Room, where Esther and Danny waited. Should he go in and reassure them? Surprisingly enough, they had both seemed to trust him throughout this morning's ordeal at the hospital. What a time they had had with the doctors and the administrators, who were thinking more of themselves than of Danny! When Dena signed the release form, in spite of all their protests, they finally threw up their hands. Although one spiteful young doctor actually tried to remove Danny's I-V and would have succeeded, if Dena hadn't become a true terror. By that time Danny was sliding in and out of consciousness. With the help of the hospital workers, they had loaded him, I-V and all, into the Healing Center van and brought him here, less than two hours ago.

When he put his ear to the door, he could hear Esther murmuring. No response from Danny, however, so Daniel opened the door, just a bit, and looked in.

"Good morning," Esther said, as though this were their first encounter of the day.

"Good morning." Daniel could now see that Danny's eyes were closed, his body terribly still as the I-V drained into his limp arm. Fear shot up from the soles of his feet, but he controlled the tremor in his voice. "How is the child? Do you need anything?"

"Nothing," Esther said pleasantly, "that you could give us. Danny is, at the moment, still alive."

"Don't worry," Daniel said, "we will save him."

"I do appreciate your earnestness," Esther said.

Once again Daniel felt uneasy. "Thank you, but...you do have faith in my power as well?" He could not help his questioning tone.

"Although I did not choose to bring Danny here or to come here myself," Esther said gently but evasively, "I realize it is necessary, for some reason which Benjamin refuses to explain."

"Oh. Very well, then." Daniel's scalp and the back of his neck began to itch. Lord, he hoped he wasn't breaking out in hives! "We should begin shortly, as soon as the last healer arrives."

"Fine," Esther said. "And now, good-bye."

Clearly he was being dismissed, so Daniel shut the door carefully and tiptoed uneasily to his private room. When he entered his white sanctuary with its round stained-glass windows, he prostrated himself on the thick, deep blue carpet. His hands grasped the tufts of wool like a security blanket.

A peal of chimes rang through the rooms.

"Excuse me," Dena said to the healers, who had begun to bicker over Omar's saffron robes.

"White," Jarvis said, "was the instruction. Even Olivia is wearing white, under all those shawls."

"Which I will remove," Olivia said, "at the appropriate time."

When Dena heard the front door chimes, she was happy to have a reason to leave the kitchen, messy with friction, sandwich crusts and orange peels. She hurried to the front door and pulled it open. "Oh." There, in a stained white robe and dusty feet, stood Danny's father.

"Hello." Clyde held out his hand. "Clyde Simmons. I'm here for the healing."

Too stunned to speak, Dena shook his hand. So he didn't recognize her! At least, not yet. She should have known when she heard the name Clyde, which was fairly unusual, but the man she had wrestled with in the desert fifteen years ago had been a gas station attendant, not a healer. How had it happened that a sexy, ill-tempered worker had become a faith healer, and not only that, but one who looked just like those cheap pictures of Jesus that David always stared at in Woolworths? Oh! She had another horrible thought. Did Clyde know he was here to work on his own son? No, how could he, if he didn't recognize Dena herself. But she had to know.

"Do you know the boy?"

"You mean Danny?"

Then he did know! Dena felt her inner structures collapsing like a building in an earthquake.

"Is something wrong?" Clyde said, when she would neither speak nor let go of his hand. "Am I too late?"

"No. No, you're just.... in time, yes, we all were...." Just before she said "expecting you," Dena caught herself and barked a grisly laugh.

Clyde hoped he was not going to be dealing with total lunatics like this during the healing. He decided to ignore her bizarre behavior. "Please allow me to introduce my wife, Harriet, and good friend, Violette."

"Your wife!" Dena said. "I didn't know."

"But I wrote to Daniel. He must not have gotten my letter. Well, please don't worry. We can always stay in a motel."

Clyde was married. Why did that hurt so much? Dena hadn't seen him for fifteen years, had never expected to see him again. Still, somehow she must have thought of him as hers, because of Danny. And because he was my first lover, Dena thought, such a wild one!

She inspected Harriet, standing uncertainly behind Clyde. Too thin, gawky really, with freckles more appropriate to a young girl. Legs too long in those little green shorts. Hardly a worthy rival for Dena. Now, if his wife had been that other one, that Violette who was fairly bursting out of her purple sundress but so strikingly beautiful that Dena could just cry, well, then, Dena would have been jealous.

"We came here," Clyde said, "with Danny's father."

"WHAT?"

"Yes, Earl Norman. Danny never mentioned him?"

"Earl is here?"

"Well, he's not exactly here; he went to a bar, although we did try to convince him..." Clyde felt himself babbling in front of this strange woman.

"We sure did try," Vi said. "It's your very own son, I said, but he's stubborn as a goat."

"I know." Dena heard her disembodied voice floating like a dead angel on the bottom of the fish tank. "I remember."

"Oh," Vi said, "then you knew him pretty well?"

"I was his wife," Dena said faintly but defiantly.

"That's nice." Vi gave Dena an ingenuous smile. "I'm his lover."

This was too much. Dena felt mistreated by the universe. Wasn't it enough to have Danny sick to the very point of death? Did she have to be the butt of some stupid cosmic joke?

"Uh." Clyde wiggled his hand, imprisoned in Dena's boa constrictor grip.

"Pardon," Dena gasped. She dropped Clyde's hand and backed into the hallway.

"Do you get the feeling," Harriet said, "that we're not welcome?"

Suddenly Daniel appeared at Dena's side. "Clyde! Thank God, you're here!" The two men embraced warmly. "And who," Daniel said, "are these lovely ladies?"

"My wife, Harriet, and our friend, Violette."

"Aha!" Daniel took their hands and planted a kiss on each cheek. "And this is Dena, my secretary, and the mother of Danny Norman."

"Oh," Clyde said. "Of course." So that was why the woman

was behaving so oddly; no doubt she had bad feelings for Earl and did not want him to see their child. Well, if Earl should decide to come, she would just have to put up with it.

"Please, come in," Daniel said. "You must meet the other healers."

They all followed Daniel down the hall to the kitchen, where the healers had lapsed into a moody silence. Even Saint Simeon was there, perched on a stool, his back to the others.

"Look, everyone!" Daniel winced at the false heartiness in his voice. "Clyde's here, with his lovely young bride, Harriet, and their friend, Violette."

"Oh, good." Olivia jumped up. "Clyde will ground us. Won't you, my dear?" She embraced Clyde and, without waiting for his response, turned to Vi and Harriet. "I hope you've been to a healing before. Otherwise, this is going to seem like a scene from a madhouse."

Finally, Harriet thought. A woman with warmth and common sense, even though she looked like a gypsy. Which was, Harriet decided, a very nice way to look, with all those shawls going every which way.

"I love your diamonds," Vi said.

"Thanks," Olivia said, "but these aren't diamonds; they're just pretty fakes." She narrowed her eyes. "Wait a moment. Where is Earl Norman?"

"Oh!" Dena shrieked and ran from the kitchen.

"Who?" Jarvis said.

"The child's father." Olivia turned to Daniel. "Did I say something wrong?"

"I don't know." Daniel's face crumpled. Why was everything so confusing, just when it was imperative to maintain an inner stillness? "What do you mean, the child's father?"

"Well," Olivia said to Vi, "didn't you bring him here?"

"Sort of," Vi said. "How did you know?"

"She's a psychic," Clyde said. "Do we have time to bathe and eat?"

"Yes, if you're quick about it." Although he still didn't know what was going on with Dena and this business about Danny's father, Daniel was relieved to focus on ordinary things. "Olivia, I'll take Clyde down the hall and leave the women to you."

As Daniel led Clyde to the bathing room, he could hear Olivia introducing the healers who, faced with "ordinary" people, were suddenly becoming civil. Besides, Daniel thought, that woman Violette was certainly irresistible. Why, if he weren't in love with Dena, he... "What a lovely wife you have," he said to distract himself as he slid open the opaque glass door.

"Yes, isn't she? She is saving my life." Clyde preceded Daniel into the bathing room and stopped in amazement. "Magnificent! Who designed all this?"

"I did." Daniel surveyed his domain proudly: the ten-foot circular pink marble tub with its fountain bubbling up from the center, the pink-tiled floor dotted with furry rugs, the giant murals of faint pink saints leading to the glass showers, and overhead, another rose skylight.

"Why don't you go ahead and clean up?" Daniel said. "I'll get some lunch for us and bring it back here."

Clyde immediately pulled off his stained robe, dropped it on the tiles, and immersed his lanky body in the cool pink water.

"Would you..." Daniel eyed the mound of dusty cloth distastefully. "...like a fresh robe?"

"Yes, thanks," Clyde said, as he disappeared under the fountain.

"Well, now I understand why Dena was so upset," Clyde said. They were eating lunch outside in the patio while Vi and Harriet were bathing. "I thought it was something about me. You do think the doctors have given up on the child?

"They don't say so, of course, but it's perfectly clear. And at the same time…" Daniel gestured vehemently with his chicken salad sandwich. "… they are completely closed to other possibilities. We almost couldn't get Danny out of the hospital."

"What a joy it will be to his mother when we cure him!"

"You're sure we will?"

Clyde rested his iced tea between his bare feet on the tiles. "Daniel, you're not having doubts? Not now!"

Embarrassed, Daniel studied the birds of paradise bordering the patio. "It means so much to me, you know. Because Dena and I are…"

"Oh. I see."

"And then there's Danny himself, an incredible boy. Talented in music and math. What a shame it would be if…"

"Yes," Clyde said quietly. "But you mustn't think like that. Especially just before the healing. I believe faith can move mountains, but doubts accomplish nothing."

"I'm afraid of the others. Except for Olivia, they're very cantankerous today."

"Just wait. I have a feeling they'll be united when they see the boy."

"I do hope so." Daniel rested his well-groomed head on his

knees. "I can't believe you brought his father here. The very person Dena would not want to see."

"I don't mean to sound harsh, but Dena is not the point. Earl came for Danny. And for himself. Even though he may not have the nerve to show up."

"What is he like?" Daniel felt an odd gnawing jealousy.

"An honest man, with good intentions. Guilt-ridden at the moment, like most of us. A decent pianist. An atheist."

"An atheist! Then I'm glad for everyone's sake he hasn't come. We don't need a cynic in these proceedings."

"Cynicism often masks the greatest faith."

"Don't be pat." Daniel resisted the desire to ask if Earl was as handsome as he was.

"We're ready!" Harriet called as she and Vi padded out from the bathing room. Freshly scrubbed, their hair damp, they were radiant in coarse white robes.

"My dear clean one." Clyde kissed Harriet sweetly.

"See how they love each other?" Vi said.

"Yes." Daniel did see. Their kiss was so intimate and loving, so different from the passion that flamed up with Dena, that he could not continue to watch them.

"I hope," Vi said, adjusting her robe over her huge breasts, "this is fun. Because I've never done something like this, and I feel a little silly in a robe."

"You look wonderful. But about fun, well, I really don't think fun is the right..." Just as Daniel took Vi's arm so he could see more clearly down the front of her robe, Dena appeared like a third eye.

"Daniel! We've moved Danny and Mother into the In-Depth Room with the musicians. The healers are waiting for you and…" Her voice faded away. "Clyde."

"Good." Carefully casual, he turned and walked to the bathing room, so Dena could not see his bulge. "I'll be right there. Please lead them in, Dena."

"No, I think you…" she said to his retreating back, but he was gone.

"Now, Dena," Clyde said. "Don't be nervous. You must have faith in us." He approached Dena and rested his hand on her shoulder. "You know, you remind me of someone."

Danny lay in the center of the In-Depth Room. Still deathly pale, his eyes closed, he breathed with his mouth open in long, hoarse gasps. Next to the Healing Table Esther, in her bright flowered dress, was perched on a high wicker chair like a delicate bird. She held Danny's hand and whispered varied but continuous instructions to his struggling spirit.

"Do not give up. Not time yet, you must wait…" Daniel heard her say. Then he lost her words in the rippling music that filled the blue room with an underwater sadness.

Except for Esther and Omar, everyone was in white. Even the cellist, violinist and pianist, playing their haunting, unfamiliar melodies so earnestly in the corner by the windows. Everywhere there were white roses. White candles burned in niches and on small, bronze tables. Incense mingled with the rich, rose fragrance.

"Let us begin." Standing behind Danny's head, Daniel raised his arms. "I invoke the Universal Spirit to be with us and move through us as we heal this child." The other healers, who were gathered about the table, lifted their arms and opened their hands to the ceiling. "Ah, yes." Daniel's voice grew stronger. At last, a sense of unity among them! "We are becoming channels. Power is flowing into our hands and down our arms."

"There, there," Esther murmured. "No need to be afraid. Not at all. This is no different from 'Time for Beany'."

Vi bowed her head and clasped her hands. "Amen." She nudged Harriet, who sat next to her by the door.

"Amen," Harriet echoed, as she watched Clyde with amazed adoration. How could she be lucky enough to marry a saint?

Daniel nodded to Dena. "Now it is time for the mother of the child to place her hands on his head."

Hesitantly, Dena came forward and smoothed Danny's damp hair away from his forehead. Her heart fluttered and sank with each of her son's labored breaths. How fragile he looked, a glass child on white sheets! Could they save him? Or would his spirit move away and leave his body broken beyond repair? She rested her hands on each side of his head. Please, please, please, she chanted, an inner litany. Please, Daniel. Let. Please let Daniel. Please. Save him. My son, without whom I… Please save.

Olivia's hands began to dance in the air. "Now the light comes down. The spirits have entered the room."

Harriet shuddered and twisted around to see who had come in. Someone had brushed her shoulder with light, forgiving fingers. Well? No one. She turned to Clyde, whose eyes were wide with shock.

"Laura," he said. "Sonora."

"Yes." Olivia smiled joyfully.

"At last," Esther said. "Benjamin, we thought you'd never

come. Although it is unlike you to be late. You see the difficulty Danny is having? Entirely unnecessary, don't you think?"

Saint Simeon began to sway and utter little wounded shrieks. Arms out to his sides, his fingers vibrating, Omar joined in with low moans. Tamara's head jerked back. "Stars, moons and suns," she wailed. "Thees are bursting inside me!" The music grew louder and slightly discordant.

"Quite a din," Esther said. "I hope it doesn't bother you, Benjamin. Please introduce me to this lovely young woman and her daughter. What beautiful black hair you have, my dear. So long and thick. I also wear mine in a braid, but as you can see, I twist it onto my head, as an old woman should."

Jarvis crossed his hands over his breast. "Louder and louder became the noise from the cataract; swifter and swifter grew the current, and the boat shot on…" He tossed his silky blond hair. "But lost in the happiness of the interior light, I gave no heed."

"Forgive me!" Clyde sank to his knees and buried his face in the bed sheets.

Esther patted Clyde's head. "Your guilt is meaningless. Why don't you just say hello? Spirits appreciate a little everyday politeness."

"I don't see anything," Harriet said. "Why is Clyde so upset?"

Esther smiled sweetly. "It's a habit."

Daniel clutched Dena's trembling body. "All hail the divinity of love, pure love!"

"All you spirits who have graced us with your presences, please help us." Olivia was beaming as she beckoned to the windows. "Come here, little girl. Don't be shy."

"Look, Danny," Esther said. "Roseanne has come to visit."

Danny's breathing suddenly grew calm. He opened his eyes and said, faintly, "Hello, Roseanne." Then he smiled flirtatiously at Dena. "Mama, I love you."

"All right," Esther said to Clyde. "Get up now, or you'll drive your wife and child away with your boring discourtesy."

Clyde lifted his head apprehensively.

"Oh!" Danny cried. "Father! You've come back!"

Startled, Clyde looked at Danny's ecstatic face.

Just at that moment a rosy golden light streamed through the rose window and illumined Clyde, Danny and Dena, who bent down to rest her head next to Danny's.

"All hail our newborn brother," Jarvis intoned. "All hail the coming of the light, for now he is healed."

"Just like my dreams," Danny said faintly. "Now.... will you.... play my song?"

"What do you mean?" Clyde said.

"He thinks," Esther whispered, "you're his father."

Dena straightened up in panic and grabbed Esther's hand. "Mother!"

"I wrote it for you," Danny murmured. "Will you?"

What a terrible misunderstanding, Clyde thought, but when he saw Danny's imploring face, he knew he had no choice. "Yes. Of course I will."

"I knew it. Yes," Danny said with a blissful smile. He closed his eyes.

"Thank you, spirits of the universe," Daniel said, "for healing this child."

Just then Dena screamed, a cry so piercing and heart-rending that Vi imagined the very temple itself had split wide open. The music stopped.

"What is it?" Daniel said.

Clyde put his hand gently on Danny's chest, just above where the tube had been inserted into his lungs. "He's not breathing."

"Impossible," Jarvis said. "We just healed the boy."

"No." Clyde could feel himself disintegrating. "He's dead."

"Yes," Esther said. "Yes, he is. Good-bye, Danny dear. Take care of him, Benjamin, and you, too, Roseanne, until I join you."

"It's my fault." Clyde drooped forward as tears gathered behind his eyes. "If I hadn't been here..."

"Nonsense," Olivia said.

"So many men choose the wrong time to cry," Esther said flatly.

"Oh, please, my darling." Harriet came to sit next to Clyde on the floor and pulled his head onto her lap.

"Your wife and child are leaving," Esther said.

"I am his wife."

"That's right." Esther nodded. "I think they're glad he found you."

Saint Simeon toyed fretfully with his orange curls. "This is the last and final straw! I was sure we were going to be successful this time."

"Eet was all your fault, with thees arguing like a child," Tamara said. "Yours and Omar's, who would not wear white."

"Saffron has a special power you wouldn't understand." Omar crossed his arms over his chest angrily and turned to the windows.

"You don't know anything!" Jarvis said. "Let me tell you..."

"STOP!" Dena raised her fist menacingly.

"My dear one," Daniel began.

"Enough!" Dena said. "Take that thing out of his arm!"

Daniel removed the I-V from Danny's lifeless arm. The tube dangled over the floor and continued its inexorable dripping of sustenance. Then Dena lifted Danny, bedclothes trailing, into her arms.

"What are you doing?" Daniel said.

"Taking Danny home."

Jarvis blocked her way. "You can't do that!"

"Let me drive you," Daniel said.

"You may call a taxi," Dena said, her teeth clenched and her face steely gray. "But don't touch me. Or my child."

"What?"

"We will wait in the kitchen. Out of my way!" she said to Jarvis, who stepped meekly aside as Dena, struggling but her head high, carried Danny out the door.

Daniel looked stricken. "She doesn't mean that!"

"Yes, she does," Esther said. "But don't worry. You'll find other women. Like that one by the door you've had your eyes on all afternoon."

"Oh, no," Vi said, "he hasn't been looking at me."

"I have not," Daniel said guiltily.

"It doesn't matter." Esther stood up slowly. "What a painful experience. But then, I knew it would be."

"I'll go talk to her," Daniel said. "She doesn't know what she's doing. It's the grief."

Earl burst into the room. "All right!" he shouted. "I figured it all out. I'm gonna stay and be a father to Danny, and Vi can stay with me."

"Earl..." Vi said.

His eyes were glowing. "I dunno how long I sat there nursing my beer. None of the old gang was there, so I had plenty of time to think. I asked myself: what do I got in my life? Nothing but Vi, I hadda answer. Sure, it's true I've been an atheist and an intellectual, but it don't give me no real satisfaction. So maybe I'm wrong, even. Who knows? Maybe living on this earth is sad a lot of the time, no matter what you believe."

"Hello, Earl," Esther said. "You received my letter."

"Yeah, I sure did. Thanks, Esther. You always were a good one for delivering a swift punch in the gut."

Esther blushed. "Well, what a lovely thing to say. That is a phrase I never would have used to describe myself."

"Yeah." Earl patted Esther affectionately on the shoulder. "You're a good woman." A crestfallen quiet had settled over the people in the room, but Earl didn't notice. "I said to myself, you know, Clyde could be right about a meaning and pattern, and where I oughta be is home with my kid. Learn to be a real father. Trust Clyde and let him heal my kid."

Still buried in Harriet's lap, Clyde gave a convulsive shudder.

"Oh, this is so sad!" Vi said.

Daniel had just left the room, but when he heard Earl's voice, he was drawn back in, magnetized by horror. He clung to the doorknob and listened.

"Well, as soon as I knew I oughta come back, the funniest thing happened. I started hearing this song in my head. I hadda rush to the piano--they got a brand new baby grand at Woody 'n Eddy's, in the lounge--and play it. When I started playing, the lounge was empty, but pretty soon all these people were standing around, like they just come outta nowhere. And you know what? I wanna play it right now, okay?"

Without waiting for an answer, Earl approached the pianist who, terrified by Earl's naive exuberance, retreated to a safe spot behind the cellist. Earl sat, flexed his fingers and began to play. A simple melody, bittersweet, filled with a longing so painful and hypnotic that everyone in the room was possessed with the desire to go home.

"Oh, my," Saint Simeon said, as he wiped away his tears with his sleeve.

Tamara wept openly for Mother Russia, even though she was from Cleveland. "I want to go back to the Czar."

"Forget it," Jarvis said. "He's dead." He returned to his own thoughts of his abandoned cabin on Orcas Island, the cool pine breezes blowing through mornings as he drank his camp coffee.

"Isn't it beautiful?" Vi sobbed. "I hope my folks are all right."

"And my grandparents," Harriet said.

In the corner the musicians huddled and whimpered.

Slowly Clyde stood up and reached down to pull Harriet beside him. "That is the song of the family," he said. "And now I know we are all together--Laura, Sonora, you and I, Danny and that little girl, Roseanne--the living and the dead, we accept each other."

"Yes." Harriet held Clyde's hand lightly. "I do understand."

Earl finished playing and swiveled to face the room. "Well, what do you think?"

"That was Danny's song," Esther said.

"I know. I wrote it for him in my mind."

"No," Esther said. "That is the song he wrote for you."

"Where is he?" Earl said. "I want to play it for him."

"You already have," Esther said. "But if you wish to look at the child, he is in the kitchen with his mother."

"No," Daniel said. "Esther, how could you?"

"Well?" Earl said. "Who's going to show me the way?"

"I will." Esther swept through the stunned and silent group. "Follow me." As she passed Daniel, she patted his shoulder. "Be calm."

While Esther led Earl to the kitchen, Daniel retreated to his study. The others wandered about uneasily, some drawn to the sunny patio, alive with birdsong and the humming of bees in the sweet peas.

Esther opened the door to the kitchen. "Here. Make your own peace. I am going to rest now." She walked back down the pink hallway and left Earl alone.

When Earl looked into the kitchen, Dena was sitting stiffly, her back to the doorway. He could just see, above the table-top, that she held something in her arms. Someone. Someone wrapped in a white sheet.

"Dena?" he said hesitantly.

She did not answer.

"Dena? It's me. Earl. I've come back to see Danny." Fear, high-pitched, fluorescent and oddly evil, hummed through the kitchen. "Aren't you gonna say anything?" He forced his reluctant body a few steps into the room. "I can understand you don't want to see me. God, I wouldn't either if I was you. But I've been doing so much thinking, see, and I realized a kid needs his father." He stretched out his arms, begging this silent statue that had once been his wife.

"I know something else now, too. A father needs his kid. So, if you could just… I mean, you don't have to forgive me or anything, but if you could just....let me see him? Then, if it's not right, if he hates me or something, I'll go away. Okay? Just let me try."

"Come here," Dena said tonelessly, without moving. "Take a look."

Earl tiptoed across the floor. When he saw Danny, he reeled back as though he had been struck. "Oh, Jesus! Oh, my God!"

"Yes," Dena said. "You're a little late."

Danny's head hung awkwardly over Dena's elbow, his mouth open, his dark, sweaty hair plastered to his forehead and ruffled out slightly by his big ears. Dena shifted, and the long fingers of Danny's right hand traced a meaningless pattern on the tiled floor.

"No!" Earl said. "He moved. I saw it."

"He's dead. You want to be a father all of a sudden? Here. Take him. Tell him all the things he wanted to hear." Dena leaned back so Earl could gather Danny into his arms.

How light he was! Surely no more than sixty pounds. Earl cradled Danny like a baby. "We're going for a walk," he said, and even though Dena stared straight ahead indifferently, he added, "But we'll be back."

He wrapped the sheet around Danny's body so the boy would be comfortable and wouldn't catch cold, because you never knew, even on a warm day, the beginning of summer, what could happen. Then he carried him down the hallway and out the front door, which was wide open, just the way he had left it when he had come running in. Years ago.

"You need to get out a little more," he said. "I'm gonna take you to a park."

As he walked slowly down the sidewalk, a young mother,

pushing her baby in a carriage, smiled at the sight of a father so devoted to a sick child. "What's the matter with him?" she said.

Earl held Danny's face close to his breast. "Nothing. Just needs some fresh air." He quickened his pace.

"Hope he gets better soon," she called after him.

"Look," he said to the boy in his arms, "there's a lotta things I gotta tell you. The first is, I left because I really didn't like your mother. Okay, I'm gonna be more honest. I didn't even like you." He peeked at Danny's face to see if there was some reaction. "I didn't want you to be sick, see, because that would make me look bad. I guess all I thought about was me, and I got restless with the way things were going. I figured you wouldn't miss me if I took off."

They had arrived at the corner park, empty in those pre-sunset moments before the sky rolls into gold. Shuffling slightly through thick pine needles, Earl carried Danny to a bench under a tall pine tree. He sat and arranged Danny's body to make him more comfortable. As he did so, he noticed the boy's mouth was now closed, his face more serene.

"I wanted everything easy, no trouble, no pain. So I took off into the desert, and you wanna know the truth? I didn't think about you much until Clyde came. Never even talked about you, and there I am, dreaming about you. Then Clyde yelled at me about growing up, which I didn't wanna hear. Not me, such a big shot, and fifty years old already, who the hell was he to talk like that? I wanted to see you, but I was mad. I got my pride, which ain't much use in the long run. Kept me from coming here in time for..."

He dusted away the film of salt that had dried on Danny's smooth cheeks and forehead. "So. Here we are, just us two, and

I wanna know about you, all the stuff I missed. Esther says you write songs? Say, didja like that song I played for you? Came right outta my head, most amazing thing, because I don't usually write songs."

Earl cocked his head to one side and waited. "C'mon, Danny, tell me something. Oh, Jesus, kid, please? See, I'm begging you. Earl Norman, your father. Dad. Daddy. Anything you wanna call me, it's okay. I come clear outta the desert to see you."

Abruptly, the tears came. He looked up into the pine branches, dark against the setting sun. "Oh, God! Do I have to live with this?"

Overhead an eagle soared, great-winged and calm in the crimson sky.

"They're what? Fakes? Don't be ridiculous. Those jewels are not only real, they're *antiques*, brought here from Russia. That woman wouldn't lie, goddammit!" Daniel slammed down the receiver. Now, what could he do? The musicians were waiting to be paid, as was the cook, and the florist. He had promised the healers a little something as well, to cover their expenses.

He sighed heavily. Everything had gone wrong. Not only was the healing a failure, but also he had overextended himself financially. What a fool he had been to invest in that crackpot piggy bank scheme! It had sounded like such a sure thing, and then, without a word of warning, the man had gone bankrupt. And there was no one to comfort him. At least, if he still had Dena...

He couldn't have lost her completely. No, she was upset,

understandably, about Danny's death, and she blamed him, even though all the doctors had given up on the child. When she had climbed into the taxi, her face blank, all she had said was, "Tell Earl to bring Danny home." She almost seemed not to recognize Daniel, even though she had been crazy about him before the healing. Opening her legs in that tempting way and showing her breasts, which were almost as nice as that woman Violette's. Much nicer than Clyde's scrawny wife, Harriet's, poor woman. He could feel the weight of Dena's breasts in his hands.

Oh, she would come back to him, if he gave her time. He would send cards and flowers, to prove his love. In the interim, there was Violette, who didn't seem all that attached to Earl. Perhaps he could… He reached for his shaving lotion, a special blend called "Tiger," and splashed some on his cheeks and neck.

Olivia stuck her head in the door. "The natives are restless, Daniel dear. If you pay them, they'll leave, and you can have a little peace."

At the sound of Olivia's voice the movie playing in Daniel's head froze at the final erotic frame; then the screen went blank. Where was he? Oh, yes, here in his study, the desk littered with opened mail, and nothing to do, nothing at all. He reached for an envelope, ripped it in half, then in quarters, then in little pieces.

"Daniel?"

He wouldn't look at her. Why should he? He tore up a second envelope, then a third. Soon he would start on the letters, because that was an old maxim: destroy the form first, then the contents.

Olivia came in and closed the door. "Are you all right?"

Perhaps he would tell her. Or perhaps he wouldn't speak at all. No difference, really. So, why not?

"I'm not going to pay them, Olivia."

"What are you talking about?"

As she leaned over his shoulder, he could smell her musky perfume. The fringe of one of her shawls brushed the back of his neck, that vulnerable spot where the blade cuts through.

"Olivia. There is no money."

"But you promised them. I don't care for myself, but the others won't leave until they get paid. I know them."

"Tell them to sue me. Or, better yet..." An ugly, whining sound, like a parody of laughter. "... tell them to sell some jewels."

"Oh, Daniel, my dear. This is not the end of the world. If we couldn't save that child, you must realize it was time for him to die. That's all. We do the best we can." She massaged his shoulders.

"But the money..."

"We'll deal with it. I'll help. I have some money."

Daniel felt his shoulders relaxing under the pressure of her strong hands. What a wonderful woman she was! All these years, and never once had he thought of her as more than a friend. Perhaps now that Dena had deserted him, he should reconsider. Yes, that would be best. A psychic and a faith healer. An unbeatable combination. As he slumped forward onto the desk, his mind drifted off into sleep.

In the Meditation Room Esther lay dreaming about Benjamin. He had come to call, in his best brown suit, with a bouquet of pink flowers, she wasn't sure what kind. Baby roses? Her family was delighted, because she was homely and certain never to be married. He sat with her in the parlor, while her mother bustled in and out with cookies and lemonade. The longer they sat, the more beautiful she became; it was quite amazing. Her mousy hair gleamed with the late afternoon light filtering in through the curtains. Her skinny body became slender, supple, a flower swaying in soft winds.

And now they were at a restaurant, some small place in the Chicago ghetto. Esther was sixteen and pregnant with Nathan, their first child. Although she wore a dark dress and her hair piled on her head, the restaurant owner teased her for being too young to be married. "Such a child!" he repeated, while Esther bit the smile away from her lips and touched, under cover of the tablecloth, the life growing inside her. Watched Benjamin through the screen of her eyelashes to see if he noticed, if he knew which night it was that he made the child begin. Because Esther knew. The night she let go and opened to a dark place, when she wasn't afraid any more. After all, at the end there is light and a meeting, after one has been alone.

Oh, look, here was Leah, with her in Paris, so many years later! Why had she gone to Paris without Benjamin? They were quarreling, but how could that be? He loved her so much, didn't want her to go until he could accompany her, but that might be years and years. So busy he was with his business, and Esther had grown a touch strong-willed, impatient to spend the money that gathered in jars in secret places. She and Leah stayed in such a fancy hotel! Esther ordered coffee from room service as though she had never been a poor immigrant, waiting in fear for the Statue of Liberty to say yes, yes. Now she,

Esther, was a rich lady with a husband and five fine children. See this one, more beautiful than Esther had ever been. Bright eyes, high cheekbones, and lustrous dark hair. Well-bred, too, and kind to everyone, even shopkeepers.

What fun it was to eat pastries with Leah in the Latin Quarter after they had bought new hats. Tried on every one in the shop, hats with bows, feathers and flowers, in straw and velvet, wide brims, cloches. All the while the saleslady repeating, "Oui, Madame, oui," because Leah was wonderful in hats. That final hat, my, how huge it was! Esther hadn't remembered, the brim so wide, wouldn't it be awkward for Leah, and the straw such a peculiar red? Blood red. Take it back, please. But no, we have paid for it.

Why was Leah wearing her wedding veil and pearls? There was no wedding in Paris; that took place in America. No, no, Esther did not want to go to the wedding, which was lovely, yes, the crushed wine glass, the hotel dinner and dancing until very late, and perhaps they had all drunk too much champagne. Leah could have had anyone, so many beaus, but she chose Myron, which was fine, let her, see how much they are in love? He twines a strand of her lovely hair through his fingers as they dance, cheek to cheek in the moonlight, because the hotel has no roof.

But after the wedding came the honeymoon. Esther refused; she would not go down that road with Leah, still holding her bridal veil although she had changed into a green silk dress. And Myron, see, he is bending to kiss her when he should keep his eyes on the road. But they are so silly, such young lovers, and Esther did not want to be with them.

Perhaps she should have forgiven Myron, because then he

might not have hanged his body from that tree in the middle of winter. She could see his frozen body, a dangling shadow over the blue afternoon snow. Why did she have to look now, when the telegram had been enough? She saw her own ice heart filled with evil gladness, because he had killed her Leah. No, not killed. Let her die.

Please, Esther begged the images that assaulted her like the broken windshield, pieces of cut glass, let me get out. Not that curve in the road! Such a screeching and a screaming, smells of burning rubber, asphalt and warm blood in new grass.

But now they were in a chapel and it was wedding time again, candles everywhere. Here came Benjamin in her dream, down the aisle toward her, and he was in white, wearing his Panama hat. Wrong for a groom, but still charming because, Esther knew, this was only a dream. She was getting married, or was it Leah? Never mind, she was mother and child both, and always, always, she was marrying her lover. Yes, she said, smiling. Yes, it is time.

When Dena opened the door of their small dark house in Altadena, Earl stood on the porch with Danny in his arms.

"I've brought him back, like I said I would."

Earl looked so hunched and pale, his hair plastered in sweat on his forehead, like an animal with its insides bleeding, that Dena felt, very far away, a flicker of pity. "You can bring him in," she said, "and lay him on his bed." She turned and walked stiffly down the hall to Danny's room, while Earl followed. At the doorway she stopped and pointed. "In there."

Earl stumbled over the doorsill, straightened and turned

apologetically to Dena. "I walked all the way." She gave no response, so he laid Danny down carefully on the bed, arranged the sheets and pulled up the covers, just to his chin, with his thin little arms hidden underneath. He looked at Dena, who stood like a guard in the doorway. "Do you mind if I...?"

"Go right ahead," she said, and vanished into the gloom.

Earl wandered around touching things: the coins in jars and albums, the foreign stamps, the math and world history books. Possessions his child had used and loved during those years when he breathed, when Earl did not know him. He thumbed through the music composition book until he came to the last piece, "Song for My Father." As he studied it in awe, he hummed, trying to catch the tune. "Wait a minute," he said. "That's not possible." He hummed the song again until he knew, absolutely, that was the song he had played, the one that had come, so miraculously, at Woody 'n' Eddy's.

"Oh," he said, "no. No, don't do that," and he knew he was imploring the universe not to be irrational. Just behind his eyes a pain began, a throbbing that crept backwards and down his neck like a marauder, finally taking over his whole body. The music book fell from his hands.

As he bent to retrieve it, he saw, on the floor by Danny's bed, a small notebook. "Dreams and Facts About Earl Norman," written in neat blue crayon on the cover. Too much, he couldn't look, but he shoved the notebook inside his leather vest. "I'll read it later," he said to the boy who had become too blurry to see, "and I'll be back. Don't you worry."

His head bowed like a penitent, he entered the living room, where Dena sat rigidly on the sofa.

"Earl," Dena said calmly. "I want you to know something. Look at me."

He lifted his head and stared into her eyes that opened into the labyrinth where a monster dwelt.

"You are not Danny's father. Clyde is."

Part Five

Pasadena, 1952

Dena wasn't sorry. She'd say it again, over and over, just to see the look on Earl's face. Who did he think he was, waltzing back here after so many years with not a word, not a cent to help her or Danny? Oh, yes, he came back ready to be a father at last. Take the boy on little trips, to see the seals in Malibu or to Knotts Berry Farm. She knew him.

Well, she cleared the air. For the first time since they had lived here, not a trace of smoke, nothing but the smell of her mother's lilac powder.

Mother. She wasn't going to think about it.

Let Earl worry about whether she'd tell Clyde he was really Danny's father. She wouldn't, of course; why should she give Clyde the satisfaction? He should be arrested anyway, running around like some plaster of Paris Jesus, pretending to have the healing power.

She supposed it was her fault for believing Daniel. How could she be so naive? That's what happened to women when they fell in love, she was sure of it. They opened their legs and their hearts at the same time and let the man fill them up with God knows what. Sperm, crazy ideas, all kinds of razzle-dazzle. Dime store glitter, that's what love was. And afterwards, sooner or later, you're always embarrassed.

Now, Daniel was going to pay. If she couldn't get him for murder, she'd get him for fraud, because she knew her mother's jewels were real. To think she gave him everything in her mother's blue satin jewel box, the one that played the wedding waltz! Every last piece. Well, not the three bird pins. Those she threw in the drawer with all the little scraps of paper she saved, like theater tickets and laundry receipts. She'd have to go through everything. But not now; she wasn't ready to enter her mother's room yet.

She wanted Daniel to suffer. Ultimately, she wanted him to want her, so she could turn him down. But for that she could wait. Her first satisfaction would be to see him in his white pants sitting in a dirty jail. Surrounded by bums. He'd be allowed one phone call, and who would it be to? Probably Dena, because he wasn't smart enough to hire a lawyer.

David had found Dena one of the best in lawyers in L.A., Ed Greer. The same one who was suing David's foreman for stealing his piggy bank pattern. Even though David, as usual, had absolutely no belief in anything she was doing. He said Dena had no case, but if she wanted to spend the last of her money foolishly, it was her choice. But how could David talk about foolish when he was practically gasping in the poorhouse?

Anyway, Daniel would call her, she knew him. "Oh, Dena, my darling," he'd plead, "how could you do this to me? After those many nights when we..." If he was making that call when nobody was around, he'd start his sex talk to make her juices run. Reminding her of how big he was and using words like "thrust" to get her going. But she wouldn't, and never mind, because even better than sex would be knowing he was suffering. Agony, that's what she wanted, his own. If she had his head on a platter, she'd nail it over the mantlepiece.

An experience like that made her understand a man like Bluebeard. Now that she thought of it, she wouldn't mind a whole gallery of heads: Earl's, Clyde's, and maybe even some of those healers'. All of them, why not? She'd keep them in a special room, and she wouldn't even clean it. She'd just laugh when the dust settled on their faces and noses, so thick they couldn't breathe.

Couldn't breathe, like her Danny. What did they know of her son, too perfect for any of them to touch? And God, too, what did he know? Letting a child like Danny get a hideous disease that made him suffer his whole life. Not a single time when they had fun but he didn't end up in bed with his inhaler, or worse yet, in the hospital. And yet he kept right on trying, believing in everything. Buying dogs and fish and birds. Bicycles and barbells to build up his little body. Entering contests and winning prizes for them all. Correspondence courses, home teachers, and that one sad attempt at college. All the music he wrote, those little plays, that concert. What would happen to it all now? What was the point, she'd like to ask God.

If she had a machine gun, she'd kill everyone, starting with God.

Furthermore. Not once did Danny complain or say a bad word, ever, about anybody. So was he just too good? Did God like to hit the good people, because they could take it? And let the bad people live in peace?

And her mother, too. Why did God kill her off just when they were starting to talk, to really communicate. Just when she might have, for once, acknowledged Dena as a human being and not just her homely, whining, sluttish daughter. That was a fine move. God must have a terrific sense of humor.

"Oh, Mother," she whispered to the cold breeze blowing through her dark house. "Now you'll never get a chance to love me, and still I miss you so. We had one thing in common, you and I. We weren't always pleasant, like David and his silly Kathleen, but we were never phony. And that, I know it now, is because we didn't live in fear of what other people think of us.

"Danny, my darling, the only one who loved me always,

how can I uncover the mirrors without seeing the shadow of your face where mine should be?"

Earl knew it couldn't be true. He watched Clyde all during the funeral and afterward, at Dena's house, and it couldn't be. Because if it was, Earl would sense it. Okay, Clyde was skinny like Danny, but that was the only way. Well, also his pale skin, and Earl was naturally dark, but Dena was pale. Other than that, Danny looked just like Earl. Same eyes, nose, dark hair.

Dena was just trying to get to him. And she did a good job, too. Earl couldn't stop thinking about it, like ghosts under the skin.

Where would she have met him?

In the desert. Clyde had told Earl he screwed a woman named Dena. But, no, she couldn't be the same woman.

What if she was pregnant when she met Earl, and that's why she wanted to get married so fast they hardly knew each other's last name? Bursting out of that tight waitress costume because she had Clyde's baby. He could ask Clyde when it was and figure out the dates. Then he'd know.

He couldn't ask Clyde. He didn't want him to claim Danny for his own son, and anyway, Earl knew Danny was his.

Earl tried to think clearly. Wasn't Dena a virgin when she came to work at Woody 'n Eddy's? She had said so, but she didn't act like a virgin.

No more, he was sick of this. Night after night, keeping Vi awake, and he was afraid to tell her. Afraid to tell anyone, because sometimes when a person says something out loud...

Oh, for Christ's sake! He needed to play the piano. Would

he wake everybody up? That baby grand in the blue room; it was pretty far away. He felt a surge of gratitude to Daniel for letting them stay in the Healing Temple, because Earl was getting short on money and hadn't wanted to mention it.

Maybe he could work on Danny's song. But how had that happened? Coincidence? No, it felt like something else. Like inspiration and a connection to his kid. Well, he reassured himself, that kind of thing happened all the time. Usually with a mother, so close to her son they experienced the same things at the same time. Earl knew a person could explain anything if he had an inquiring mind.

Except the weight of Danny in his arms.

What the hell did that mean? Okay, he'd get up, out of bed, careful not to wake Vi. What an angel she was, with those mascara smudges like a raccoon under her eyes. *Shhhh*, he thought. *Pull back the covers, don't touch those breasts glistening in moonlight. Silver pears, so ripe. No. Nestle the sheets around her lightly.*

He tiptoed down the hall, remembering the way he carried Danny, sheets falling loose until Earl wrapped them around his fragile body, still warm and damp. Then he knew the connection was real. Who could tell him he wasn't the father?

Earl felt a cord from his chest to his son's, like heart to heart. He knew Danny was out there, somewhere. If he was, there was more to life than he and Spinoza had figured out yet. Which gave Earl the crawling creeps, he had to admit.

Like that letter Clyde got from Pete, saying his eyeball grew back. Probably a joke with the gang. So why did Pete write to Clyde about it? To make him feel good?

Suddenly Earl heard piano music, very faint, like a tease. Somebody playing Danny's song.

"Shhhhh," he whispered, as he turned the knob of the Blue Room door. "Don't make a sound, you creaky door." He entered the shadowy room and reeled backward. "Who's that at the piano? Danny? Hey, it's me, yer dad. Turn around, lemme see you. Oh, my God, he's got my face!"

No, there was nobody there. What was the matter with him? He had the jitters, like his mind was racing down the wrong track with no conductor.

He needed a cigar. Where did he leave them? Oh, yes, right next to that golden Buddha in the garden. In the incense tray. Daniel had said Earl needed to smoke outside, which was fine. Nature never bothered Earl, not even when it was fixed up so fancy.

Ah, he felt good in California, close to the ocean. Maybe he and Vi would settle out here, find a house, and she could take her singing lessons. Who knew, maybe Clyde and Harriet would stay too. They could share a house. So what if Clyde was a faith healer, who didn't save his son? Earl didn't blame him. They were falling through the same darkness, both of them too late to save anybody.

If he could get to know David and Kathleen again, and those little girls, maybe he could learn how to love. Maybe they could be a real family. Except for Dena. She'd never open the door to Earl, he knew, not even to hand out Danny's music.

That melody again. Clyde heard it in his dreams like background music. When he woke up, it continued faintly, an underground stream. The rippling of sacred water in which he must purify himself, make himself a vessel for the oracle.

He felt his body becoming lighter, almost translucent, as he waited for the revelation. Some word had been conceived and was growing like Harriet's child. Their child. Waiting to become flesh.

Sometimes he felt the child inside his own body, and he knew the child was both Sonora and Danny. The children he couldn't save. Who had forgiven him, as had Danny's father and Sonora's mother.

Esther saw his ego, and she knew. Who can save anyone? It was difficult enough to save themselves from titillation and trivia. Clyde imagined his mind lost in a maze of trash, his feelings cheap, unreliable. Whenever he saw someone stumble up ahead, he'd rush to help, but the light was dim. If he got there at all, he was usually too late. Such vain heroics.

He wished to learn how to love. As he curled around Harriet, sleeping on these moon-washed sheets, he could feel the child in her belly. Feel the children within himself.

There was no more blood on their faces. Death had washed them clean, Clyde knew it. The tragedy was finished, and all that remained was a mourning in the blood that must be acknowledged. A memory of loss running under, like Danny's music, making new moments precious and possible.

What was this connection he felt for Danny? His face was so much like Clyde's, and his body was just as thin and pale. And why had Danny thought he was his father? The boy was delirious, of course, and that was why Clyde had finally said yes. Because Earl hadn't come, and Danny was longing for his father.

Time to come out of the desert. They needed to stay in California now, although Clyde wasn't sure why.

He would like to open a bookstore again, to feel the solidity of books around him. A small one, quiet, where he could read. In the evenings he could bring stories home for the children. After dinner they would sit around the wooden table, push aside their blue plates and take the children on their laps. He and Harriet would read aloud, taking turns in the growing darkness.

Dena had decided. The mirrors would stay covered and the doors would stay closed. She had disconnected the phone. The last call she made was to the contractors. They had started the work already, making the walls of the house two feet thick. Solid concrete. Then around the house a concrete wall, as high as the building codes would allow. She had said seven feet, so even Clyde couldn't see over, but the man wasn't sure that was possible. If you can't do seven feet, she told him, then make it six. At least that would keep Earl out, and David and his family, they were all so short. Make a great gate, she said, with a lock on my side.

She had been in her mother's room, and now she knew Daniel was right. All those pawn tickets with different dates on them, starting soon after they arrived in California. She must have sold everything, and where did the money go? To David? But even then Dena couldn't understand it. Her father left them so much, and Nathan and Samuel sent some each month, a generous amount. She knew, because she took the checks to the bank.

And there was another mystery: why didn't she tell us the jewels she let the children play with were fakes? But she never told Dena anything. So all she had now was her life insurance and the money Nathan and Samuel would continue to send, because they were good brothers, and she was sorry she ever thought a bad word about them.

She would be fine. The house was paid for, she didn't need a phone, and she ate very little. Less and less, because now she wasn't trying to get Danny to eat, and she had no mother in the house. There would be gas bills, but she had turned off the electricity. She didn't need it; she could use candles if she wanted to see in the evening. Although she probably wouldn't.

Earl could come around the house all he wanted to, but he wouldn't get Danny's music. The music was Dena's, just like Danny was, so Earl might as well stop fooling himself. Scratching at the windows like a restless cat, all hours of the night. She heard him, even though she pretended she didn't. She would keep the curtains closed, the blinds as well, so no light could enter. No cheap alley cats, their bedraggled fur and cat breath smelling of half-digested rats.

She would be so thankful when that wall was finally built. Thick and solid. You could always count on a wall to be there when you turned around quickly. Not vanish when you went into the kitchen for a drink of water. You didn't have to love a wall, and it would never die on you.

If Daniel should come around, ha-ha, is all Dena would say. Because he would, now that her phone was dead. Probably at that very moment he was too heartbroken to speak, and he did have his pride. So she'd let him have it. By the time he arrived, crawling the whole way on his hands and knees, his white pants ripped, her wall would be up. The gate closed and locked.

Daniel would stop, astonished, because he thought if he was penitent enough he could come right into her house. Right into Dena herself. Men were so clever at making women feel sorry for them; she was sure that was one of the best kinds of foreplay. *Oh, the poor things*, women always said. *They feel so terrible, all sackcloth and ashes*. Suddenly the juices were running down women's legs, and they would crawl right onto the ash pile with the men. When what they should do was say, *take a shower, straighten up, and maybe I'll be home later*.

He wouldn't be able to sleep for missing Dena and wishing he could get in touch with her. Touch her. Hah! So, whenever she woke up at all odd hours of the night, she'd know he was staring at his ceiling, drenched with the sweat of loneliness. That would comfort her when she followed those paths that led down into the tunnels. *And don't let anyone kid you*, she thought, *there is no light at the end*.

There was only one light in the house, on the mantel, just under Danny's gold-framed picture. Dena kept an eternal candle burning for her son. That was why she couldn't leave the house, not even for groceries. She couldn't let the flame die out.

The night after the funeral Jessamyn saw them all in a dream—her grandfather, her grandmother, Danny and Roseanne. They were eating dinner in a big house that had huge windows with lots of panes in them. The house was on an island way out in the ocean somewhere.

At first the ocean was red, so she knew it was made of blood. Then it turned clear black. She could see all the way to the bottom, where odd flowers were growing, the kind of flowers that eat fish. In her dream the ocean looked like a painting decorated with fish of all colors: green, blue, orange, yellow, purple, and some with stripes and polka dots. Some of the fish were so stupid they made Jessamyn laugh out loud, the way they'd swim right into the open flower mouths.

Everyone seemed to be expecting her, because the door was open and the house was just blazing with lights, so she went on in. In every room there were lamps, crystal chandeliers, candles and fires in fireplaces. *Too much light*, she thought. *Why does anybody need this much?* But it was really pretty.

As she went along the hallway, she could hear them in the dining room. She knew just where it was, anyway, because she'd lived in that house before. It was sort of her house.

They were all having a terrific time, and they were glad she came. Everyone was eating strawberry Jell-O in glass bowls on a glass table. And drinking red wine, even Danny and Roseanne. They gave Jessamyn some of everything, which was nice of them. Her grandmother raised her wine glass and said, "To the children."

Jessamyn raised her glass. "To the grownups," and they laughed and laughed, because they knew there were grownups hiding in the children's bodies and children hiding in the grownups' bodies.

Then they each ate a small glass cake and a mirror. Jessamyn worried at first that they would cut on the way down, but they didn't. Although she did wake up the next morning with a small stomachache.

As they were eating, Jessamyn heard chanting from some other room, just as though they were in church. "Who's in there?" she said.

"Angels," Danny said, so seriously she knew he was making a joke.

"God," Roseanne said, but she didn't even pretend to be serious. She slapped the table, bounced a little and laughed so hard she turned bright red. Then all of a sudden she stopped. "See?" she said, "I don't cough any more. Neither does Danny."

"That's good," Jessamyn said.

Danny sat down at a huge glass piano and played the song he wrote for his father. As the music rippled through the rooms, the crystal chandeliers swayed and tinkled, the candles flickered, while Jessamyn watched through a blur of tears.

"Don't cry, Jessamyn," Danny said. "This is a love song."

"What do you mean?"

"For my father."

"Do you still miss him?" she said.

Danny turned around and smiled. "No. He came back just in time."

"That's not true. He came back too late!"

"He carried me in his arms and told me he loved me."

"But you were dead!"

"Oh, that doesn't matter," Danny said. "He came out of the desert to find me. That's what counts."

Her grandmother stood up, took three gold combs out of her white hair and let it fall down her back. "Well," she said, "it's time to set the house on fire."

"No!" Jessamyn said. "Wait a minute. You can't do that."

"Of course we can," her grandfather said. "We do it every night." He took off his Panama hat and laid it on the table.

Then he and her grandmother and Danny and Roseanne took long matches and went around lighting the walls, furniture, carpets and curtains. Jessamyn watched the flames scorch things, then grow brighter and hungrier, until they were billowing through the house, eating it up.

As she moved back across the water, she could see the whole house was made of glass. The flames shot up, golden red and hot. *This house is going to burst*, she thought, but it never did. In the very center of the fire stood her grandmother, her grandfather, Danny and Roseanne, burning, but never burnt.

The Last Line

(for Danny)

We played on your mountain of magic
high enough to split the sun,
dressed up for your stories
in our mothers' fine lace and pink
pearls, spun to your music,
young Mozart. The grownups sighed
and laughed at my flying feet
pulling you in my red wagon.

At twelve, you ate nothing, carefully,
and your shadow wasted, while you
wrote jokes and jingles for your silent
mother, won her a year of salted peanuts.
Professors reached for your math problems
and with empty hands sent you, coughing,
from their colleges. We fingered
your old coins in glass jars, rode
the gold camels on your bright stamps.

At fourteen, you listed doctors
in your small, precise journal, no
thoughts of God, just medicines
and birthdays, or hospital times,
new doctors and notes for a play.
We blamed your mother and took you
to heal in pine trees, taught you
how to descend the stairs, face first,
on your stomach, too small now for
peanuts. But we had three years

of secrets, red-faced in giggling
corners. When you could breathe, I
teased the life out of you, till
you smiled sorry one day and your lung
collapsed to a real, flat line, no
point. I was eleven, waiting
your return from the ashes, and
the jingle's on me now. I've got you
in a gold frame, smiling a thin sorry
in your blue and brown striped shirt.

Jessamyn Singer

AFTERWORD

I began *The Candle of God* as a memorial to my cousin, Jimmy Meikel, who died of cystic fibrosis when I was fourteen. I realized I was the only living member of my family who still remembered him, and I used direct quotes from his journal in the novel. But the characters, though some were loosely based on my family, took on a life of their own, as characters tend to do.

I wish to thank the Tucson Historical Society for helping me with research for the sections on Tucson.

CPSIA information can be obtained at www.ICGtesting.com
Printed in the USA
BVOW071804300512

291389BV00001B/2/P